INSIDERS

INSIDERS

MARVIN H. MCINTYRE

iUniverse, Inc.
Bloomington

Insiders

iUniverse books may be ordered through booksellers or by contacting:

iUniverse
1663 Liberty Drive
Bloomington, IN 47403
www.iuniverse.com
1-800-Authors (1-800-288-4677)

Because of the dynamic nature of the Internet, any web addresses or links contained in this book may have changed since publication and may no longer be valid. The views expressed in this work are solely those of the author and do not necessarily reflect the views of the publisher, and the publisher hereby disclaims any responsibility for them.

Any people depicted in stock imagery provided by Thinkstock are models, and such images are being used for illustrative purposes only.

Certain stock imagery © Thinkstock.

ISBN: 978-1-4620-2264-9 (hc)
ISBN: 978-1-4620-2265-6 (ebk)

Library of Congress Control Number: 2011908512

Printed in the United States of America

iUniverse rev. date: 06/29/2011

To Jo Anne

I never knew *Grace* before you.

PROLOGUE

GEORGE GRANT WAS A universally loved man. It was a label coveted by many but assigned to only a few, and he would have disagreed with the assessment. He was extremely uncomfortable with praise directed at him. A positive, consistently cheerful man, he created a very successful company built on the premise of mutual respect. He gave credit as easily as most people dispense unsolicited advice. Even his competitors could not conjure up a criticism of this generous, humble man.

George Grant was also a creature of habit. Ever since his heart attack two years before, he had applied his business discipline to his health. He had lost thirty pounds, and now at five feet nine inches tall and 160 pounds, there was no beer belly and no old-man softness. With his resolve, he didn't need a trainer, but he could well afford one, and he liked the company. Consequently, wherever he was, he worked out at least three days a week with a personal trainer.

Here in Bethany Beach, Delaware, it was a cute, young girl who put him through his paces. But at eighty years of age and after fifty-four years of marriage, his wife, Mildred, still laughed and encouraged him when he teased the young ladies.

Although Mildred would not walk on the highway and worried when George did, everyone at the beach walked or rode bikes on US Route 1. The city had ample bike and walking lanes, and after Labor Day exercisers often outnumbered the cars. However, at five thirty on the morning of October 30, 2008, there was just George and Butch. George had on light blue Nike warm-ups, which were Mildred's favorites because, she said, they matched his eyes. He had added fluorescent strips to lessen her concerns. Butch, as usual, was au natural.

All during his working years, George had never needed an alarm clock to wake him up in the morning. Even though he still had no need for prompting, Butch, who George was convinced was part rooster, provided it anyway,

Butch was a six-pound Maltese and not the type of dog that George ever dreamed he would own. Mildred's only concession to George was to let him name the little white piece of fluff Butch. As reluctant as George had been to get the dog, it was love at first sight, and he wasn't sure he could sleep at night without Butch in their bed.

The limit of Butch's tiny bladder was invariably reached five minutes before daybreak. His gentle, but persistent, licking of his master's face would stir George to action. Because Mildred was a light sleeper, his initial response to the licking was a whispered plea to his wife. "Not again, Sweetheart," he would murmur. "A man my age needs to pace himself." Her predictable giggle assured him that all continued to be right in his world.

For George, the morning walk with his ferocious sidekick was a perfect time to say his gratitudes. Good advice had prompted him to classify his Palm Beach, Florida, condo as his permanent residence in January of 2000. Then in February of that year, he sold his company at a very attractive price. Interest from AAA tax-free bonds more than provided for his lifestyle, and the sale of the company allowed him to donate most of the proceeds to his family's charitable foundation.

George and Mildred's famous open-door policy at their lovely oceanfront home in Bethany Beach assured a constant stream of relatives and friends. The Grants loved every minute of the confusion. Finally, George was grateful that at his last physical, his doctor had declared him to be in excellent shape and said that he should live to be at least one hundred. George knew how blessed he was, and giving thanks was as natural to him as breathing.

As they turned out of the neighborhood into the exercise lane, Butch strained at his leash, excited at the prospect of making fresh territory his own. Butch's enthusiasm always put a smile on George's face; the two were more alike than he cared to admit to anyone but himself. The two alpha males shook off the cold air and enjoyed the crimson sunrise together as they began to pick up speed.

Butch's head turned first toward the squeal of tires that seemed way too close. As George swiveled toward the black town car barreling toward him, he knew it was going to end his life. The sickening thud and shattering of bones resonated inside his body. The leash flew from his limp hand, and the extra inch of lead spared Butch's life. George's last thought was that the damn doctor had been wrong, but Mildred had been right.

About one hundred yards ahead on Route 1, the car idled. The driver appeared indecisive, with eyes fixated on the rearview mirror. Moments passed. Then slowly, almost painfully, the car pulled away, blood and tissue dripping in its wake.

Two minutes later, from across the highway, a young woman saw an elderly man lying in the road. Pulling over, she called 9-1-1, and tears streamed down her face as she watched the tiny white dog try to lick his mangled master back to life.

CHAPTER 1

ON A NORMAL DRIVE to the beach, my wife, Grace, and I would be listening to a book on CD. More accurately, I would be listening intently, and Grace would be driving. According to our agreed-upon rules of the road, that gave her control over the temperature and all audio functions. Consequently, whenever a random thought crossed her mind, she had the power to stop the disc and share such thought with me, Mac McGregor.

On those rare occasions when a quick trigger finger might be annoying, I knew that a simple offer to drive would result in my gaining dictatorial control, a thought that was often considered but never implemented. I prefer to not have to think about where I'm going when I'm in transit. In every other waking moment of my life, I tend to focus on exactly where I'm going. Besides, when her cute little fingers become too twitchy, I can bring out a massive eye roll.

Funerals, even ones that successfully serve as a celebration of a person's life, are nevertheless draining. Inevitable thoughts of our own mortality and that of our loved ones are interspersed amid memories of the deceased. Grace and I had been close to George and Mildred Grant for over twenty years, and the three-hour drive was weighted with memories.

By unexpressed consent, we had shared the ride in silence. Both of us instinctively understood the need. I reached over and touched her arm tenderly as she pulled into the church parking lot.

Nestled between the crowded, often boisterous confines of Ocean City, Maryland, and the more cosmopolitan, progressive inhabitants of Rehoboth

Beach, Delaware, is Bethany Beach, "the quiet resort." Serving as a microcosm of the resort town in which it resides, the Mariners Bethel United Methodist Church is located on Route 26, almost within walking distance from the town center.

As those coming to pay their respects almost reverently searched for parking spaces, we paused in the sunlit beauty of this late fall day, part of us wanting to remain outside. The idea that death is allowable if the person lived into his eighties did not console me. The bizarre and callous circumstances of George's death overrode all platitudes.

Yet the tired gray headstones in the church's cemetery were strangely welcoming. They wrapped their uneven arms around the house of worship. I took Grace's hand as we walked into the large narthex of the recently renovated church. On two separate occasions, when our friend Jean Pusey sang a solo, we had attended services. Memories of her clear soprano voice, backed by the praise choir, took me momentarily away from our purpose here.

Arriving early had allowed us to absorb the church's changes and still feel the nostalgic pull of sameness. The stained-glass windows we remembered from the old church had been used to create new ones. Grace and I shared a smile as we read the ancient deed on the wall. It was signed by the founding Christians who had pooled their money to purchase the land for one hundred dollars.

As we entered the sanctuary through one of the two sets of double doors, our eyes were immediately drawn to the front. Brilliant light was shining through the two majestic, life-size stained-glass windows flanking the pulpit. One portrayed Christ walking on water, and the other showed Him calming the seas. It was hard to dispute that God was there.

It was forty-five minutes before the scheduled time for the service, but the church, built to hold more than five hundred people, was almost full. David Grant, George and Mildred's only child, saw us and excused himself from a small group of mourners. As he walked toward us, unspoken emotion moved through us like an electric current. Our eyes welled with tears. He hugged Grace and then me. We looked at each other, and I was struck by the fear that any words I said would be insufficient. David nodded in silent understanding. Motioning us forward, he took Grace by the arm and ushered us to seats right behind the family.

With a wan smile, David turned and walked over to escort his mother to her seat. Almost as if choreographed, a reception-like line of people formed. We watched as they blended into a pattern of concerned faces, tearful embraces, and gentle expressions of love. Not just Sunday faith but everyday faith lived here. I wiped my eyes with a tissue, ran my hand over the smooth edge of the oak pew, and took a long breath. I bowed my head and stared absently at the thick, gray carpet. I closed my eyes and prayed.

From the large stage, the minister's message was meaningful, heartfelt, and uplifting. When the choir, about fifty strong, sang "How Great Thou Art" and then "Amazing Grace," I sang with them like I wanted George to hear me.

There were no formal eulogies, yet the parade of friends and family who wanted to speak, offer a humorous anecdote, or just give thanks for George's friendship seemed endless. With David's help, the minister would scan the room and call on the next person to speak.

Earlier, I had raised my hand and felt sure that my request had been noted, but others were chosen, so I was content to listen. Besides, I would have ample opportunity to share my thoughts with David and Mildred at a later time. Finally, the minister raised both hands and said, "We have one final tribute to our beloved friend." He paused and then pointed at me. "Mr. McGregor?"

I had nothing prepared, but I believe that if I speak from my heart in God's house, I will be guided in my words. I smiled at Grace as she squeezed my hand, and I stood. David motioned for me to come to the pulpit. I made my way to the front, turned, and faced the congregation. I felt a tug as I saw a smile emerge from Mildred Grant's tear-stained face. My heart raced. This was one of the biggest stages of my life. I began. "Why aren't you here?" The words hung in the air. "There is enough love in this church right now to guarantee world peace! But you're not here." I gathered myself.

"Who is going to call my office at two in the afternoon and ask if I'm awake? Who else will ever try to convince me that he became a Florida resident not to save taxes but because, in Florida, his vote would count?" The congregation's tittering of laughter grew to warm chuckles.

I looked around at the congregation and raised my voice. "Some of us *still* need your guidance on how to be a great husband, a great father, and a great Christian. But you're not here," I said with tears streaming down my face. "And we miss you."

CHAPTER 2

LEAVING FROM POTOMAC, MARYLAND, before seven in the morning normally makes the commute to Washington, DC, tolerable. After thirty years of experience, I could make this trip in my sleep. Only the black coffee resting in the cup holder of my 2001 Lexus hardtop convertible prevented me from testing my theory that day—that and the adrenaline-filled anger that I was unable to will away.

Gliding to a stop at the light at River Road and Falls Road, I glanced into the rearview mirror. The man staring back with clenched teeth, hunched over the wooden steering wheel, should have been enough to shock me into an attitude adjustment. I forced a few long breaths, released my death grip on the wheel, and watched as the blood returned to my fingers. One final glance before moving resulted in a mirthless laugh as I thought of my carefully sculptured image.

I am a thirty-year Wall Street veteran and head of the High Net Worth Group of a prestigious regional brokerage firm. I have been a frequent commentator on radio and television, and I've been ranked as one of the top five investment advisors in the country by *Barron's* magazine for the past five years.

Mentally listing my alleged street creds, even in my present funk, was no help. A recent newspaper article credited me with being "cool, calm, and collected, always in control." That was yesterday's hero, not the fraud who was very reluctantly driving to a breakfast meeting. The only control I was currently exhibiting was over my bladder. And if I ran into serious traffic en route, that control would be in question, too.

How could I be in control when the whole freaking economic world was out of control? A financial advisor cannot stick his head in the sand. Scared clients need to know what to do. I had two options: one, pretend I understand the global panic, and more importantly, have a sliver of confidence that our leaders will take the necessary steps to solve it; and two, shout from the rooftops, "We are on the brink of a depression, and we can only pray that they will figure it out!" Lady or the tiger; fraud or Chicken Little.

Added to this horror film that was pinballing around in my mind was the frustration that I had been bullied into this breakfast. By all rights, I should have been in my office counseling scared clients and trying to figure a way out of this mess. But Sam Golden, who was the Securities and Exchange Commissioner under President Clinton, is one of my oldest friends. In truth, this breakfast had been on my calendar for two weeks, but that hadn't stopped me from trying to postpone it twice. Under normal circumstances, I would enjoy having Sam pay for breakfast and trading barbs with my friend.

But Sam was insistent, even though he knew that I needed to get ahead of this tsunami. Between spending all day talking clients off the ledge and spending half the night trying to divine the future, a social hour just seemed wrong. Unfortunately, my arguments fell on deaf ears. Breakfast at the Hay-Adams— I was going, but I was definitely not happy.

I was not slowed down by traffic, so I soon pulled into my office parking lot. Our nation's capital is not an early city. It may be because there is no easy commute from the suburbs or because the city has an overpopulated army of lawyers and government workers who are not early risers.

I tabled my surliness as I gave the veteran attendant my keys. With an exaggerated look of admonishment, I cautioned him that I had checked my odometer and would know if he drove women all over town in my car. My comment, plus an early tip, resulted in the full facial smile I was seeking.

The distance from my office on Pennsylvania Avenue to the Hay-Adams Hotel is about eight blocks. I hoped that the brisk walk in the early morning sunshine would give me time to exorcise my demons and be at least semicivil to Sam. He is consistently annoying, but it is impossible to stay angry at the goofy bastard.

The Hay-Adams Hotel is located at16th and H Streets. This classic, historic hotel was named after John Hay, a private assistant to President Lincoln and later a secretary of state, and Henry Adams, an acclaimed author and descendant of two presidents. It offers unparalleled views of the White House, Lafayette Square, and St. John's Church, which is proudly referred to as the "Church of Presidents."

The ever-present doorman acted like he actually knew me as he opened the door to the opulent lobby. Although to me the hotel feels a bit pretentious, it remains a tourist's dream.

Often, breakfast at the Hay-Adams is an opportunity to see powerful people. This was not one of those times, as I spotted Sam Golden sitting in a chair facing the entrance, half-reading the *New York Times*. When he saw me, he jumped up like a kangaroo, and the paper fell from his lap to the floor. My eyes followed its disheveled descent. The man has always had difficulty walking and chewing gum at the same time.

Sam's hand shot out, and then in a voice too loud and too enthusiastic to come from a former SEC commissioner, he said, "Angus 'Mac' McGregor, my man! So glad you could make it." His poop-eating grin revealed his satisfaction in the fact that I had kept the appointment. Rewarding neither his salutation nor his victory, I ignored his hand and walked right by him into the dining room.

Impervious to embarrassment, Sam stumbled after me. I greeted the hostess and asked for our table. Sam followed me. I still had not acknowledged his presence, and I faked a surprised look as he sat down across from me. Our table would have been considered a premium table, except for the fact that this high-profile restaurant was only at about 10 percent capacity. It was sad evidence of the state of our declining economy.

I looked around. If this recession continued, the waitstaff could be cut in half. The more I studied the causes of this financial earthquake, the more frustrated I became. In my mind, a catastrophe increases in magnitude when the wounds are self inflicted. Unfortunately, greed rarely has a conscience and has no regard for collateral damage.

"I don't get a handshake? I don't get a hug?" Sam whined.

I leaned forward. "Consider yourself fortunate that I didn't do an about-face and head back to the office. You beat me up to meet you and then you lay the 'Angus' crap on me," I replied evenly. "You've known me for forty years. In that period of time, how often have you heard me refer to myself as 'Angus'?"

His smile began to leak confidence. "I'm sorry. I'm sorry. I *really* appreciate your having breakfast with me, and I know that being called 'Angus' pisses you off." He paused and looked at me for forgiveness. I remained unmoved. Like a puppy dog that has been disciplined and then instinctively tries for your affection again, he began, "So how about I turn on my charm full wattage and you remember why you love me?"

The over-the-top exhortations, coupled with his lopsided grin, forced me to cover my mouth with my hand to mask a reluctant smile. "That statement presupposes facts not in evidence," I countered in my best lawyer voice.

Sam laughed, and when he did, it seemed like the laugh traveled all the way up his six-foot-four, Ichabod Crane–like frame. Sam is one of those disgusting types who doesn't exercise other than run his mouth. He eats constantly with no regard to fat or carbs, and he has about 6 percent body fat.

He looks almost the same at fifty-five as he did forty years ago, except that his still-black hair is a bit thinner and his nose is slightly more prominent. His pale face becomes alive with the intensity of his steel-gray eyes. He sees everything. A few minutes with Sam Golden, and you know he is scary smart.

Still trying for a light mood, Sam snatched a menu from the approaching waiter. He scanned it like a speed reader on Ritalin and said, "My friend is in a hurry. I'll have three eggs over easy, bacon, grits, and an English muffin. Coffee and orange juice also, please."

I rolled my eyes at Sam and then told the waiter despondently, "I'll have the granola parfait and an iced tea."

My choice of a healthy breakfast was met with a grimace. "Do you have a cholesterol problem?"

"Do you have an MD to go along with your JD and PhD?"

"I already know the answer," Sam said with a dismissive wave. "You don't." He moved his head from side to side and started looking at me like he was picking fruit. "You haven't changed since high school. No wrinkles, brown hair. Why, you're probably still at your wrestling weight."

Ignoring that obvious attempt at flattery, I replied thoughtfully, "It probably would cheer me up if I leaped across this table and pinned your bony behind."

Sam, who is often easily amused, laughed again. "Well, I'm glad to see you in fighting form, even if you do eat like a wimp." He paused and studied me again, only this time the intensity was uncomfortable. I began to feel like a defendant in a courtroom.

Finally, he spoke. "Mac, you manage money for your friends, family, everybody you care about in the world. Markets are plunging out of control. How do you cope? How do you feel?"

For a moment, I refused to let the question register. My conditioned response was to offer a stock answer: investor Valium. But Sam was not a reporter trying to interview a victim after a tragedy; he was a long-time, caring friend. His earnestness and his concern were palpable.

I stared at him in silence. I took a deep breath, closed my eyes, and then opened them. "Every nerve ending in my body feels like it's on fire. Serious doubt was previously a stranger to me. Now worry, fear, and anxiety are constant companions."

I paused. "It's not about me. I worry for my clients." I looked at Sam like he was the enemy. "And for my country." I turned away, disconcerted by my self-revelation.

Sam leaned in closer. "I know you. You've protected your clients." He stopped, perhaps sensing that my regurgitation had not been complete.

I slowly turned my head back to look at him and measured every word. "Yes. We gave them financial air bags, but their psyches are being raped."

Sam looked down at the table. It was if he had pushed a witness to the breaking point.

After a few minutes of contemplation, Sam spoke again. "You aren't capable of dispassionate care. No matter how well you've protected them, you blame yourself because they're scared. No one predicted this economic collapse."

I was touched by his words and the gentleness with which they were spoken. Logic was normally an antidote for frustration and anxiety, yet I had been self medicating with it for a while with no relief. I held up my hand like a stop sign. I needed to exit this conversation. "Sam, you've always been a gentle soul. In fact, that may be the reason that it was always so hard for you to get laid," I said softly, with a well-meaning smile.

I took another deep breath. "However, my guess is that you didn't require my presence to be my therapist, even though you suspect I'm in urgent need of one. So what is the real purpose of our breakfast?"

"Mac, if I thought it would help to prove to you beyond a shadow of a doubt that it wasn't your fault, I would argue it before the Supreme Court. But let's face the facts. We've been here for twenty minutes, and you haven't eviscerated me." He shrugged, adding a palms-up gesture. "Does that seem natural to you?"

That warranted a chuckle. I do abuse those I love. The planets must have been improperly aligned. "More lawyer talk—your industry's aphrodisiac. Meanwhile, you've deftly avoided my question. Are you sure you're not running for office?"

In one continuous motion, he smiled, rolled his eyes, shook his head vigorously from side to side, and raised his right index finger. "Allow me to eat first. Without nourishment I will surely wither away."

He spotted the waiter, who conveniently arrived at the end of his plaintive plea, so further pressing was useless. Sam is single-minded when it comes to food. From previous encounters, I knew that he would attack his multiple courses like a buzzard on carrion. I would not have to wait long for my answer.

I scooped a mouthful of parfait and tried not to gaze too longingly at his feast. With a mouth not yet devoid of food, Sam spoke. "You do know that I'm head of our newly elected president's task force to clean up Wall Street."

I nodded. So far, this was the only positive that I had seen from the new guys in town.

"Our mission will be to bring transparency, oversight, and accountability into your industry." He said this with a passion that sounded like a politician with a campaign promise, yet thankfully he offered this with a bit less undigested food.

In response, I simply raised an eyebrow of skepticism. This was a problem for a global army of forensic insiders, not a plethora of bureaucrats seeking sound bites.

Noting my dubious look, he increased the volume. "Unregulated competition doesn't work. Winning becomes just about outperforming the other guy. There is no concern for the greater good. When greed is involved and there are no boundaries, self-discipline is an illusion. Thus, some hedge funds use not only tactics that are permitted but also whatever the hell they can get away with."

Sam looked expectantly at me for a response. He was either interested in my thoughts or dying for me to take over the conversation so he could continue shoveling food.

My parfait had already disappeared, and this was an area in which I have strong opinions. My objectivity was likely colored by the fact that I was spending considerable time doing damage control for this problem. Fortunately, with Sam, there was no need for me to filter my response.

"Only the uninitiated or financially motivated would think that hedge funds don't need to be regulated. They've turned the stock market into a casino. The most common positions for investors now are cash and fetal." Bitterness was a definite by-product of my candor.

I leaned in close to him and lowered my voice. "The whole system is broken, Sam. You and I both know that it's not just the crooked hedge funds. What's the first thing that a politician does when he or she gets elected? They start running for reelection. I don't want my representatives to represent my district or my state. I want them to represent my country!"

I shook my head in frustration.

"The government can't control the capital markets or the stock markets or the mortgage markets. But they can monitor the markets and punish abusers. Screw the special interests; adopt logical rules, and enforce them. It's not rocket science. It just takes courage." I paused and looked him in the eye. "And it starts at the top!"

I sat back and rubbed my forehead with my hand like I had a headache.

Sam was just staring at me intently and not eating. It almost totally broke my train of thought. "Sorry. I didn't mean to monopolize the soapbox." I took a breath and got back on track. "Hedge funds are like the CIA, except they make a lot more money. Some of their computers have as much power as the government. Their proprietary models are called black boxes, and they operate in total secrecy."

I let out a breath, leaned forward, and said through gritted teeth, "Regulate is my second choice. My first choice is incarcerate."

Sam and I unintentionally played "eye chicken" for a few minutes. Then he looked down and ate the last few bites of his breakfast.

I was still in the dark over the purpose of the meeting, but I knew Sam would enlighten me. Wasting time is anathema to both of us. Sam wiped his chin and folded his napkin. He put both elbows on the table, steepled his fingers, and rested his chin on his hands. As he looked at me, I could almost hear the thoughts churning. Abruptly, he spoke. "Mac, would you consider joining our team of economic advisors?"

He was serious. In order to give substance to my response, I waited a few beats. "I'm flattered. Even the possibility of affecting policy would be exhilarating." Then I shook my head in a negative gesture. "But in this environment, I need to be there twenty-four/seven for my clients."

Sam's face pinched up into what appeared to be a look of reluctant resignation as he digested my answer. "I thought that would be the case, but damn, you would be great. Your industry knowledge, your integrity, and the fact that you would have no hesitation about expressing your opinion—well, it would be inspirational. I wouldn't even make you play nice."

I smiled. The waiter ventured over and broke up the love fest. "Can I get you gentlemen anything else?"

"Maybe you could bring a pastry basket," Sam suggested. "I'm going to try and tempt my friend, and we have a little more talking to do."

"Tempt my friend?" I asked.

"Well, there's a chance. The English muffin just didn't do it for me," Sam confessed. He continued after the waiter left. "Let me also tell you the main reason I need your help. I believe we'll be able to uncover most of the strategies that the hedge fund managers have used. Although it'll be like pulling teeth, we'll be like pit bulls on a pants leg. One of the few positives of the market crash is that we have a mandate from the president, Congress, and the Fed to investigate the ass off these computer terrorists."

Sam's excitement was contagious. I felt like I had received an invitation to the Playboy mansion and my clients wouldn't let me go.

Sam's concentration was momentarily broken by the arrival of the pastry basket. He grabbed a blueberry muffin and looked at it with the affection generally reserved for a newborn child.

"Is it hot?" I asked.

"Yep," he said as he stuffed it greedily into his waiting mouth. Reluctantly, I reached over and grabbed a steaming muffin. Sam politely ignored my inability to resist temptation. "We'll have authority and interagency cooperation. I've chosen all the members for our task force, and I have some of the best minds in the business working for me. All I care about is protecting our country," Sam concluded.

I felt an involuntary flicker of hope. If no politicians were involved, and if civil liberties became secondary to the integrity of our financial system—did my by-the-book friend really mean that the gloves were off?

Sam looked at me with a pained expression. "Mac, I should have forewarned you. I'm bringing you over the wall. I need you to keep our conversation confidential." In the brokerage industry, being "over the wall" means that you've received nonpublic information that you are not allowed to exploit. It is similar to an off-the-record conversation with a reporter.

This was starting to sound like Sam had some serious juice. "No problem," I replied and watched his face relax.

"You used to work with Jeremy Lyons." It almost sounded like an accusation.

Although it wasn't a pleasant memory, I nodded.

Abruptly, Sam lunged forward as emotion bled into his voice, "We need to find him!" he whispered with eyes ablaze. "We need your help!"

CHAPTER 3

FROM THE HOTEL, I cut through Layette Park, distancing my mind from Sam's request and allowing myself to absorb the city that I love. I turned right on Pennsylvania Avenue, and my eyes naturally pivoted to the home of every president except George Washington. It is hard to imagine Sam Golden shooting buckets with the new leader of the free world. I took a deep breath of the still-chilly morning air and mentally buckled up for the rest of the day.

On snow days, or days on which traffic is inexplicably snarled, there is a temptation to move my team to the friendly confines of the Village of Potomac. The commute would be a layup for me, and the tantalizing Congressional Country Club would be only five minutes away. Still, the thought does not linger with me even long enough to reach the category of fleeting.

Washington, DC is electric. If I look to the left when I exit my building, I see the White House. When I cross the street and walk by it, the history of 1600 Pennsylvania Avenue grabs me like a long lost friend. If I run through the maze of lobbyists, I will end up at either the Hart Senate Office Building on Constitution Avenue or the Rayburn House Office Building for members of the House of Representatives on Independence. If I want to weave through a gaggle of lawyers, I can arrive at 1st street, which houses the Supreme Court. If power is indeed the ultimate aphrodisiac, then this city is the world's largest power generator.

Our complex is a very large rectangle with open offices on the outside and individual workspaces on the inside. There is considerable natural light from the large windows overlooking Pennsylvania Avenue, and when someone cleans off the top of my desk, all appears neat and efficient.

"Where were you this morning?"

Senior partner, chief rainmaker, and issuer of the only greeting I received as I walked past my partners and associates was a bossy munchkin with her hands on her hips. I gave her a bored stare, removed my suit coat and placed it on the back of my chair, sat down, and logged on to my computer. In most businesses, ignoring someone who works for you is admittedly rude, but as a rule, there are no repercussions. However, ignoring Lena Brady can be hazardous to your health.

Lena is much more than a glorified secretary. She oversees the administrative associates, works with clients, and organizes my business and personal obligations. Her round face, short brown hair, big brown eyes and pug nose resemble Charlie Brown's friend, Lucy. And to our clients, she is respectful, charming, and extremely helpful.

I kept my head down, concentrating on my computer screen. I didn't need to look to feel the dagger-like lasers shooting from her eyes. She now stood in front of my desk, her hands still on her hips. She didn't move a muscle and probably didn't even blink. As the computer was finishing the log-in process, I raised my head and spoke with slight disdain. "I always keep my calendar up to date, and I believe that you have access to it."

She responded in what could never be considered a subservient manner. "I have access to everything in your business and personal life, *Boss*."

Her sugary sweetness was not a good sign. I should have remained mute and patient and first looked at the calendar before I got obnoxious. Instead, I had panicked under the withering stare. She walked around my desk and moved the chair that was beside it until it was right next to mine. "Why don't we look together?" she asked innocently.

With no desire to prolong the pain, I ignored the computer and instead looked at her with half-lidded eyes. "Tell me again why I keep you around."

She smiled back smugly. "You would be a train wreck, and Grace would divorce you. She already likes me better than you." I sighed. A breakfast I didn't want to attend, stock futures down more than two hundred, and I am so off my game that I'm not even able to annoy Lena.

Piling it on, she added, "So when your largest client called this morning looking for you, I said, 'I don't know where he is. He won't answer his cell and refuses to *ever* use his BlackBerry. He is off the reservation.'"

I felt the lurch in my stomach. I hate not being available during a crisis, especially for Rod Stanton. "Did he say what he needed?" I asked despondently.

"No!" she cried as she jumped out of the chair like a jack-in-the-box. "Because he didn't call."

My mouth opened. That was probably a good thing because it allowed her to take the hook out more easily. She executed a perfect about-face and sashayed away from my desk. Calling over her shoulder, she said, "But he might have. Always tell Momma Lena *everything*."* * * * *

"So, Grumpy Pants, how was your day?"

"Grumpy Pants?" My raised eyebrow and tone should have been sufficient to have Grace correct her insulting and inaccurate characterization.

"Oh, I'm sorry. I should have said Sammy Sunshine." Her sweet smile is not always appealing.

In a marriage, certain debates should be ended before they begin, particularly when one party may be bereft of ammo.

"Speaking of Sam," I said, mirroring her sweet smile, "I had breakfast with Sam Golden this morning."

"Oh, how is he?" she asked.

"Even more annoying than usual."

"No way. He 's a sweetheart. I can't believe that he's still your friend, considering how much you've picked on him over the years."

"That may be in question now"

"Why?" she asked with a concerned look, as she leaned over the coffee table that separated us.

I gave her a self-righteous look in return. "Because he asked me, actually pounded on me, to do him a favor, and I refused."

My reply was greeted with silence and no change in her concerned look. There are times when I feel that I should have opted for a wife who would have agreed with everything I said. "Do you remember Jeremy Lyons?" I challenged.

"Of course," she responded with a look of near-rapture. "He's every woman's fantasy."

"What?" I stammered.

She laughed. "Just lightening the mood, my darling. He was scary."

"Yeah, well, Sam wanted me to find him," I said, giving my summation.

Grace considered this for a moment and then shrugged her shoulders. "And you said no?"

"What!" I exclaimed for the second time, only there was a little heat behind this one. "I know I don't bring my work home. However, you *do* know what is going in the world. I need to spend every waking hour reassuring clients and figuring out strategy to fight this financial earthquake.

"The last thing I need to do," I said, leaning closer to her, "is to go on some fool's errand for Sam Golden and try to find some evil hedge fund manager. With all his government resources, he should be able to find Jeremy Lyons himself!" I could have added, "The defense rests," but Grace mistakenly views that as a sign of arrogance. I sat back, feeling that my articulate serving of justification had been sufficient.

She studied me in silence for a few minutes. "Honey," she began softly, "you may want to reconsider."

I started to interrupt, but she was clearly not finished. She held up her index finger and gave me a smile that asked for patience.

"Sorry," I said. "Go ahead."

"Thanks," she smiled. She looked me in the eye. "Mac, you've been a mess for a while now. I know you feel that this time is different. I believe you. And no one could take better care of their clients than you." She paused. "But waking up every night and spending hours on the computer is just not healthy. It's like you're addicted to financial porn!"

I felt the weight of her words. Her comments were not stream of consciousness. She had thought about this for a while.

Grace was silent, looking at me for my reaction.

I gave her a begrudging nod.

She moved almost eyeball to eyeball with me and spoke even more urgently. "I see you going through this, and I want to walk into your office, twist your head around, and make you reread the serenity prayer framed on your wall. If you're not 100 percent, how can you help the people you care about the most? Are there really any answers at three o'clock in the morning?"

I closed my eyes for a moment before speaking. "No, but you get mad at me if I practice other forms of self-abuse."

She smacked my arm. "I'm serious, Mac. You need a distraction. Have your mind go in a different direction. You don't joke around as much, you don't pester me about sex as much …"

"Okay, okay!" I raised my hand in surrender. "I give up."

"And," she leaned forward, now about two millimeters from my face, "can you imagine Sam Golden ever refusing you anything?"

She had softly thrust the dagger of guilt into my body. I lowered my head and took a deep breath. Defeat and I will never be friends. I sighed. "I'll call Sam tomorrow, courtesy of my adorable shrink."

"Good," she said with a self-satisfied smile as she settled back in her chair. She looked me up and down. "In that case, you may get lucky tonight."

CHAPTER 4

ALTHOUGH THE SENATOR'S ICE-BLUE eyes were having difficulty focusing, he would have to be blind to not know that the woman sitting next to him at the bar was exquisite. The fact that she was two or three generations younger and that he was a sip of whiskey away from being stumbling drunk were not impediments. Women and whiskey were his favorite food groups. He pursued both on autopilot.

"Young lady, I am Heywood Cunningham," he said with the warmth and the smile that had made Democratic opposition a total waste of time. "I hope that you'll allow a former devoted public servant to buy you a drink."

*   *   *   *   *

A black-gloved hand was pinching his nostrils. Heywood coughed and jerked his head free, and the grip released. Shock and pain ripped through his head as adrenaline pushed through his drunken stupor like a fire hose—not that clarity was a gift.

A man dressed totally in black sat cross-legged on his bed. Risking a furtive glance to assess the situation, Heywood saw light behind his louvered shutters—an unwelcome morning. He vaguely remembered having been rebuffed by an extraordinary woman, staggering home, and somehow managing to get his key in the apartment door. He must have left the door open! How else could this son of a bitch have gotten in?

Heywood blinked his crusted eyes into focus. Hoping to stop the pain that threatened to come right through his eyes, he reached up and vigorously massaged his forehead. "What—? Who—? How the hell did you get in here?"

The stranger remained motionless, his tar-black eyes expressionless. He appeared relaxed, unresponsive, almost uninterested. Although Heywood didn't sense aggression emanating from the man, he couldn't shake the feeling that he was in bed with a rattlesnake.

Misjudging the man's look of passivity, the former senator from the great state of North Carolina challenged, "Are you fucking deaf?"

The intruder sighed. "No, Senator, but I am not a patient man. Do you need a shower to be in full possession of your faculties, or will this cup of Starbucks suffice?"

Heywood glanced at the cup on his nightstand. Hopefully, the offer of coffee reduced the probability of violence. "Who the hell are you?" he asked, increasing the volume. How did you know that I'd be alone? I double-lock the doors, so how did you get in?"

Patiently, as if talking to a child, the man responded, "Max is my name, the girl is one of ours, and it is not relevant how I got in. Coffee or shower? You need to be able to make a quick decision."

"Coffee, and let me get some Bufferin," Heywood moaned, now realizing that he was probably not going to die. "And I've got to take a leak." He walked painfully to the bathroom and closed the door. He unzipped his wrinkled suit pants and relieved himself. The medicine cabinet mirror made him wince. A really old, red-eyed drunk looked back at him. As he ran the water to wash his hands, he quietly picked up the phone next to the toilet. No dial tone—shit! Maybe he *was* going to die.

When he returned to the bedroom, Max reminded him, "Remember, Senator, patience is not my strong suit."

Heywood swallowed three Bufferin with the coffee, grimaced, and looked at the intruder. At first glance, the man seemed rather ordinary: short, gray-black hair; a slight, wiry-looking body; somewhere between forty-five and fifty-five in age; and a forgettable face. On closer inspection, the wrinkles around his black eyes, the fading scar that seemed partially hidden by his shirt, and the fact that he still wore the black gloves were disconcerting.

Heywood had spent his life reading people, and his best guess was that Max was a bully. Well, you hit bullies in the nose. He sat back on the bed, towering over Max, and leaned forward. "How about you just kiss my patient ass, Maxie boy. I am a former US senator, and our security system already has your criminal face on record. Now I want some answers, and I want them right fucking now!"

Instantly, Max's right hand shot out and clutched Heywood's throat, pressing it with painful, persistent force. The strength of Max's grip paralyzed the senator as he fought to push air through his restricted passageway.

As Heywood's face reddened, his adversary spoke in the same unemotional voice. "I do not like nicknames or filibusters." As he spoke, Max's chokehold increased in intensity.

"Two choices: if you promise to remain mute and attentive while I make a proposal, I will answer your questions. On the other hand, if you interrupt me, we will repeat this exercise, although I cannot promise to be as gentle. Blink your eyes if you understand."

Heywood blinked his eyes like the wings of a hummingbird. Max released him and continued as the wide-eyed former senator fell back and started rubbing his throat. Heywood coughed, cleared his throat, and tried desperately to regain his equilibrium.

Tears had appeared in the corners of his eyes, and Heywood could feel, as well as see, the annoyance of the stranger as he waited for the senator to collect himself. Not wanting to further antagonize the man, Heywood nodded weakly at him to continue.

Matter-of-factly, Max began. "Sixty days ago, you had $5,120,000 in cash equivalents. Today those assets are worth only $4,600,000. If you continue this rate of spending, you will run out of money in less than four years. Your business has evaporated. You do not see your children, and you do not see your grandchildren, because their mother has convinced them you are scum.

"Most of your friends do not want to be with you, because they know that you are a self-destructive drunk who will soon be broke and probably asking them for money. Please nod if you feel that my analysis is correct, Senator."

Heywood's mouth was open and his eyes were watering, but he nodded as if he were a puppet and Max was pulling his strings. Heywood struggled to speak. Max raised a gloved finger and cautioned, "Not yet. I am going to give you the opportunity to be on top again. I will be explicit about the benefits of this opportunity and the conditions required for acceptance. This is not a negotiation; it is a unilateral offer. If you decline, we will allow you to continue to flush yourself down the toilet."

Max leaned forward, fixing the senator with a stare to make sure that he had Heywood's full attention.

"The opportunity is specific. First, you will invest all of your liquid assets except for $100,000 with us. In return, your account will receive a wire for $100,000 monthly for the rest of your life. Upon your death $5 million will be paid to your designated beneficiaries. Obviously, any money that you save from your monthly stipends is yours to keep."

Heywood stared in amazement. According to his quick math, that was more than a 25 percent annual return on his money. Those kinds of numbers would make his hangover an afterthought.

"In order to give you assurance of our legitimacy, we will hand you a letter of credit from J. P. Morgan Bank, which enables you to terminate our relationship on a moment's notice and have $5 million returned to you. The conditions of this arrangement are as follows: No drugs. We are aware this is not one of your vices. No drunkenness, and no discussion with anyone about the nature of our agreement.

"One of the reasons that you have been extended this generous offer is that you were unique in the Senate. In contrast to your colleagues, who ran their mouths whenever they managed to cop a feel, you did not discuss your peccadilloes."

Questions were running through Heywood's mind like *Jeopardy!* on steroids. Just how deep was their investigation of him? How did they get access to his financial information? How the hell did they know that he had never bragged about his exploits while he was married? And who the hell were *they*?

"Penalties for noncompliance are severe," said Max as the senator abruptly refocused. "We may stop you for a random breathalyzer at any time. The first time you fail will cost you $10,000, the next time $100,000. On the other hand, if you discuss our arrangement with a friend, lover, or anyone else, the consequences are terminal."

Max paused and looked at Heywood with uncompromising eyes. "Your investments with us will be confiscated, and our contract will provide that the letter of credit simultaneously expires. Obviously, we need concrete proof of your breach of contract, but we will have recorded evidence of your noncompliance." Max looked at him calmly. "Please, Senator, ask your questions."

Heywood paused, collecting his thoughts. "How would you be able to get recorded comments?"

"We have dedicated, resourceful employees, plus we are experts at electronic surveillance," Max replied.

"Well, if I didn't brag about the women, it sure doesn't make sense that I would tell anyone about this crazy deal. How much checking can I do?"

"None. Basically, you will check on the authenticity on our letter of credit. You are a lawyer, and the contract is one page, easily understandable."

"Aw, shit," said Heywood, looking up quickly to make sure they were having a conversation and that he was allowed to interject. "There has to be a catch. No free lunches today."

Heywood stared at Max when he didn't respond. He leaned slightly forward and asked, "How many commandments do I have to break to get in bed with you?"

Max flashed a hint of a smile. "You are already in bed with me."

Heywood blinked.

"Be assured, Senator: you will not be required to break any laws."

"What will I be required to do?"

"Any requirements we have for you will be revealed when you have a need to know."

Heywood put his hand on his forehead, trying to absorb what had transpired. "If I can't get drunk and I'm not working anymore unless you call me, what do I do when I'm not fulfilling your requirements?"

"That is your choice. We would suggest that you write your memoirs, with no reference to us, of course. Your friends and family will be curious as to why you will be sober, seemingly not concerned about money, and occasionally off to mysterious places. If you tell them that you have gotten a sizable advance to write a book and that it is a secret, your status will rise exponentially. Also, your friends will no longer disparage you; instead, they will be envious and afraid of your portrayal of them in print."

Heywood studied this intimidating man who spoke like he had memorized the answers to a test. Everything he said was robotic, yet logical. Still, Heywood felt a prickling instinct that the man was not the type to leave loose ends. On the surface, the financial inducements of this opportunity were mind boggling, but Heywood suspected that this was truly an offer that he could not refuse.

Manufacturing a look of impressed bemusement, Heywood asked, "Are you going to help me get laid, too?"

Max nodded as if he had been told to expect the question. "Yes. Part of your recruitment process may be to entertain a potential client in a controlled venue, and we have a number of beautiful women who will be grateful for your contributions to our organization. In fact, after you have had the opportunity to validate the letter of credit and execute the contract, I believe that a certain young lady would like to come here and cook you a celebratory dinner."

With a subtle sleight of hand, a card appeared in Max's fingers. He handed it to the puzzled senator, who thought that the last thing this man would carry would be a business card. He was right—it contained the name and cell number of the woman he had met last night.

"You have forty-eight hours to make a decision," Max said with finality.

Heywood stared at him and let two minutes of silence pass. Then he straightened like the statesman he used to be, looked purposefully into Max's eyes, and said, "I need to read the contract and call the bank, but I've already made my decision."

CHAPTER 5

IN THE ILLOGICAL WORLD of financial advice, procrastination does not work. Delayed gratification may be pleasurable, but delayed suffering can be terminal. If you need to make an unpleasant call, listen to Nike and "just do it." An unhappy client can turn into a complaint, and then you can end up on life support.

It was 7:45 a.m., and I was walking the walk. It would have been nice to come to the conclusion to help Sam independently. However, marital harmony requires a cart full of compromise and an ark full of acquiescence. I was halfway through leaving Sam Golden a rude voice mail when he picked up. "Mac," he said with emphasis. "I'm delighted that you called." The fact that he was so damn cheerful made this chore even more odious.

In an annoyed voice, I began. "I have no idea why Grace is so fond of you." He apparently couldn't figure this out either because he was silent—then, a sign of life.

"Beats me, pal. Her judgment in men has always been questionable."

The world is really upside down, I thought. *Sam Golden is not this clever.* "Do you want to be cute, or do you want some help?"

"Help, please!"

"That's better. In fact, a sincere grovel would be even nicer. We're going to do this by my rules." Since I had been emasculated at home, it was important to assert control here, to restore balance in the universe.

Sam was respectfully quiet. Good start. I went into due-diligence mode.

"After you asked for my help, you indicated that Jeremy Lyons is running a clandestine hedge fund. How do you know that?"

"We believe that he is managing a large hedge fund."

"Believe? Not know? You're not even *sure* he runs money?"

"Here's what we do have, Mac. As you know, hedge fund managers are secretive in their methodologies, but they all know who is who. We're squeezing them, and they're all singing the same tune."

"The 'Eve of Destruction'?"

"No," he laughed. "Good memory, though. They swear that some maverick is running big money. And it's smart money."

I was getting exasperated. This was beginning to sound like a wild goose chase. "How does that point the finger at Lyons?"

"Three different managers all mentioned the name Lyons and promised on their nine-figure incomes that was all they knew."

"Any kind of GPS, domestic or international?"

"Nada. Shadow trades come from both US and foreign houses. And yes, we did try to pressure the clearing firms, but they wouldn't be intimidated."

I considered Sam's information. It made no sense at all that a hedge fund manager would want to stay under the radar—unless he was a stone-cold crook. Make the cover of *Barron's* or *Business Week* with a world-class track record and investors would be throwing money at you.

"I have another question for our all-seeing government," I said. "All hedge funds are limited partnerships. If he worked with corporate clients or endowments, you would have already used moral suasion and found something out. So his target client has to be megarich if he's trading size. Where are the tax forms, the K-1s? Why not ask your big brother partners, the IRS, to take a peek? Tax returns are the easiest way to determine who would be qualified to invest. Find an unknown manager posting big returns, send out the dogs ..."

Sam sighed and hesitated for a few long moments. "Mac, you wondered why I pressured you to help. In one conversation, you have encapsulated our list of possible leads. I promise you that it took a lot of people working together a lot longer to come to those conclusions. Even though your last suggestion was unethical, and the administration would never cross that line, assume that if we had, we would have come up empty."

I accepted the flattery and the not-too-subtle message, but still I gave him a shot. "Nice try, Sam, but you're not after me just because I'm a pretty face. You want me to prostitute myself with every industry contact I know until we find your man."

No response. Then, "Guilty, Mac. I really feel that this guy is off the reservation."

I remained silent because I knew it would make Sam nervous.

"Why did you really change your mind, Mac? Why are you helping me?"

I thought for a minute before answering. "Because you needed me," I admitted quietly.

"Really?" he replied with childlike wonder

A nicer guy would have left it there. "That, and Grace promised me sex."

*   *   *   *   *

Time is finite. That's not a news flash, but in order to be responsive to my clients and also make a credible effort in the fantasy search for Jeremy Lyons, I needed some serious help in time management.

During the ride to our headquarters in Baltimore, Maryland, I had two scheduled conference calls. For me to have a business call while driving would have been the proverbial accident waiting to happen. Fully aware of my motor limitations, I had arranged for the car service that I used for airport runs and for bringing elderly clients to our office to transport me.

I had finished my second conference call with about five minutes to spare when the driver pulled up in front of our firm's headquarters. I popped the door open and jumped out. "An hour and fifteen, max!" I shouted as I ran up the stairs to the glass doors.

The wait at security was minimal, even with the ID flashing and sign-in sheets. The zaftig African-American woman securing my admittance gave me a brilliant smile of recognition. I needed more. I leaned down and whispered loudly, "Act like you don't know me. I'm afraid that the big boss is becoming suspicious." Her resounding giggle was music to my ears as I entered the elevator that would take me directly to the Center Club.

If I had stopped first at the office, it would have cost at least another ten minutes of glad-handing because I have a lot of friends there. I would love to have visited and commiserated with them, but time was not on my side.

Fortunately, I was a few minutes early; there was no chance that my boss, Jim Wellons, CEO of Johnston Wellons, would be late.

"This day could not get any better!" Jim exclaimed with the over-the-top enthusiasm that is his trademark, yet he is ironically genuine. He pumped my hand, gave me a big hug, and we sat down. "I was so excited that we were having lunch that I told Brenda. Now I'm in big trouble because I wouldn't let her join us."

"I do love that woman."

"That's only because of all the women we saw you with, she picked out Grace and told you that she was the marrying kind."

I smiled. "If that story is retold in mixed company, the 'all the women we saw you with' part should be deleted to prevent certain injury to your favorite financial wizard."

"Of course," he said, laughing.

We spent the next few minutes talking about the market and what strategies I was using. When the waiter arrived, we both ordered the restaurant's signature item, the crab cakes.

I looked at Jim and couldn't help thinking about Sam's comment to me about looking the same. Jim had hired me, and he had been my friend for thirty years. Without question, he continues to be the poster child for positive thinking. About three inches shorter than me, he sits ramrod straight, so he seems taller. A former airborne Ranger, his thin, light silver hair is still cropped close. Fair skinned, with a kind face that flushes with excitement, he has blue eyes that are electric with enthusiasm.

From exercise to diet, relationships, and faith, he is the most disciplined man I have ever met. In spite of his success, there is not an arrogant bone in his body. He loves everyone he knows, and he encourages everyone he meets with a smile that is incapable of artifice. Even with fifteen hundred advisors in his firm, he always calls each one on his or her anniversary with the firm.

"How can I help you?" Jim asked as he leaned toward me. I had no fear of distraction or interruption, for he is an extraordinary listener.

"I have an unusual request." I paused. "I need to find Jeremy Lyons." I paused again, noting that his intent expression had not changed. "You can save me a lot of trouble. Do you know where he is?"

He shook his head, shrugged, and said "No."

I took a breath. "I need anything you can remember that can help me locate him. I promised someone close to me that I would try my best." I did not try to hide my pained expression while he seemed to mentally open computer files.

"He was not our type of person." Jim began.

*　　*　　*　　*　　*

On my way back to my office, I called our firm's compliance officer, Charlie Corvato. When I'd asked Jim to fill me in on Lyons's legendary exit from the firm, he suggested that I call Charlie. Although I had gotten significant background information during lunch, Jim had assured me that I would get explicit color commentary from Charlie.

"Corvato." This was the gravelly voice of a former Golden Gloves winner, the prototype no-nonsense Italian capo, and the most feared man in the firm.

It probably took me twenty-five of my thirty years with the firm to conquer my fear, but now we were friends. And my friends expect a certain standard of behavior, regardless of market conditions. "Charlie, I'm innocent!" I squealed. "They are trying to frame me! I'm clean, man! You gotta believe me!"

As expected, my high-volume stream-of-consciousness shtick brought forth a hard-earned chuckle. "Hold on! We haven't gotten the mail yet, but so far no customer complaints for you today."

We exchanged a few pleasantries, and then I said, "Talk to me about Jeremy Lyons."

I was greeted by silence and then a grunt. "I shoulda popped that asshole."

"Do you know how I can find him?"

"Did you check the local meetings of Assholes Anonymous? Why? Who'd he screw?"

"Give me your version of Lyons's infamous last day," I coaxed.

He thought for a minute. "I'd been riding his ass pretty hard, so I'm sure it wasn't all about you."

I blinked in surprise. "Whoa! I have recollections of him bolting, but how did I become part of the problem?"

"He traded stock like a madman," Charlie continued, "and not your household names. We didn't have a lot of firm capital, and I felt he was an accident waiting to happen. Each time I'd slap his hand, he'd look at me like I was an idiot, but it's my job to protect the firm."

"So how did my name get into the mix?"

"Jim made you head of the firm's advisory council, and Lyons went postal, demanding that the boss tell him why he chose you. Jim told him that you were a natural leader and that the brokers liked you. He screamed that we didn't know what we were talking about. He said his people would take a bullet for him. That pissed me off. I said, 'Just who the fuck are your people?'

"The crazy bastard slams his hand down on the top of Jim's desk, sweeps all the picture frames to the floor. I step toward him, ready to take him out. But Jim grabs my arm. Then this asshole gives me a look that tells me if he were carrying, I'd be Swiss cheese. He glared at both of us. Mac, he was begging to go at it, and I was dying to oblige. He leans forward and says, 'My people are the ones who will help me rule the financial world.'"

"What happened then?"

"Nothing. He looked at us like he dared us to argue. Jim wouldn't let me pop him, so I was done. He bolted from the room and took nothing with him. No personal effects. No books. Not even any of his clients. Dis-ap-peared."

I thought for a minute. "Anything else?"

"Yeah. If you find him, lemme take a shot at him."

I forced a laugh. "Sure, Charlie. It's nice to know you don't hold a grudge."

CHAPTER 6

I CROOKED A FINGER for R. J. Brooks to join me in my conference room and close the door. R. J. had become one of my partners. When I first met him, the twenty-one-year-old infant was our branch office coordinator. At that time, he bore a strong resemblance to the Pillsbury Doughboy. His dark hair looked like it wanted to curl, and because of his scholarly glasses and honest-to-goodness dimples, I automatically smiled when I saw him.

Affable, intellectually insatiable, soft spoken, and respectfully clever, R. J. grew on me rather quickly. When he told me he was leaving the firm to attend Harvard Business School, I offered that he might get a more practical education with me.

Our offices are situated in a trading floor design. In our large, U-shaped configuration, the partners' offices frame the work stations of the administrative associates who actually do the real work. From my vantage point, which is the far left corner, I can eyeball all of the beloved miscreants who work with me.

My conference room is to the immediate left of my desk. A dark wood table, which seats six people on its best day, sits in the center of the room. Against the left wall is a small rectangular table that holds a speakerphone and a big bowl of candy.

On the wall opposite the Pennsylvania Avenue window are assorted reprints, including one of a *Barron's* interview with me and my ranking as a top advisor. Across from the table is a wall of photographs in which I am with famous athletes, politicians, authors, and entertainers. I should be embarrassed by this shameless self-promotion, but it is effective with prospective clients.

As we sat down at the table, I noted that R. J. had not purchased his lunch that day. I removed my salad from its brown paper bag and inquired dryly, "And what did the missus make for her stud muffin today?"

He pondered for an instant. "It might have embarrassed Janice if I had asked her," he replied. "However, she made *me* grilled salmon, asparagus, zucchini muffins, and mixed berries for dessert."

"Do you remember in grade school when we used to trade lunches?" I offered.

"I'm sorry, but I don't believe I had been conceived when you were in grade school."

I laughed. "The amusement factor does compensate for your many other deficiencies."

We ate in silence for a few minutes, and then I put my fork down and leaned forward. "I had breakfast the other day with Sam Golden, former head of the SEC. Do you remember him?"

"Sure. You were actually proud of the job he did."

"Having a good friend run the SEC is not like knowing the chief of police. But we've been friends since high school. He was a smart, geeky looking guy who kept to himself. I found out that he was shy but really interesting when you brought him out of his shell."

"Hmm," said R. J. as he put his hand on his chin and looked around. "Have you noticed that most truly extraordinary people fit that description?"

I raised an eyebrow. "You've never even been *introduced* to shy. Anyway, he is now on the Obama transition team. By the way," I cautioned, "this stays with just you and me."

R. J. cocked his head curiously.

"Sam and I chatted for a bit, and then he got me going with the axis of evil, that is, the SEC and hedge funds. After I had spewed out all of my venom, he hit me with one out of left field. He offered me a position on the transition team."

I paused. R. J.'s head moved back, but his look of surprise did not slow down his reaction time. "Damn, Mac, you definitely ought to take it," he responded enthusiastically. "You know what's going on better than anyone else, and you're not afraid to say what you believe. You could really help create change for our industry."

I nodded, amused that he continued to drink the Kool-Aid.

"In any other market climate, I would be all over it," I admitted. "It's very flattering, but we're nowhere near out of the woods."

"We can handle things here. You know you have great people."

I paused so as not to devalue his statement. "I know, but until this nonsense is over, no new committees, no new charity boards, no distractions." I gave R. J. a knowing smile. "When Sam offered me the opportunity, the real incentive to me was how it would mess with Rod Stanton's mind."

Rod Stanton and I have been friends ever since I started in the business. His politics are slightly right of Attila the Hun's. If I had signed on with the Obama transition team, he would've had a stroke.

"Mr. Stanton would have the last piece of incontrovertible evidence that the world as we know it is coming to an end," added R. J.

I fixed him with a stare. "I believe that Sam's job offer was not planned. It was sincere, but he knew that it was a long shot."

"So what was his agenda?"

"Sam asked for my help in what he considers to be a very serious endeavor." I shook my head. "Apparently, despite all of their resources, they can't find Jeremy Lyons. They have reason to believe that he's running a large hedge fund. I know you've heard of him. Jeremy had exited stage left from Johnston Wellons before you joined us, but he left an indelible mark."

"He probably operates out of another country. Surely the government could track him down in the United States without your help."

"Just because you and I agree on something and it happens to be eminently logical, we cannot assume that our government would share our conclusions."

He gave me a strange look. "You didn't tell them you'd do it, did you?"

"Not originally," I admitted begrudgingly .

I paused, but R. J. was going to wait me out. "She who must not be denied convinced me to help."

"Why would Grace care?" he asked, dumbfounded.

I sighed. "It's a nonissue. I'm in, and so are you."

He studied me as if trying to figure out when he had enlisted and whether or not he had an escape route. Always a quick processor, I could see R. J. mentally determining the futility of argument.

"You went to Baltimore?" he said, putting the pieces together.

"Background."

He nodded. "What possible logic went through Mr. Golden's mind to think that you or, more accurately, we could add any value in this situation? Personally, trying to find someone who doesn't want to be found exceeds the limit of my risk tolerance."

The look on my face showed him that we were in total agreement. Nevertheless, I shared my thought process. "I've examined this," I said as I checked off the points on my fingers.

"First, I agree that the odds are against us shedding any light on Lyons's whereabouts. It's not like we're exchanging holiday cards. Second, I believe that Sam has seriously overestimated my contacts and influence. Third, on the off chance that we are helpful in this endeavor, we know that Lyons is not local, so our involvement would be covert. Fourth," I said smiling, "how dangerous could a fifty-five-year-old be?"

*   *   *   *   *

It had not been my intention in 2006 to bring another principal into our practice. However, not unlike the NFL draft theory of grabbing the best athlete available, when I had a chance to acquire Arthur J. Cohen, Esquire, I pounced.

Up until June 1, 2006, Artie had been a tax partner at Ernst & Young in Washington. He was a legend in the city. Whenever anyone needed answers, someone would lovingly suggest, "Ask old Artie." The humorous coincidence of the phrase preceding his name only previews what you would get if you met Artie.

The first distinctive feature on his pleasant-looking, egg-shaped head is the thin fringe of fine brown hair that made me think of a slimmer Friar Tuck. Artie's contention is that the lack of hair could be attributed to either his excess brains or the repeated banging of his cranium on the headboard. Credence might be easily attributed to the first theory; however, the second supposition is fantasy.

At sixty-two, his skin is still as smooth as a baby's, his hazel eyes are perpetually twinkling with mischief, and he reminds women of their fathers, so they all love him.

Neither Artie's diet nor his exercise regimen contributes to the fact that he looks much younger than his age. Instead, it is his boundless energy, enthusiasm, and genuine willingness to help anybody at any time. He is never off the clock for a friend.

"Artie, I need to go to Cleveland. Can you drive me?"

"Sure. You ready to go now?"

"Artie, you mind if I use your house for a poker game while you're on vacation?"

"Not at all. Tell me what you guys like to drink and eat, and we'll have it ready."

"Artie, my wife left me. Can I fool around with yours?"

"Sure. Someone ought to."

You get my drift—the nicest guy on the planet.

Proving our lack of culinary versatility, my newest partner and I chose to go for a quick lunch at the cafeteria on G Street. Mostly, I eat my lunch in my conference room, but Artie gets claustrophobic when he eats in the office, and besides, I needed to pick his brain.

Here's the picture: two alleged movers and shakers in Washington eating off plastic trays with plastic plates and plastic utensils. The older one had some Chinese concoction that was eerily familiar, and the younger, more imaginative one had a vegetable plate with two hard-boiled eggs for protein.

Younger and more imaginative spoke first. "Arthur J., I have a conundrum. I want to hide in the USA from everyone. I will pay my taxes, federal only. So I will have to live in Nevada or Florida or Texas or somewhere else that has no state tax. I have no debts, no credit cards, no bank accounts, no stocks or bonds in my name. What should I do?"

He looked at me thoughtfully. "Marry me."

He garnered a smile for his cleverness, but I was buying lunch, so I added an impatient glare.

"Okay. Your tax return would have to have a P.O. box address. You would not avail yourself of any government services. No social security payments, no voting, no driver's license. Obviously, you would not own any property in your name; everything would be hidden in a maze of corporate shells."

"So even in this age of Big Brother, it is not impossible to disappear."

"True. But you would eliminate a considerable number of our modern conveniences, and you would be a cash-only customer. It would be much easier and less expensive to hide out of the country."

"Thanks, pal. That was helpful. Let's walk back and check the carnage."

"Why did you want to know, Mac?" Artie asked as he stood and handed me my raincoat.

"Intellectual curiosity."

"Hmm. I believe that is the code for 'nonya.' Just promise to take me with you."

"I wouldn't leave home without you."

CHAPTER 7

JEREMY LYONS FIRST MET Max Parnavich two weeks prior to his abrupt exit from Johnston Wellons. It had been under unusual circumstances. After concluding a ninety-minute workout with his sensei, which ended with a thirty-minute sparring session, Jeremy had gone to the Third Edition, a bar in Georgetown, for a late dinner. It was early on a Monday night, so the bar was almost deserted.

As Jeremy sat at a small table, eating his bland pasta with vegetables and sipping a glass of mediocre red wine, he studied the only other customer in the bar. Aside from an ugly scar on the left side of his throat, the man was unremarkable. Dressed in jeans, boots, and an often-worn sweatshirt, he nursed a beer as he sat alone at the end of the bar. He engaged in no conversation with the bartender, nor did he look around; he simply stared straight ahead at nothing.

Jeremy studied people. A great portion of his success could be attributed to his ability to read them. He didn't really care about people, but he believed that his talent gave him a competitive edge and allowed him to manipulate people to his advantage. He also believed that practicing analysis helped him further hone his abilities, so at this moment he was theorizing about the man he would soon know as Max. Jeremy's first impression was that the stranger at the end of the bar should not be underestimated.

As Jeremy was noting the absence of any extraneous movement from the man at the bar, two very large men entered. With two pairs of small, weak eyes; bulbous noses that were veined and misshapen; atrocious plaid shirts tucked into mud-splattered jeans; and big feet enclosed in worn, brown work shoes invariably dipped in cow dung, they provided an easy study. The burly pair of farm boys looked like brothers. The bartender waved; they were obviously regulars. Laughing and punching each other, they stumbled to barstools and ordered two beers.

Jeremy watched the man at the end of the bar with interest, because for some reason the two behemoths sat right next to him. Max turned his head forty-five degrees and gave them a short, "Don't fuck with me" glare.

The men were oblivious and just kept laughing, yelling, and clowning around with each other. The bartender placed the first beer in front of the man farthest from Max. Yet the man next to Max grabbed the glass and, in snatching it, spilled beer on Max. Jeremy was intrigued that Max had remained immobile when the beer splashed on him. The men laughed, and the one next to Max said, "Sorry, pal," as he fished a five-dollar bill out of his pocket. "Let me just buy you a drink."

"No. Just move," Max said evenly.

The man put his hand on Max's shoulder, and Jeremy speculated that he was about to ask an asinine question such as, "What's your problem, pal?" but the only sound that emerged was an anguished howl of pain. In a blur, Max had grabbed the man's wrist and wrenched it 180 degrees. Jeremy raised an eyebrow when he heard the crack. As gravity pulled the man forward, Max rammed a knee into his face, breaking his nose. The large man had been totally disabled, and Max had not left his seat.

Enraged and moving quickly for a big man, the other man grabbed his beer bottle, broke it over the bar like he had seen in movies, and thrust the jagged edge toward Max. Max seemed to float off of the barstool as he moved in slow motion to avoid the bottle, and with a vicious side kick, crushed the second man's knee. As the man was falling, Max kicked him so hard in the groin that Jeremy looked to see if his testicles had come out of his mouth. As the man hit the ground, writhing in pain, Max dropped to the floor with his elbow poised over the man's larynx for a killing move.

"Stop!" Jeremy commanded from his seat at the table. Max held his position and glared threateningly at Jeremy. Jeremy wiped his mouth with his napkin, came over and knelt down next to Max, and said quietly, "I can take care of maiming but not killing with witnesses. Come with me." They locked eyes, and Max stood up.

Jeremy walked over to the bartender, who was standing with his back to the wall and holding a baseball bat. His eyes were frantically looking from Max to Jeremy.

Jeremy spoke with an ethereal calmness. "I know they're friends of yours, but they put their hands on this gentleman and provoked him, and the one who is now a eunuch had a lethal weapon."

"But, but, he almost killed him," stammered the bartender. "He was going to!"

"Pure speculation. In less than a minute's worth of action, it is difficult to see clearly," Jeremy said soothingly. He pulled out five one-hundred-dollar bills and handed them to the bartender. "In the worse case, it's your word against mine, and I had never met either party before tonight. You might make it temporarily uncomfortable for me, and then we might have to meet again." Jeremy's gaze held the weight of certainty. The bartender averted his eyes.

Jeremy continued staring at the bartender until the man pocketed the money and quietly retreated, with only one more guilty glance at his moaning friends.

"Thank you for your hospitality," said Jeremy. He turned and nodded to Max.

As Jeremy walked out of the bar, Max was a step behind. Neither said a word until they entered Jeremy's apartment. Jeremy motioned for Max to sit down on the black leather couch across from his chair. Both Max's efficiency of movement and his silence appealed to Jeremy, and he said, "I am Jeremy Lyons. Who are you?"

"Max Parnavich."

"Do you have any questions for me?" asked Jeremy.

"Why did you interfere?" Max asked, still without emotion.

"Because in jail or dead, you have no value to me. And I intend to make you very valuable to me. In time, I will need to know everything about you, and when I do, you may receive a very valuable gift—my trust. Very few are capable of earning it. But for now, I need to know why you have given up and obviously seem to have a death wish. A quitter will never earn my trust."

"And will I learn everything about you?" asked Max combatively.

Jeremy paused, considering. "Not until the end, when I have accomplished what others cannot even dare to dream. But you will know enough to be loyal, wealthy, and powerful."

Jeremy met Max's unflinching gaze with the confidence of a man whose success was assured by divine plan. Gradually, Jeremy's stare seemed to reach inside Max's brain and reactivate a switch that had been long dormant.

Max lowered his head, rested his elbows on his knees, interlocked his fingers, and began. He had been a Navy SEAL. The brutal training, the ruthless competition, and the danger had been like oxygen to him.

A few too many incidents had caused him to become an ex–Navy SEAL. Two citations and one court martial for excessive force, and he was ousted with a dishonorable discharge.

Jeremy listened patiently until Max finished. "Your training will be invaluable to me. And your proclivities toward violence," Jeremy said, smiling provocatively, "will make you interesting."

C H A P T E R   8

ROD STANTON WAS SITTING at what would be his favorite table in the Jefferson Hotel's five-star restaurant, Lemaire, if that sort of thing held any importance for him. If it is possible for a man who owns an airplane that seats twelve comfortably not to be pretentious, he achieved it. Wealth to him had merely been a way to keep score, and he did like to win. To his credit, he was extremely philanthropic. As much as he liked to win, he liked to give it away more.

One of the rare successful baby boomers without a college degree, he was the prototypical self-made man. While his contemporaries were frolicking in college, he was mastering computers in the Air Force. He started his own company, borrowed about three times his limited net worth from permissive banks and family, and worked twenty hours a day. Predictably, he later sold the company for $10, million, and he was on his way.

As CEO of two public companies, he capably disguised the fact that he was basically an introvert. A facile mind gave him the ability to be charming, but he had very few close friends and preferred to keep it that way. His attention span with uninteresting people was nonexistent. However, as he scrolled through the messages on his BlackBerry, waiting for the former senator from North Carolina, he was intrigued.

Of course, Rod had taken the senator's call because Heywood Cunningham had been one of the "good ones." Rumored to be not only a larcenous bastard but also a lascivious one, he had nevertheless understood what it meant to be a fiscal conservative.

Rod had enjoyed reminiscing when he Googled some of the senator's past speeches. "Spend, spend, spend. Don't my esteemed colleagues know how to live within this country's means?" When he read it, Rod thought about how appropriate the senator's past comments were for the present economic morass.

As chairman of the prestigious House Ways and Means Committee, Senator Cunningham had been one of the most powerful men in government. When he retired after four terms, he apparently became one of the most sought-after lobbyists in Washington.

As he finished e-mailing what he considered a rather amusing rejoinder to his friend Mac McGregor, Rod glanced up to see the attractive, tuxedoed waitress leading the senator to his table. He turned off his phone, put it in his jacket pocket, stood up, and extended his hand. "Senator, what a pleasure it is to meet you."

"Sir," the senator said, covering Rod's hand with both of his in the customary politician's handshake. "I promise you that the pleasure is all mine." Still holding Rod's hand, he turned his gaze to the waitress. "And young lady, your southern hospitality is like a ray of sunshine to an old war horse like me."

She gave him a surprised look, which indicated that she did not think he was that old. Heywood smiled at her reaction, while Rod mused that he used to think McGregor was full of shit. There was a new leader in the clubhouse.

"Have a seat, Senator," Rod said, as he motioned him to the beautifully upholstered chair.

"Thank you, sir. I will," the senator responded as he smiled broadly. "What an elegant restaurant. Can you tell me any of the history?"

"History never was my strong suit," Rod began as he returned the smile. "But I do know that Lemaire is located in what used to be the ladies parlor of this century-old hotel."

The senator chuckled. "No wonder I feel right at home."

Rod had always believed that the only thing that made a lech tolerable was if he knew he was a dirty old man. He guessed that Heywood had charmed away sexual harassment suits more than once.

The waitress reappeared at the table, smiled, and gave them each a menu. Both men were fine with tap water, and Rod had an iced tea, while the senator settled for a Diet Coke. They scanned the menus for a few moments. "What would you recommend, Mr. Stanton?" asked the senator.

"Please, Senator, call me Rod."

"All right, Rod, and I would appreciate it if you would call me Heywood."

"That works. I must confess that I am more of the sandwich-in-the-office kind of guy, so I don't eat here often. But if you like peanuts, they are famous for their Virginia peanut soup."

Heywood nodded, and Rod continued. "I'm going to have the crab cake sandwich. I understand that another popular item is the filet mignon Black Angus burger with Maytag blue cheese."

"I will follow your lead," Heywood said, "and I would love to try a cup of the peanut soup, also. Before I called you, I must admit that I did some serious reconnaissance on you. What I would really love to follow is your business acumen. Your history of investment success is quite extraordinary," the senator concluded warmly.

Rod was impressed that the senator maintained uninterrupted eye contact during the conversation. His professional flattery sounded sincere, and his ready smile was supported by an ever-present twinkle in his eyes. Add the low southern drawl, and you had one charismatic old rascal.

"I would also be remiss if I did not thank you on behalf of the party for your substantial contributions," added the senator.

"I am still writing checks, Heywood." Rod spoke the name rather stiffly. "But it seems like our guys have lost their way."

"Sadly, I cannot contradict. I think that we had to get the hell beat out of us to realize how badly we screwed things up. But I do believe that we will rise from our ashes smarter, leaner, and more focused on core values." Heywood cocked his head at his host. "I have a few up-and-comers that I believe would really benefit from getting to know you and getting your take on things. Would you be amenable to visiting with them if I brought them to Richmond after the New Year?"

Rod looked at him curiously. If the purpose of this visit had been to have some young legislators visit with him, Heywood could have accomplished that with a phone call. Rod's strength lay in analyzing problems and opportunities, not in the dance. He waited until the soups were served and the waitress had left the table before he spoke again. "Heywood, if you have someone that you would like me to meet, of course I would take the time. But your ulterior motive has to be more devious than setting up future meetings."

The senator laughed. "I see that rumors of my dastardly nature have preceded me. And they were right when they told me that you like to get down to business. If you will allow me to partake in this sumptuous repast that was just served, I give you a politician's promise that I will need only about fifteen minutes after the meal to present an offer that I hope you can't refuse."

Rod nodded, marveling that the senator had taken no breaths during his monologue and had told Rod that he would tell him what he wanted when he was good and damn ready, and here Rod was, smiling like a fool back at him.

Over lunch, conversation remained benign as the senator probed about areas of industry that interested Rod. In return, the senator shared a few amusing anecdotes that highlighted the self-deprecating humor that had been his trademark. Rod still had no idea what the agenda was, but he had wasted time with much less interesting folks in the past.

After both crab cake sandwiches were mere memories and both men had declined coffee and dessert, the senator rested his arms on the table, clasped his hands together, looked earnestly at Rod, and began.

"Again, Rod, I do appreciate your hospitality, although I would have felt better if you had let me pick up the check. At least bring the missus to Washington some time and let me return the favor."

"Thank you, Heywood. That would be nice."

"Great. I will hold you to it. Now I will get right to the point. I am aligned with extraordinary investors whose returns, quite frankly, have been a lifesaver for me. Each year they add a few new clients, and only after they have thoroughly researched the candidates. Obviously, it is my job to invite you to participate. I hope that after you hear my description of this opportunity, you will consider it compelling."

Rod saw no nervousness or tells that indicated that the senator might be part of a scam, but he believed in the Reagan doctrine of "trust, but verify."

"The characteristics are as follows," Heywood continued. "One, we would like you to lend $30 million to the Franklin Corporation. Two, on the first of each month, $500,000 will be wired into your bank or brokerage account. Three, you will have a letter of credit from J. P. Morgan Bank that you can call at any time, and full repayment of your loan of $30 million will be wired to your account within twenty-four hours. Four, exercising the letter of credit will terminate the relationship. And five, disclosure to family, friends, or advisors about your relationship with us will result in the termination of the agreement and the return of your funds. It may seem extreme to have this privacy clause, but the managers are concerned that their proprietary strategies and methodologies could be compromised." The senator sat back and waited for a response.

Rod digested what sounded like the classic "free lunch."

"So I give someone I don't know $30 million, they pay me 20 percent guaranteed annually, and I have no risk as long as Morgan is solvent?" he asked with heavy skepticism.

"Actually, Rod, we would probably both know in advance in the unlikely event that J. P. Morgan would be unable to pay, and we would replace the letter of credit with one from a firm that we deemed to be a more stable institution."

"And these mysterious managers who have discovered the holy grail of investing want to invite me to their party for what reason?"

"It's not just because of your support of the Republican party. The managers feel that your instincts, business knowledge, and analytical skills could be quite valuable to them. They would hope that you would be agreeable to sharing these attributes on occasion—industry overviews, opinions on executive talent, prospective trends. Total time commitment would not be over one day a month and could be done by either audio or video conference, or in person, if you prefer."

The offer to visit in person added a measure of legitimacy. "Heywood, do you have a prospectus or a description of the types of investments that your gurus will make?"

"No, sir," replied the senator, who was considerably more business than charm at the moment. "The downside for a sophisticated investor like you is that your monies will be in a blind pool. However, the fact that the interest rate is extraordinary and that your loan is 100 percent callable may take some of the sting out of the investment uncertainty."

"You would know better than I, but isn't it similar to buying a corporate bond? In that instance, do you know how the corporation will invest the funds?"

Rod nodded and said, "It's somewhat similar, but at least I have an idea with the corporation. Your boys would need to have Morgan as their prime brokerage to induce them to guarantee the loan," he added, thinking out loud. "And a loan is more favorable from a tax perspective for them, but …"

He stopped in midsentence, stroked his chin, and waited a long moment. "That's a secondary benefit. The primary is that with a loan there's no K-1 partnership return required, and they never have to divulge whatever the hell they're doing."

Rod waited another few moments and then he said, "But why $30 million? Why not ten or fifty? Could I start with less money and add later?"

"I'm afraid that the amount offered is not negotiable," Heywood answered. "Research indicated that this amount was sufficient to get your interest and make it worthwhile for you to offer your insights when asked."

Rod looked at him appraisingly. It was disconcerting to think that some stranger could pinpoint an amount that would be a suitable investment for him. Still, it wouldn't have been hard to add up the publicly disclosed stock that he held on boards of which he was a member. That would be a good start. "Your research is accurate. What kind of information can you give me on the Franklin Corporation?"

"Again, none, and I'm afraid it would be difficult for you to find much information on your own. The principals are more secretive than the Swiss. If too much money is invested in their models, they become inefficient. Consequently, offers are extended to only a few individuals, some of whom know the others. If a client begins probing into their organization, they terminate the account and return the funds."

"So I really can't discuss this with my advisor?"

"Absolutely not, Rod. The offer would go away."

"But I would validate the authenticity of the letter of credit," Rod said, leaning toward the senator.

"Yes, sir. Here's the bank contact information and the bank chairman's information, but you may already know him," Heywood said, sliding a business card across the table.

Rod glanced at it and said, "I do," as he sat back.

"Also," the senator added, "you cannot withdraw any principal. Upon your death or loss of mental acuity, the corporation will repay your loan in full and terminate the relationship."

"Loss of mental acuity? Who determines when my IQ disintegrates to that of a Democrat?" asked Rod with a raised eyebrow.

"Only the courts, Rod, not us," said the senator with a laugh. "I'm at my time limit. I'll give you the loan documents. If you have further questions, my card has my cell phone and personal e-mail."

"I may call you with another question or two," Rod offered, "but it does sound damn interesting." The two men stood up and shook hands again.

The senator looked Rod in the eye. "We really would love to have you with us, Rod. Please let me know your decision as soon as possible."

"I will," said Rod, "and thank you for making the trip."

The senator smiled and said, "I can find my way out, and it was well worth the two hours from Washington to get to know you. You are a true American."

His parting comment was said with such sincerity that even Rod's finely tuned BS meter was silent. If he made the direct loan, he had no risk of loss or potential involvement if the operation was fraudulent. Thus, it really was a no-brainer. Nevertheless, he would have to concoct some feasible story for wiring $30 million from Mac. It was a close call, whether a guaranteed 20 percent per year return was worth the mountain of abuse he would get from his favorite financial wizard.

CHAPTER 9

GEORGE AND MILDRED GRANT'S son, David, was a former investment banker with Merrill Lynch. At the end of 2007, he retired and cashed in his chips. He subsequently opened an account with us, and with frightening foresight stayed liquid. Needless to say, he is our current market-timing hero.

"R. J.," I called over the glass separating our spaces. "Are we prepared for Mildred and David's meeting?" He raised one finger, took a minute to conclude his call, and then walked over to my desk.

"We have them scheduled for Friday at eleven o'clock. I thought we could order sandwiches from the Bread Line. By the way, Artie has reviewed the trust documents, and since David is the executor of his father's estate, I think that it would be good for them to meet."

"I agree. Anything complicated or out of order?"

"Not according to Rabbi Cohen."

"Did DeMarco get back to you about any residual benefits from George's former company? I think he may still have been a board member."

Danny DeMarco, who is often referred to as Danny Demento, is our least politically correct partner. It is a victory that was hard won, and he wears it like a badge of honor. At five feet nine, with a body type that could be affectionately described as moderately chubby, he is a mischievous moving target. His fine, blond hair starts at his ear line, rises only two inches north, and frames crinkly, constantly moving light blue eyes, an infectious grin, and a constant stream of one-liners.

"No," R. J. answered. "He did not get back to us. Can we fire him?" R. J. was a frequent target of the DeMarco humor.

"Call him on his cell and put him on speaker."

My lines had calls, so R. J. called from his line.

Danny picked up immediately. "Is Mac there with you?"

"Yes," answered R. J., looking at me strangely.

"Wait for it, wait for it … ahhh." The flushing sound left no doubt as to his location.

"Thanks for sharing. The whole office now knows the benefits of speakerphones," I admonished. "On to other matters that do not make me cringe. Did you get info on George Grant's former company?"

"Yes. The PR lady was quite helpful. George left the board last year. No pensions or health insurance, but there was a $50 million key man life insurance policy that the company paid and was portable. George took it, but they don't know if he kept paying or not."

R. J. and I exchanged concerned glances. When David Grant called and briefed us on the meeting, there was no mention of the insurance policy—not a detail he would normally overlook.

"Are you sure it was $50 million?" I asked.

"Yep. I double checked. Two people at his old company confirmed it."

It was puzzling, but I hoped David would be able to give us clarity.

"Okay. Thanks. Please wash your hands."

*　　　*　　　*　　　*　　　*

Nowadays, our clients are met at the fifth-floor reception desk and escorted up a flight of stairs. Normally, a more junior member would have greeted Mildred and David Grant, but Lena Brady volunteered for this because she wanted to personally express her sympathies before the meeting.

In order to give us more room to spread out, Lena brought them into the large conference room that is also in our space. In contrast to the coziness of my personal conference room, this room is more typical of a brokerage firm, complete with a large rectangular table and identical black-leather swivel chairs surrounding it. Matching wooden serving tables make this the preferred location whenever we're having lunch.

Mildred looked a little smaller, or it might have been just my imagination, but her eyes glistened when she saw me. Her smile was warm but resolute. It wasn't just George's death; it was the circumstances. When I thought about the cowardly hit-and-run driver, bile came to my throat, but this wasn't the time.

"Mildred," I said, as I opened my arms and embraced her. I held her until the soft, muffled sobs subsided. I held her hand for a few moments and then stepped back and moved to hug David.

R. J. had held back at a respectful distance, but he moved forward and hugged Mildred when she looked up at him and smiled. Two of his best traits are his empathy and his genuine concern for others. R. J. shook hands with David, and I motioned for everyone to take a seat.

"Mildred, I really appreciate your coming in to see us today, and I promise that we'll make this relatively painless. I sort of feel like George is watching us now, and if it gets tedious, he will find a way to berate me."

David smiled and nodded as Mildred said, "He always hated to be left out, and he loved how you teased him, so I'm sure he's here."

"I'm not sure who teased who the most," I replied gently.

"I know that I couldn't keep up with him," David added.

"Well, if he were here," Mildred said with surprising conviction, "he would say, 'Let's first figure out what we're having for lunch and then get down to business.'"

Her George imitation made us all laugh and relax. It reinforced the fact that behind her super-successful husband was a remarkable woman. And when I'm given marching orders from a remarkable woman, I comply.

After we ordered lunch, Lena joined us to go over the required estate paperwork with David. The process for retitling assets and accounts can be daunting, but Lena has considerable experience, and her charm makes the process much more tolerable.

With impeccable timing, Artie J. Cohen poked his head into the room, and I introduced him to both Grants. While Mildred was signing new account forms, Artie caucused with David for a few minutes, and they agreed that everything was in order for a smooth transition.

Lunch was delivered soon after Lena and Artie went back into the main office. As I would expect, Mildred assured us that she would not be making any precipitous moves with any of their homes. They had planned a family vacation after Christmas, and that would not change either. Fortunately, their family was extremely close, and Mildred had almost too many friends to count.

When my dad died, I learned from my mom that staying busy does not eliminate the terrible emptiness, but it can make it more bearable. Lunch conversation was not business oriented and included sharing our favorite George stories.

After the lunch dishes were cleared, R. J. asked David about George's key man life insurance policy.

As we had anticipated, David went to his insurance file and pulled out the perfectly organized information. He read from his notes. "Dad's company purchased a universal life policy at age seventy-four for a $50 million death benefit. It was targeted for a zero cash value at age eighty-five. Dad's notes indicated that this strategy reduced the premiums."

David looked up. "I would just give you the file to read, but it has taken me years to decipher Dad's hieroglyphics," he said apologetically.

"This works for us," I replied. "Go ahead."

"Dad was proud of the fact that he was preferred, nonsmoker, because Mom had chided him for being pleasingly plump."

Mildred smiled lovingly, her eyes full of memories.

"The company paid annual premiums of $1,416,339 until Dad sold the company and retired. Shortly after he sold the company, Dad had his heart attack. As you know, it was a mild attack, and he became a seventy-seven-year-old gym rat. After passing a rigorous physical with flying colors, he decided that he didn't want to keep paying the premiums."

David looked up again. "He writes that Mac and R. J. have made sure that the family and charity will be in great shape, so it didn't make sense for him to keep paying the premiums. He told his insurance agent to find a buyer for the policy, as the cash value was only $1,455,026. You'll note that there was no rounding with my father. At age eight, he gave me my first wallet, and engraved inside was 'Be precise.'" David smiled at the memory.

David continued, "The insurance agent ended up selling the policy for $15 million to the Washington Group. I Googled them, but I couldn't find anything. His notes say that they were the highest bidders.

"Because he loved a challenge, Dad managed to find out that his new life expectancy was six to eight years." David looked at me and smiled. "Mac, it's almost like he knew that I would be reading this to you. Listen to this. 'I do hereby intend to kick the insurance company's ass, but on the off chance that I don't, Mac, it's your job to turn fifteen into fifty.'"

I smiled and wiped away a persistent tear with the back of my hand. "Hopefully, he did not include a time frame."

"He gave you a break. That's it," David finished.

I wasn't going to discuss it now, but I did know enough about the practice to be dangerous. Since the buyers kept the cash value, George's policy cost them $13,500,000. Most companies would convert to a minimum-level premium to age one hundred. I estimated that their costs for the annual premiums would be between $2 million and $2.5 million.

According to my off-the-cuff evaluation, by George's dying after only two years, an $18 million investment turned into $50 million. For the investor, it doesn't get any better than that.

It smelled funny. "Thanks, David," I said. "That was really helpful. Mildred, do you have any questions for us, or is there anything you want us to do for you?"

Mildred looked at each of us as if she were trying to remember something. Her faint smile seemed to hide the sadness that she wore like an invisible cloak. I felt myself tense as I leaned forward.

"There is one more thing, gentlemen," she said. "If you could pass me one more piece of Grace's homemade peanut brittle, we will get out of your hair."

The lightness of her tone was like a soothing balm. "And Mac, please," she added," I would love it if you and Grace would join me for dinner one night at the beach. Please thank her for the peanut brittle and her sweet note, and give her a George-size hug for me."

This brave woman gave me a smile that would melt an iceberg. R. J. and I both teared up with her, and only David saved us from the faucets going full blast. As we hugged her good-bye, David said, "I hate for Mom to eat alone," as he eyed the peanut brittle.

*   *   *   *   *

Throughout the day, when my mind wandered from my work, I tried to think of ways to reconcile the troubling aspects of George Grant's death. With limited investigative skills and no access, my best option became Larry Pusey.

In his off-duty hours, Larry is a city councilman. Both he and his wife, Jean, are retired elementary schoolteachers. Also, they are long-time residents of Bethany Beach, Delaware, and very involved in church and civic affairs.

Without question, everybody in the ocean-side resort town knows Larry Pusey.

At sixty-five, Larry insists that he has the body of an eighteen-year-old. A receding silver buzz cut frames a weathered face accented by a too-often broken nose and blue-gray eyes always seeming to crinkle with the joy of life. It is hard to dispute his claim of six-pack abs because he works out excessively, a prerequisite for his "job." When you have a four handicap, you are probably working more than a forty-hour week on your chosen retirement vocation.

For the past twenty years, Larry and I have been close friends. He may not qualify as one of my high–net worth clients, but he is definitely one of my high-quality clients.

I didn't know if Larry's job that day was a four-hour stint in the morning or the afternoon, so I decided to call him from the car on my way home.

"Larry ..."

"Mac Attack!" he interrupted excitedly.

"Larry." I had to stop him before he started. "Sorry, but I'm running and gunning—no golf, no joke. I need your help."

"Okay," said Larry.

"My friend George Grant was recently killed in a hit-and-run accident."

"I know," he interrupted again. "Jean and I were at his funeral. Great guy."

I should have figured that out. "I'm sorry, pal. I didn't see you there."

"We saw you, but we didn't come over because you were with the family. But we loved what you said. You made us cry."

I blinked. "Me, too. Anyway, I'm guessing you know the chief of police."

"Sure."

"Do you think it would be possible for you to take a look at the accident report?" I asked.

"Remember, this is lower, slower Delaware. Anything is possible," he responded.

"Great, and maybe you could even visit the scene of the accident if that wouldn't be too much trouble."

"Sure. What are you looking for?"

"Theories. Something to explain what feels unexplainable. I know that there's no logical explanation, but any impressions or hunches you might have … you're a fiction junkie like me, so maybe you'll figure something out."

"I'll give it my best shot, Mac. I'll get back to you."

"Great. Thanks again, Larry."

"Uh, Mac, one more thing." After a moment of silence he asked, "Are we all right?"

I paused. This was not a year for flippancy. "You or the country?" I asked.

"Both."

"You guys are in good shape. No matter what, your lifestyle is protected." I paused again. "My gut and history tell me the country will be fine, but we're in desperate need of a logical plan."

"Like what?"

"First, the Fed has to pump money into the financial system. Big banks and life insurance companies need to stay working. Second, you round up all the senators and Congress folks who put their agenda ahead of the country's and put them in a time-out. The few remaining may actually help. Finally, put some of the clowns who are on the firing line in the financial industry in a room with the head of the SEC. When the bombs are going off around you every day, even a knucklehead like me can figure out where you really need change." I took a breath as I finished.

"I'm ready!" shouted Larry excitedly. "You've gotta run, Mac. I can guarantee you Delaware's vote."

I laughed and stepped off of my soap box. "Sorry. I hang out with too many unsavory characters."

CHAPTER 10

ROD STANTON'S ENERGIZER BUNNY assistant, Liz Granger, picked up my call on the first ring. "Liz, the offer still stands. I'll pay you twice what he pays you to come to DC and work with me."

She laughed, "You're like the relentless suitor."

"You know that if I weren't married, a ring would go along with that deal."

"Well, my husband sometimes does threaten to trade me in."

"Now we've ventured into the twilight zone. I would never buy that."

"You're probably right," she conceded, "but I could never leave Rod. He needs me."

"I heard that. I'm returning his call. Is he available?"

"For you? Always."

"Hey pal, what's going on?" An opening comment from Rod that did not include an insult always made me suspicious.

"Nothing new. I just continue to wallow in self-pity."

"Listen, I called because I need you to wire some money," said Rod, abruptly getting down to business.

Not a good sign—this was usually done by e-mail.

"Please reread our contract. Money can only come *into* the account." I tried again to lighten the tone.

"It will, every month—a nice check."

"How much do you need?"

"Thirty mil."

"Are you kidding me?"

"Nope."

"What the hell for?"

I heard him take a breath and reply robotically. "It's a fully collateralized demand loan that's for an excellent purpose and pays an acceptable rate."

"Demand? So you could get your money back at any time?"

"Yes, but it would have to be an extraordinary circumstance because there is no ability to re-up."

I mulled it over. "This sounds strange. What's the purpose of the loan, and what's the rate? I assume that you and your forensic CPA have confirmed its creditworthiness."

"We did. The rate is exceptional, and the purpose of the loan is partially connected to national security, so I can't really give you details."

I gave a sarcastic laugh. Rod was being way too vague. "It would be more fun if this were a video conference so I could see your eyes shift guiltily aside with that last assertion," I said tauntingly.

"You don't believe me?" Rod spoke with a slight bit of indignation, solidifying my hunch that his reason was bogus.

"This 'I can't tell you because of national security' crap is too reminiscent of 'I did not have sex with that woman,'" I replied with an edge.

He was quiet. Because we had been friends for so long, our conversations were often in the no-holds-barred category. The awkwardness of the moment was palpable.

"So, do I get the feeling that I'm being a bit stonewalled for the first time in our relationship?" I asked seriously, not backing off.

The question hung out there. He knew that I wouldn't say anything more.

He finally broke the silence. "Mac, I promise that it will be okay, and I'm sorry that I can't be more transparent with this."

I was not happy, and I hoped that my silence would increase his feelings of guilt. I don't like feeling excluded. "Okay. We'll send the wire," I said with resignation. "But Rod, my scam senses are off the chart. This sounds like the classic free lunch. Be careful, man."

He sighed. "Always, pal, plus I know you've got my back. Thanks again."

His reassurance did nothing to calm the sinking feeling in the pit of my stomach.

*   *   *   *   *

Steve Mosberg was an arbitrageur. When he entered the brokerage business in the late seventies, the term was spoken with reverence. These were the people who had the sole discretion to invest a portion of the firm's capital for the purpose of making short-term gains. In today's market, technological advances have marginalized the profitability and the necessary skill set required of the arbitrageur. Now algorithms, computers faster than the speed of light, and MIT grads not old enough to shave rule this world.

Seeing the proverbial handwriting on the wall, Mosberg had taken a two-year sabbatical in 2002. In less than a week of not working, he was bored to tears, so he started a hedge fund. He had neither the patience nor the temperament to market it to outside investors; consequently, it was a small but efficient vehicle.

Mosberg was five feet six inches tall with tight, curly, still-black hair; a swarthy complexion; and an addiction to Diet Coke and pizza. Born and bred in New York City, he was blessed with great market instincts. Most important for my purpose, he had ears everywhere on the street. If anybody could get a read on Jeremy Lyons, it was Steve Mosberg.

"Big." The strange nickname that Mosberg assigned to me coincided with my initial ranking in *Barron's* magazine. Since then, he never used my given name.

"Got a minute?" It is important to talk in bullet points to a man who has phones in both ears.

"Always."

"Jeremy Lyons?"

"Two weeks ago, heard the name."

"Really?" It sounded promising. "Do you know where I can find him?"

"Hold."

Terrific. One of the downsides of talking in monosyllables to Mosberg during market hours is that he is constantly executing orders to buy or sell stock. And money trumps friendship. I understood perfectly.

Mosberg's voice came again. "Sorry, no. Big trade. Short side, stock options, credit defaults—whole nine yards. Right as rain. Wish I'd piggybacked."

"You're sure it was Jeremy Lyons?" Fortunately, I could understand his verbal shorthand.

"Nope. That's the word. No first name, just 'that fucking Lyons.' Maybe an urban legend."

I winced. "Did you hear it from one source or multiple?"

"Hold."

It must be nice to be that busy, and he calls *me* "Big." At least the hold music was sixties soul.

"Heard it before—multiples," he said, coming back on the line. "When it's a pure trade and the usual scumbags are not involved."

Feeling like a timer would go off on my questions, I pulled another one out of the air. "When you were running money, did you ever hear of any other man of mystery?"

"Nope. Just this guy."

"And no one has ever found out where his base of operation is?"

Silence. I thought it might be a precursor for the hold button. "About seven years ago, a guy was fired from Tucker. Wanted to follow the smoke and try to join Lyons."

"What happened?"

"Disappeared."

I mulled this over. "Do you remember his name?"

"Yeah. Sal Seminara." I heard someone call him in the background. "Big, gotta go. Call me later on the cell if you need me."

Sure that I was being overly cautious, I had asked R. J. to e-mail Sam Golden from his personal computer. It was a long shot, but I wanted to know if Sam could track down this Sal Seminara. Although I would deny it under oath, I had to admit that, so far, Grace had been right. My cloak-and-dagger snooping had been an interesting distraction. The fact that I had only moved forward a few baby steps just increased the challenge.

CHAPTER 11

COMING IN THROUGH THE garage, I opened the door to my house. Immediately there was a face in my crotch. Grace is good but not that good. It was Harry, my older son's golden retriever puppy. We were dog-sitting while he and his wife were away on a long, romantic weekend. Grace was already laughing as I opined, "Jamie hasn't been married long enough that he should have to train his dog to do that."

As anticipated, this did nothing to stop her mirth. "I think that Jamie wanted to give you something to get your mind off the market," she giggled.

"You're my antidote for the market," I said, grabbing Grace in a bear hug and expertly cock-blocking Harry at the same time. We smooched as I looked into the blue eyes that have hypnotized me for over thirty years. "Now keep this horny dog away from me while I change my clothes."

"Come here, Harry," she said sweetly, and like any male would, he docilely followed orders.

After dinner, with Harry banished to his bed in the basement, I turned to Grace. "I need some help, O Fount of All Knowledge."

Grace gave me a slight eyebrow raise and nodded approvingly that I was finally getting it.

"With the ultimate carrot of forbidden pleasures, you coerced me into this wild goose chase for Jeremy Lyons."

She nodded, as if agreeing with my assessment of her power, so I continued. "In addition to Sam's A team, I have a few people I know beating the streets for me. But I need to expand the search. Who else might be able to shed some light on our hero's whereabouts?"

She looked at me liked she used to look at our kids when they got a good report card. "Mac, it sounds like you've really gotten into this," she said innocently.

My responding glare fell as harmlessly as a gumdrop thrown against bulletproof glass.

"Let me think a minute," she added, still smiling.

Selfishly, I did not expect Grace to add anything. However, in the event that I couldn't track Lyons down, I did want an accomplice to share the blame. In fact, I had already practiced the "Well, you made me do it and you were no help" speech.

I watched with affection as she wiggled her cute little nose and squeezed her eyes shut in concentration. "Ron Judkins," she announced triumphantly.

My initial instinct was to dismiss her idea—not because the idea didn't have merit but because her tone was annoying. Nevertheless, it's my responsibility to preserve domestic tranquility. In addition, in the past, the majority of her ideas have tended to pan out. Thus, I nodded wisely.

She continued. "Pam always called him Tonto, and she called Lyons the Lone Stranger."

"Pam?"

"Judkins's wife—well, ex-wife now. I can probably get his number if you want."

Surrendering with dignity, I replied, "That would be wonderful, my sweet. What would I do without you?"

*   *   *   *   *

It is counter to my DNA to accept the possibility that being distracted can be a good thing. My aversion to this concept is due to the fact that I am a broken record when it comes to advocating focus. Also contributing to my certainty is that I believe that multitasking is alive and well in the McGregor household. For example, I can watch television, read a book, and at the same time sagaciously respond to my wife's queries. Ergo, I am not easily distracted.

Still, the previous night, I had allowed myself to be distracted from both business and my "Where's Waldo?" mission. As a result, my decision to be completely distracted by my beloved proved to be not only enjoyable but also therapeutic.

Consequently, there was no death grip on the steering wheel or face furrowed in worry the next morning as I maneuvered down Canal Road to my home away from home.

My window was open as I embraced the crisp, early morning air. When traffic slowed or stopped, I searched the towpaths of the canal for brave joggers. Even the bare tree branches seemed to be waving good morning. Simon and Garfunkle's "Bridge Over Troubled Water" was cranked up, and I'm sure that the duo appreciated my robust sing-along. Ah, sex. Man's pacifier as well as his sleeping pill.

In spite of Grace's assurance, Ron Judkins's telephone number was not easily obtained. Advisors often leave one firm for another. In fact, some nomads make a career of moving. Like the similar hollow denial of a spouse leaving because he or she has found someone else, the ulterior motive with advisors, in spite of what they say, is invariably money.

Do not expect that to be accurately conveyed to clients. There is a parallel in the world of free agency in sports. Not that it made him a bad guy, but Ron Judkins was a brokerage harlot.

When he came on the line, I said, "Ron, this is a voice from your past, Mac McGregor."

"Are you shitting me? I get a call from the famous Mac McGregor. Be still, my heart."

"I note that time has not mellowed your sarcasm. Do you have a minute?"

"All day for the top broker in DC. What can I do for you?"

"I'm having some fun writing a novel, and a character that I want to portray is based on Jeremy Lyons." R. J. and I had previously concluded that this would be reasonable cover for our nosing around. If anyone we spoke to communicated with Jeremy, they would be less likely to discuss our curiosity.

"In that case, I know who the serial killer is. I can give you some good shit, but if it comes back to me, you've gotta get me into the witness protection program."

I laughed. "Was he really that bad?"

"Dude, outside of his staff, I was the only one he ever spoke to. You probably heard about the knuckle push-ups he did in the nude and his doo-flicky hitting the floor."

"Yes," I replied, grimacing, not really requiring an instant replay.

"True story—not an urban myth. I had to squeeze my eyes shut. The only reason he tolerated me was that I was no threat and would do whatever he asked, and because he really wanted to bang my secretary. Do you remember Margo Savino?"

"I was married, so I have no recollection of a dirty blonde, five-foot-two, about 110 pounds, killer body, full lips, wearing no bra."

Ron gave a wry chuckle. "I'm surprised you never noticed her. Anyway, you're right. She was hot, and she just ignored Jeremy, which drove him batshit. Oh, let me tell you about my strangest conversation with this psycho. By the way, he was such a friggin' neatnik that I would have sworn he was a fag. Oops. It's *gay*, now. How could that dude have been gay and not made a pass at me?"

I laughed again, remembering that Judkins's strength was neither focus nor continuity. He could change from topic to topic like a Mexican jumping bean; nevertheless, he was always entertaining.

"Meanwhile, back at the ranch, just the two of us are having drinks at a bar. I'm sneaking up on wasted, but, of course, the robot is still in full control. He looks around to make sure that no one is listening and says to me, and believe me, he's serious as a heart attack, 'I will own this city.' Then he looks right in my eyes like he's trying to sell me something and says, 'If I fulfill your every financial desire, and if it became necessary, would you take a bullet for me?' No bullshit, Mac; it sounded like an offer from Satan himself."

The train was close to being off the track, so I interrupted. "What did you say to him?"

"I looked at him like he was from Mars and said, 'Fuck, no.' Can you believe that was the last word the son of a bitch ever said to me? He looked at me, paid for the drinks, and left."

I believe that the self-preservation instinct in nonwarriors when things start to get scary is to raise their hand and shout, "Check, please!" Suppressing that urge, I persevered. "And no one has heard from him since?" I asked. "Do you think that Jeremy is the type to try and change his identity, change his name or appearance?"

"No way, Jose. He loved his name, King of the World, and all that shit, and he loved to look and flex in the mirror."

"Would he live outside the US?"

"Not in this lifetime. The son of a bitch was a hermit and hated travel."

"Whatever happened to Margo?" I asked without a bit of prurient interest.

"She fell off the map for over twenty years and then just called me about a year ago."

"When did she leave?"

"Let me think. Hmm. I guess about a month after Jeremy bolted. Said she had a better offer but wouldn't say with who or where. Then she calls me from Sarasota, Florida, opens an account, sends me half a million, but says she only wants hot IPOs."

"Doesn't she know that the last hot initial public offering was almost a decade ago?"

"Yes, if she's been paying attention. We had a cordial conversation, but her zip was definitely gone. She seemed burned out. She's not a dumb blonde. She's real risk averse, and she's patient. She's been in short-term CDs, just waiting."

"Do you have a number for her? I'm sure she could add some color. I would like to know some of Jeremy's lame pick-up lines."

"Sure. I'll e-mail you her contact info. But" he gave a dramatic pause, "I do want a quid pro quo for all my help."

I winced. I had almost been home free. "What can I do for you, Ron?" I asked, trying to figure out where this might be going.

"I want to be in your book. You can just use my initials so that I know it's me. Make sure that I have an impossibly large dick."

"Done," I chuckled. "It's a good thing it's fiction. Thanks for your help."

*　　　*　　　*　　　*　　　*

I wanted to at least log a call in to Margo Savino before I left for the day. I was surprised when she answered on the third ring. "Margo, you may not remember me, but it's Mac McGregor."

"I remember," came the monotone reply.

"Did I catch you at a bad time?"

"It depends. What do you want?" Her tone left no opening for pleasantries.

"Actually, I have a rather odd request. I'm writing a novel, and I want to base one of the characters on Jeremy Lyons. Ron Judkins told me that you knew him better than anyone else and that you might be able to help me with some background or characterization."

Total silence. It went on so long that I wasn't sure if we were still connected.

Finally, she responded. "Are you still a big-shot broker?"

"Only in my wife's eyes." Another very pregnant pause.

"Meet me at the Ritz Beach Club in Sarasota on January twenty-third at noon. If you're there, I'll give you plenty of information. If you're not, don't call me again."

CHAPTER 12

IT WAS AFTER FIVE, the phones were mercifully silent, and R. J. and I were in my conference room calling Sam Golden. I partially adhered to Sam's cautioning by using R. J.'s cell when we called his office.

Sounding somewhat agitated, he said, "What's up?"

"I need to know how far you want me to take this."

"All the way."

I sighed. "That's exactly the precise instruction I was seeking …"

"Sorry," he interrupted.

"Hey, if you're too busy for a report or to help me make a decision, I'll just go back to my *real* job." My retort had a little more sting than I intended, but in a safe environment we tend to lash out, particularly when we're in a state of frustration to begin with.

"Mac, I really am sorry."

Enough flagellation. "First, did you find anything out about Sal Seminara?"

Uncomfortable silence. "Yeah, Mac. He turned up in Georgia."

"Did you interview him?"

He paused. "No. He drowned a couple of years ago."

I felt a shiver. R. J.'s eyes widened. "Circumstances?" I asked.

He hesitated again. "Accidental drowning."

"In a bathtub? On a toilet? Under a sprinkler? How the hell did he drown?"

"Sorry." I could feel his grimace over the phone. "In the ocean."

I closed my eyes, absorbing the information. I processed it and tabled it for another time. "A woman in Sarasota, Florida, who used to work for our firm and knew Lyons well indicated that I should go to Florida to see her."

"Great! We'll pay. Stay at the Ritz. Take R. J. with you." Sam sounded relieved with the subject change.

"I'm not concerned about the money, but she may have nothing." I looked at R. J. as if the second part of his statement had just hit me. "Why should I take R. J. with me?"

"You are ill-equipped to travel alone. Grace or R. J., take your pick," he answered matter-of-factly.

Although most men would be annoyed at this slap at their capabilities, I am at all times a realist. I assert that my lack of logistical competency is attributable to the fact that my mind is too busy trying to solve the problems of the world. Unfortunately, no one who knows me has bought into that theory.

What was annoying me was the fact that R. J. was nodding at the phone as if Sam had actually said something profound. I also sensed that Sam's conscience was bothering him because we had advanced far beyond routine queries in our search for the elusive hedge fund manager. Sending me for a few days to a sandy beach might make him feel less guilty.

"Okay," I said, relieving the tension, "but only if you bill the DNC for this boondoggle."

*   *   *   *   *

Most red-blooded, sports-crazy guys believe that working in a sports agency is better than working in a brothel. Consequently, numerous clients over the years have asked us whether we might be able to provide an introduction for their sons.

It's a delicate situation because I don't want to take advantage of my relationships in the industry and because I know that the job sucks. It is probably easier to make it in the NFL or the NBA than to become a force in the agency business.

In spite of the warning signs that I give the parents and the children, it's hard to burst the dream of courtside seats or standing next to the newest Michael Jordan wannabe as he signs a gazillion-dollar contract. Those who do matriculate to the industry soon get tired of being glorified gophers with no access to the fame and fortune they envisioned.

From the perspective of financial advisors, managing assets for athletes also seems like the pot of gold at the end of the rainbow. Entry into this segment of the population is extremely rare, partly because of the scarcity of top agents and partly because of the past incompetence and lack of integrity of a few advisors.

Our access into the world of professional athletes came courtesy of Paul Parker, perhaps the original sports agent. At our first meeting, I determined that he was the most full-of-shit person I had ever met. Consequently, we were destined to work together. Admittedly, this may not have been a case where opposites attract.

At six feet two, and hovering around 220 on the scale, Parker's attractive face was framed by pistol-grip ears. A sartorial abomination, complete with a seventies vintage blue blazer, a striped shirt cleverly unmatched with a striped tie, and gray pants that actually had a hole worn through on the right leg, his style somehow seemed to work for him. In his youth, he had been a great athlete, but his energy, intellect, and off-the-charts self-esteem made him a charismatic leader. Most important, he could be trusted.

After he became a disciple, having him recommend us to athletes readily became his idea. My picture and bio were soon featured in his company's brochure, and as long as I was out of earshot, he would strongly endorse us. So, not only were we able to work with some outstanding young male and female athletes, but we also got to scam some primo seats to sporting events.

Just as I was leaving the office, I got a call from Parker. "Tell him to stay

off the phone for three minutes and I'll call him from the car," I told the associate who had answered my phone.

As I got in my car, I hit the speed dial for Paul Parker. Very few clients make my speed dial, but Parker was the only guy that I could whip in golf, so I needed him for my self-esteem. Uncharacteristically, he answered his own phone.

"Why am I still at work and you are sashaying your way home?" he inquired, seeking pain.

"Because I am infinitely more efficient than you, exponentially smarter, and because it is ten o'clock before you drag your dead ass into work."

"Yeah, yeah. Well I'm embarrassed to admit that I actually need you to help figure something out."

"News flash," I said with resignation. As bright as this man was with his business, both R. J. and I had explained the same elementary stock market strategies to him until we were blue in the face.

As expected, he ignored my shot. "I called Lenny Cramer as you suggested, and we had dinner when I was in California."

Lenny Cramer had been the chairman and CEO of Bay Savings & Loan. A victim of a plethora of subprime loans, the company filed for bankruptcy a few months ago. I had suggested that Parker get together with him because they were friends. In addition, the filings indicated that Cramer still had a huge stock holding in Bay Savings, which was now worthless. With the public outrage over the excesses of greed, the odds of Cramer receiving any golden parachute were negligible.

"I waited until he was on his fourth Macallan and water before asking him whether he would be all right financially," Parker went on. "He slurred a reply and said that they thought they had beaten him, but he had an insurance policy, one those assholes would never find. Then he looked at me smugly and said, 'I can live real well on five mil a year for the rest of my life.'"

"Even to a market scholar like me, that didn't make much sense, so I told him so—nicely, of course," Parker added.

"Nicely?"

"Okay, I told him he was full of crap. Anyway, he became indignant and almost shouted. Did I think that he would have all of his money in his piece-of-shit company? Did I think he was an idiot? Actually, I did think he was an idiot, Mac. Even you could have helped this putz."

I shook my head. True love is often disguised. I think the clown was actually trying to give me a compliment.

"Thanks for the vote of confidence. He probably just has a tax-free bond portfolio," I replied.

"Not unless it pays 20 percent," Parker said triumphantly.

This caused but a moment's pause. "There is no vehicle that pays a consistent 20 percent annual return," I replied confidently.

"I know the man was either drunk or close to it, but he swore that he had been making 20 percent a year for five years, including this year. Then he turned white, looked around furtively, and swore me to secrecy. He said he might lose it all if I told anybody."

"And now you're telling me. The vault has sprung a leak?"

"Nah. You know that I'm good for a secret, but it was not a valid contract. He had already told me. No consideration."

For some strange reason, I thought of the Shakespeare quote, "First kill all the lawyers."

"Besides," he continued, "if I hadn't promised not to say anything, the poor sucker would have had a heart attack. Maybe there is something that my brilliant financial wizard doesn't know?" I could feel the smirk over the phone.

"Paul, although I don't know every financial strategy available, I do know that the only guy who could give you a consistent 20 percent return was Charles Ponzi."

"You mean like a Ponzi scheme?"

"Your financial erudition amazes me. Yes, a Ponzi scheme. I do understand why you brought it to my attention. If it were true, it would indeed be the answer to the investor's prayer."

"Okay, check it out, and when you find out that I'm right, I want in. Plus, I will expect an eloquent apology from you."

CHAPTER 13

JEREMY AND MAX WERE in the smallest of Jeremy's three viewing rooms. Jeremy's taste in old movies had motivated him to create access only through hidden panels in an elaborate bookcase in his personal office. Unlike secret rooms in films, where you could open a passageway just by pushing a wall or moving a book, entry into this space required fingerprint and retina scans. The only individuals who had access to the room were already in it.

Small was a relative term, since the room measured twenty feet by sixteen feet, larger than most home theater rooms. There were no windows or visible doors, and, out of necessity, the room was soundproof. It was often used for interrogation.

Jeremy and Max were sitting in two black leather chairs and watching a surveillance tape from Lenny Cramer's home. Both were silent as they watched Lenny walk into his house. He was white as a sheet, sweating, and looking all around.

A rather mousy man with thin, reddish hair, and a pale face covered with pockmarks signifying an unsuccessful battle with acne, Lenny hid his insecurities in impeccable suits and glibness. However, nothing was hidden in his current demeanor. He looked frantic and afraid for his life.

"What's wrong?" his equally mousy and equally unappealing wife asked.

"Nothing, nothing," he said nervously. "Let's go to bed. I don't want to talk."

Lenny appeared to be on the verge of tears and seemed a heartbeat away from a total breakdown. His wife silently put her arms around him and helped him into the bedroom.

Max turned off the video, pointed to the screen, and said, "That's it."

"Where had he been?"

"Out to dinner with Paul Parker, who's an old friend. Parker's a big-time sports agent," added Max.

"Did we have ears in the restaurant?"

"No. He left his house apparently in good shape. No indications of possible leakage."

Jeremy cradled his chin in his left hand with his left index finger extended. "So there could be many factors outside of our interests that could have caused his condition. Parker could have called him a crook for mismanaging the S&L." He paused. "Does Parker have connections with any regulators?"

"None, unless they're jock sniffers. Curiously, the only connection is that he works with Mac McGregor."

Jeremy looked at Max with an annoyed expression. "McGregor does get around in the baby pool," he said thoughtfully. "Tap Parker's lines for a few weeks."

"Should I make a house call on Cramer?" asked Max with a touch of eagerness.

"Please, Max, the man did make us a few hundred million dollars," Jeremy said with feigned indignation. He looked at Max and shook his head as if he were truly disappointed. "Wait the two weeks."

*   *   *   *   *

Jeremy's pleasures were well contained in his building. First-run movies, vintage wine, exotic foods—all were brought to him. His gym rivaled any other in the world. He felt that outside sports such as golf were insipid, and the idea that he might have to wait on someone was laughable. Only one game mattered: amassing what others might consider obscene amounts of money.

Most hedge fund managers have limited resources to achieve superior returns. For short periods of time, it appeared as if some people had discovered the key to the mint, and their astronomical returns became the envy of the industry and any institutions or billionaires that were not using them.

Each new "black box" genius is flooded with money and then eventually self-destructs. Regardless of how sophisticated their models, hedging systems, or proprietary strategies are, it is just a matter of time.

To escape the inevitable fate of lesser hedge fund managers, Jeremy preferred to stack the deck. He hated notoriety, not because he was a recluse but because in his world, one could not be both rich and famous. His picture on the cover of *Forbes* magazine would have been a death sentence.

Most hedge fund managers covet the Harvard and Yale endowments of the world. Fame, yes, but also scrutiny. That allows you no chance to run deep under the radar. On the contrary, the only accounts that Jeremy would accept were well-connected individuals with public companies. Here, lack of exposure was minimized by greed and fear—two very predictable emotions.

Fortunately for his business model, Jeremy was not constrained by ethics, legality, or conscience. The extent of the collateral damage was never part of his analysis, only how much could he make and the possibility that he could be caught.

Added to this disciplined, emotionless logic was what he liked to call his "secret sauce." Like all truly innovative financial strategies, duplication or exposure could render it useless.

Although a true academian might appreciate the simple brilliance of his strategy, the world would be too quick to label it barbaric or heinous.

*　　　*　　　*　　　*　　　*

Richard Hwang and Milton Peterman were lovers. To Jeremy, that simply meant that they were easier to control. An unlikely security breach by one would result in the certain torture of the other, a useful deterrent. They had graduated from MIT summa cum laude in successive years.

Contrary to what the advertisements say, it is the skill of the trader, not the technology, that determines ultimate gain. Milton and Richard, under Jeremy Lyons's intense scrutiny, had assembled four additional gifted, yet disciplined, traders. Nevertheless, the equipment on their trading floor was always state of the art.

Although traders did not have a forced tenure with Jeremy, their burnout tended to occur between seven and ten years. While they were in his employ, Jeremy maintained audio and video records of each one whenever they were involved in illegal trades or acts. After their departure, the threat of exposure, a generous pension, and the possibility of extinction ensured their continued silence.

Until two years earlier, Jeremy had resisted having a female trader on his team. His initial reservation about female traders was that they could be a possible distraction. On his trading floor, there was no banter. Meals were power bars, Diet Cokes, Red Bull, coffee, and, for the purists, bottled water. Bathroom breaks were accomplished with record speed.

Jeremy's first female trader, Alegria Lopez, had immigrated to the United States from Cuba as a child. Recognized early as a linguist and a math prodigy, she had a full scholarship to any university in the United States or abroad.

She chose Rollins College in Winter Park, Florida, which did have a stellar record for academic excellence but was certainly less recognized than the most ardent of her educational suitors. When she chose to complete her graduate work at Rollins, too, the Ivy League schools that continued to pursue her became even more frustrated.

Two years prior, a newspaper article extolling her unique intellectual gifts had intrigued Jeremy. He waited for an opportune time to contact her. On a hunch, he had Milton, who had no experience in sales or recruiting, approach Alegria.

Jeremy knew that the CIA would be making a full-court press to recruit Ms. Lopez. Her mastery of both Chinese and Arabic would have been sufficient to have the agency salivating. The addition of her math and computer skills would have pushed them over the edge.

From Jeremy's perspective, the competition for Alegria's services was between two professional, clandestine opportunists. Although he appreciated the irony, he did not expect it to be a contest. All Milton had in his arsenal were the script from Jeremy that he had memorized, a five-year contract, and a check for a $500,000 signing bonus. As Jeremy had sensed, the lure of working with a financial genius to outwit the capitalist markets was his most compelling argument. She agreed to meet.

Two days later, after flying in on Jeremy's private plane, Alegria was escorted to his trading room. There was no question that she would salivate at the sight of the pristine, ultra-high-tech equipment. Jeremy figured that thirty minutes with the other traders should be sufficient to convince her of their extraordinary skills and singular mind-set.

Jeremy appeared and directed her to his private office. Within minutes, he knew that his messianic magnetism had mesmerized her. Still, Alegria had one request. She asked Jeremy if she could submit original ideas for stock trades and be assured that he would seriously consider them. Jeremy pondered a moment as if it were a difficult request. In reality, it was a promise easily given because she had not asked for a minimum size of the transaction.

Now, two years later, Alegria was Jeremy's pride and joy. She was a recluse by nature, and she was content to live in his building. Random analysis of her video-recorded life indicated a singular passion for learning. She called her family religiously once a week, sent them money, and attended Mass on Sunday. She had no time for friends, romance, or hobbies. Every waking hour away from the trading floor was spent on her computer or with her Kindle, on which she read voraciously.

Best of all, after only six months with Jeremy, she had begun to produce trading ideas. To humor her, Jeremy began small, with investments in the $500,000 range. While the ability to ascertain privileged information about public companies is invaluable, it is only actionable when unexpected news, either positive or negative, is known. Consequently, in flat markets, Alegria's intuitive selections, while not the illegal sure thing, filled the gap with consistent profits.

Although normally distrustful of anything left to chance, Jeremy's confidence in his protégé increased with each successful trade she made.

Another benefit was that a thorough examination of his books, something he deemed impossible as long as he was alive, would reveal a significant number of legitimate trades in among his questionable ones. Currently, the single-minded Ms. Lopez's ideas warranted between $30 million and $50 million per investment. As an aside, she had become a very wealthy woman.

As he waited for the market's opening, Jeremy studied Alegria with what was, for him, almost a paternal instinct. She was painfully thin, with dark eyes that might have been arresting had any makeup ever touched her face. She had black hair, cut short at a barbershop only when it became a distraction, and fingernails bitten down to the quick. It was as if she never wanted anyone to see her as a person.

The opening bell sounded, and his focus became all encompassing yet laserlike. The glow from the monitors created a sinister look over Jeremy.

There was an overwhelming amount of data available to the people in front of the screens; it would give the ordinary person information paralysis. Jeremy's traders, however, focused intently on the displays like submarine sonar men. They knew exactly where to look and what to look for in the dizzying number of dynamically updated charts, tables, and live video feeds.

Jeremy, as the totally engaged conductor, seemed to see everything that his six traders were doing. It might make one wonder whether, if he had twelve hands, he could work his magic unassisted. These traders were the best at what they did, but under his control they were simply marionettes doing his bidding.

C H A P T E R   1 4

SOMEPLACE ELSE IS A rigidly enforced private club. The main lounge is a large, circular room with a stunning center bar. Along the outer walls of the spacious room are booths that allow for smaller private gatherings away from the main bar area. Between the main center bar, elevated above the rest of the room and the booths that ring it, is a magnificent dance floor with a laminated, hard polymer, ultra-gloss surface.

By design, the dance floor was rarely crowded. Unlike most night spots, the background music consisted predominantly of soft, familiar love songs. The hard beat of hip-hop was an infrequent interloper, only appearing for a specific audience. Occasionally, beautiful women would dance briefly together to a more upbeat tune as if to tease the onlookers, Shortly, the music would segue seamlessly back to the slow, soulful melodies.

Radiating from the outer walls are spokes that extend at every two hours, if the room is viewed from above and seen as a clock face. The main lounge entrance and the coat checks are at six o'clock. At four o'clock, a passageway leads to bathrooms and massage rooms.

Hallways leading to private rooms are at eight, ten, and twelve o'clock. The two o'clock spoke is a restricted passage for staff that leads to a state-of-the-art kitchen. Between the spokes are booths for seating. Flat-panel, high-definition TVs surround the center hub of the main bar.

Directly above the main bar is the visual focus of the room: an elaborate dome lined with mirrors reflecting colored lights around the lower circumference of the dome. The lighting is computer controlled and moves slowly while changing. Programmed into color mood charts, the tantalizing lights create a progression of moods.

Early evening sequences may be in a blue mood chart. Light blue crystals such as aquamarines , blue quartz, and blue lace agate relate to creativity, peace, joy, and tranquility. As time moves on, the scientifically designed modulations of colors become more stimulating, suggesting excitement, sensuality, and passion. As a result, the kinetic artwork feels like an artificial aurora borealis.

Hanging from the center of the ceiling is an exquisite piece of blown-glass artwork. Imported from Murano, Italy, its delicate translucent branches seem to reach out and wrap the room in calming light. Although the dome is stunning and considered a tour de force, the lower portion of the dome is a two-way mirror.

Above the lounge area is a private second floor known only to a select few. From this vantage point, there is a panoramic view of the main lounge, as if the watchers are looking at an aquarium below. The second level houses a bank of flat-panel monitors and computer equipment that digitally records all of the activity beneath them.

High-end cameras are hidden in all private rooms, booth areas, massage rooms, and bathrooms. In order to augment the "eye from the sky" view through the mirrors, directional and steerable microphones cover all areas of the first level. This affords the watchers the ability to eavesdrop everywhere.

Jeremy knew that if he had not possessed extraordinary financial acumen, he could have been a successful architect. Even though he had made it impossible to verify, Someplace Else was his vision, and he was also the sole owner. While other billionaires competed with one another for fine art or charitable bequests, Jeremy owned a place that everyone wanted to visit but no one could enter without his explicit permission. It was his biggest vanity, but, of course, it did serve a financial purpose.

Because divulging inside information is punishable by jail time, corporate executives of public companies assiduously resist the temptation to discuss nonpublic information. Not only is it illegal to tell someone inside information, but if you are the recipient and you act upon it and get caught, your ass is in the slammer, too.

On the other hand, if you had access to this privileged information and could take advantage of it without getting caught, the financial rewards could be staggering. Such a challenge was irresistible to Jeremy.

In Jeremy's mind, the equation was simple. Most corporate insiders are men. Men are ruled by their dicks. Feed the perversities; feast on the inside information.

In addition to his cadre of bright, stunning, sensual women, Jeremy employed six articulate, charming, highly attractive young men. The maximum tenure of any of these young men was ten years or age thirty-five. If the vetting and monitoring processes were not so extensive, he would have preferred to get rid of them after five years. Not unlike the Marines, he was looking for a few good men and women.

Generally, the young men's functions were more interesting. In fact, most men would have killed to have their job, which was to recruit perfect women. Vince Lombardi once said, "Perfection is not attainable, but if we chase perfection, we can catch excellence." Jeremy admired Lombardi's discipline and total commitment to winning, and he accepted no less from his people. As with the legendary coach, if you crossed Jeremy, you were done. As a result, his male persuaders had a precise profile for the potential candidates.

Arresting beauty had to be coupled with intellect and a fun sense of humor. No tattoos or disfigurements were allowed, which made it mandatory that the men complete a full-body examination of their prospects. Each woman would have to be single and ultimately agree not to get married until no longer associated with the organization. Women with past alcohol and drug problems were disqualified.

Similar to any analytical investment process, in a final interview the benefits, duties, and absolute requirements of placement were agreed upon. With all candidates, Jeremy would join the meticulous Max in the final interview. Max's role was to thoroughly explain the organization's expectations. If all the conditions were satisfactory, Jeremy, who usually studied in silence, would make the decision.

The men who were charged with procuring the extraordinary women had the freedom to look anywhere. However, this uncharacteristic latitude did not give them a false sense of security.

By the time these men brought a woman to stage three of the process, they were required to know everything about her. In addition to their personal due diligence, the men were afforded access to the organization's computer experts for a technological forensic check.

Watching from the second level of Someplace Else, Jeremy was focused on the private booths. The predators where confined to the booths because they were told that it guaranteed anonymity. It was a continuing source of amusement to Jeremy that successful CEOs believed whatever you told them. Each private booth had a two-way glass into the dance floor for their voyeuristic pleasure, yet it never occurred to them that their every movement was being watched and recorded.

Specifically, Jeremy was monitoring the booth where Congressman Floyd Caldwell from Tennessee was dining with Claude Hensley, the CEO of Pharmatech. Congressman Caldwell, who was only forty-two, was a minor player who thirsted for the big leagues. He was afforded the opportunity to visit Someplace Else because he had been vocal in asserting that regulation of hedge funds would destroy free enterprise. If he could help them turn Hensley, Jeremy would consider putting him on the payroll. For the time being, Caldwell was just in it for the challenge and the girls.

When Jeremy's newest acquisition, Sabine, entered the club, time and motion seemed to stop. She was an African beauty with long, dark hair and almond-shaped eyes the color of milk chocolate with flecks of gold. With her full, bee-stung lips and regal nose, she looked like royalty.

All five feet ten inches of her slowly glided through the crowded bar as if she were a snake slithering into sight from the jungle. She wore a short, simple, dark-brown halter dress that showed off her toned arms; still, it was impossible not to be drawn to her long, exquisitely shaped legs. Sabine was an arresting vision with gold bangles spiraling down her arm and Manolo Blahnik shoes that would make Imelda Marcos proud.

As Caldwell had been instructed, he pointed through the glass at Vanessa, another thoroughbred in Jeremy's stable. She was swaying rhythmically to the slow beat of the music. When Vanessa saw Sabine, she stopped dancing. In an almost exaggerated slow motion, she turned to greet the newcomer. They hugged briefly. Caldwell had been with Vanessa previously, and Hensley almost tripped over his tongue agreeing to have Vanessa and Sabine join them for dinner.

To Jeremy, no Broadway play could compare with watching the black widow spiders bait the trap. He rubbed his hands together as he watched the elegant seductress set out on her maiden voyage. He liked everything about Sabine.

Whenever he could add irony or perversity to his arranged assignations, Jeremy felt an additional rush. He believed that he could identify with Hitchcock and other great Hollywood directors who were honored for their artistry. Hensley's daddy, or for sure his Southern great-granddaddy, had to have been a member of the Klan. He laughed out loud. From days of Adam, forbidden fruit has always been the sweetest.

Both girls would leave tonight without having sex with either Hensley or Caldwell. Hensley would be hopelessly fascinated by Sabine. In this private setting, he would feel comfortable with his light banter and impure thoughts because of the security of the venue, the quality of the ladies, and his trust in his friend the congressman.

When he returned home to his family, Claude Hensley would try to resume a normal life. He would rationalize that the evening had been innocent and that there had been no adverse ramifications. Ultimately, he would call his friendly congressman, and the trap would shut.

*   *   *   *   *

Chris DeMarco bent over his computer. His fingers moved so quickly over the keyboard that it seemed like he was playing the lightning round of Whac-a-Mole. A trancelike smile graced his fifteen-year-old face as he warmed to his father's challenge.

Chris was either a prodigy or a superb hacker in the making. Up until this point, he had just danced on the sidelines of illegality. And as long as his mom, Amy, was in the house, that was as far as he would venture. But when his dad said that no one in his office could get any information on the Washington Group, Chris's eyes lit up like the Fourth of July.

"Would you like me to try, Dad?" Chris asked innocently.

"Sure, pal. Give it all you've got."

"Any restrictions?" Chris softly inquired. His mom was out playing Mah Jong, and his dad, after a couple of beers, was, well, extra cool.

"Dude, show me anything that I can print and take to the office, and you get a ten spot!"

It had taken thirty-five minutes, much longer than Chris had imagined. The entire time, Danny DeMarco sat proudly behind him, wondering for perhaps the hundredth time how he and Amy could have spawned this kind of talent.

"Got it!" shouted Chris excitedly as a website appeared. In one fluid motion, he hit Print and turned toward his father.

Danny looked at the screen, and his mouth gaped open at what he saw: "WARNING! THIS IS A RESTRICTED SITE! IF YOU DO NOT EXIT THE SITE IN 30 SECONDS, YOUR COMPUTER WILL BE FORCED OFF. ALL PREVIOUSLY STORED DATA WILL BE ERADICATED."

"Chris! The computer!" Danny said with alarm.

Chris turned on a dime, read the message, gave it a skeptical look, and asked his dad, "Do you believe them?"

"Get off!" shouted his father, who was now standing behind him. Chris tried to exit the site, but he was too late. He and Danny stared transfixed in horror as Chris's computer was no longer under his control.

*   *   *   *   *

Everyone who buys or sells a stock would like to have an edge. Insider trading is the ultimate edge, which is why discovery results in criminal charges. It is like betting on a boxing match when you know that one of the combatants is going to take a dive.

Under normal circumstances, Alegria Lopez would have been repulsed by her boss's illegal practices. But Jeremy had given her an opportunity. As he had promised, whenever her research dictated that she should buy or sell short a stock, Jeremy executed the trade without question. Even when a few trades went against her, she closed the trades immediately, and there was no second-guessing about the loss.

To Jeremy, trading was war. You take no prisoners, and how you achieve victory is irrelevant. So although Alegria did not approve of his methodology, she remained respectfully silent.

Real research was done on the ground. Of course, Alegria devoured all the virtual research on any situation she was considering. But whenever possible, she wanted to see the whites of their eyes before she pulled the trigger on a stock.

In addition to her intellectual gifts, Alegria was pragmatic. She had heard herself described as mousy and nerdy. Those were the nice comments. Fortunately, no portion of her self-esteem was tied to her appearance. Occasionally, that gave her an advantage.

In order to evaluate the leadership abilities of a company's management team, Alegria needed the individual attention of her subjects. She was definitely not just a pretty face; thus, she brought backup.

It was the last day of the three-day boondoggle of home builders in Boca Raton, Florida. For the first two days, Alegria sat alone, ate alone, and engaged in no conversation. She listened, studied, and took copious notes. It was not surprising that no one had approached her. In a sea of blustering white males, she was invisible.

Upbeat speeches piled on top of rosy predictions. Encouraging terms such as "temporary dip" and "housing always increases in a low interest rate environment" were only white noise to her. Her instincts told her that their ebullience would be punctured like a balloon that is stuck with a pin.

Still, while Diogenes searched for an honest man, Alegria needed only to find a cautious one. She needed confirmation of her conclusions regarding the industry.

On cue, Vanessa Meyers walked over to an attractive gray-haired man who appeared to be in his late fifties. A genuine tan darkened a solid face accented by intelligent blue eyes and a nose that had been broken more than once.

Alegria had studied him and watched as he listened intently to all the presentations but retained a look of skepticism. His name tag read "Bill Kirkland," and he was the president of DZ Homes, which was the most conservative home builder on the NYSE.

Vanessa asked him if he would like to have a drink with her and her friend. He quickly tried to hide his look of surprise as he shrugged his shoulders and agreed with a smile.

When he walked out with Vanessa, every eye in the room followed. Noting the attention, Kirkland blushed, looked at her, and said, "I hope none of those clowns shot a picture of me."

"Why not?" came a teasing reply.

He raised his eyebrows. "My wife trusts me, but you would be hard to explain."

Vanessa laughed, took his arm, and whisked him into the bar. When Kirkland saw Alegria waiting, she smiled at his look of relief. If she had been as beautiful as Vanessa, he would have needed somebody to restart his heart before he could utter a sound.

After the introductions and drink orders, Alegria began asking questions. "What made you decide to go into a defensive mode?"

Kirkland raised an eyebrow; this was not a social question. "In 2005, we determined that 40 percent of the homes we sold were bought by investors. We only build in communities. So that 40 percent became instant competition as the investors tried to flip the properties."

She nodded. "Where do you see the mortgage market?"

The drinks were delivered, and Kirkland took a grateful sip. "I don't think I caught what you do." He looked at Alegria and then back at Vanessa.

Vanessa patted his arm and said with a smile, "We're interested investors and big fans of your company."

Kirkland stopped for a moment, seemingly disconcerted by the vague answer. After a moment's contemplation, he apparently decided that he was not divulging any nonpublic information, so he turned back to answer Alegria's question.

"As you know, we got out of the mortgage business. Politicians, Freddie Mac, Fannie Mae, and market strategists all encouraged us to make mortgages. They claimed that 70 percent of people should own a home; they believed it would stabilize society."

Kirkland shook his head like he wanted to dismiss the lunacy. "We took a short-term earnings hit, got some crap from analysts. But screw them. We're going to take care of our company."

Smiling, Alegria nodded her assent. "I agree with your decision. It was prudent, and I believe it will prove prescient. Yet I'm still curious as to your analytical process. What made you arrive at this decision?"

"Just simple arithmetic," he answered with a modest shrug. "Three trillion dollars of mortgages written. Imagine that—three trillion. Our industry did that four years in a row. That's a total of $12 trillion worth of mortgages, sports fans."

Kirkland was just getting warmed up. He leaned conspiratorially toward Alegria. She smiled and gave him a look of awe. The man was a natural storyteller. The least she could do was play the part of the rapt listener. "No matter what the politicians tell you," he said in a low voice, "only 60 percent home ownership is sustainable. So 10 percent of the loans are pretty much guaranteed to go in the toilet. That's $1.2 trillion worth of bad loans!"

He sat back, looked at Vanessa, and gave her a smile filled with both knowledge and sadness. She agreed with his vision of severe pain for his industry, but she sensed his sincere regret that he was powerless to stop it.

Alegria allowed the silence to continue as if it were all sinking in and was a lot to absorb. To the contrary, her linear mind had processed it all before he had finished speaking. She asked a rhetorical final question. "And wouldn't liars' loans, no doc loans, and 100-percent-plus mortgages just exacerbate the problem?"

Kirkland turned to Alegria with a smile reserved for the professor's favorite student. "Exactly, young lady. Exactly."

As she walked to the elevator, Alegria's fingers moved like a blur over the keys of her BlackBerry. She had faked an urgent call she had to take, and Kirkland offered no resistance to her exit. Devoid of prurient curiosity, she never considered whether Vanessa and Kirkland would get together. She acknowledged Kirkland's foresight in curtailing home building and in divesting himself of the mortgage business. However, it was doubtful that he had the courage or the cunning to do more than build a cocoon around his company.

Opening the door to her hotel room, she noted the one-word response from Jeremy, "Call."

CHAPTER 15

BECAUSE FOR MAX PARNAVICH the anticipation was even more of a rush than the action, he followed the subject for two weeks. The fact that he had no assignment and no assurance that one would come was irrelevant to him.

The preparation and the delicious chill Max got when he was inside an empty house analyzing a mission were indescribable. He could close his eyes and visualize the entire operation. If Max had decided to be a Hollywood director, his staging, movements, and predictions of actions would have been unrivaled. Instead, he was a willing, efficient killing machine.

For Max there was more juice in a justifiable execution than in one done strictly for profit. When the order came to terminate this particular victim, he was pleased that it would also have aesthetic appeal. Historically, Max's instincts on which loose ends would be eliminated had been 100 percent accurate. He liked perfection, and although he was proud of his error-free analysis, in truth he was often able to subtly influence the decision.

Carmel Highlands reeked of affluence. Yet for Max, who had no interest in huge homes, fine art, or manicured landscaping, his subject's house did have appeal. Looking out the floor-to-ceiling wraparound windows, he was mesmerized by the panoramic view of the Pacific Ocean.

When he joined the SEALs, his motivation was not only fueled by the rigor of their training and their reputation as being the toughest bastards in the military; it was also driven by the lure of the water, particularly the ocean.

This house, located on Yankee Point Drive, was about sixty feet above the ocean. It was ultra contemporary, and its open, precise lines would have intrigued Jeremy. In the mammoth common room, large river rocks were embedded in the floor, and huge redwood beams were spread on the ceiling, which was over twenty feet high.

More than likely, Max thought, this house had been on a decorator's tour. He smiled, knowing that notoriety would also increase the interest of the masses in the event that it became necessary for a tragic death to occur here.

A normal recon would have taken Max no more than thirty minutes, but he had been inside for over forty. Very few breaking-and-entering felonies occur at noon in a neighborhood where houses are close to one another. Within twenty-five minutes, he had learned every inch of the home, but he still sat cross-legged, looking out at the ocean.

In this case, his skills were almost wasted. Because all the houses in the area were oriented to the magnificent beach view and surrounded by giant hedges, Max could have marched a platoon through the front door and no one would have noticed. Reluctantly, he stood, and in spite of the slight risk of exposure, opened the sliding glass doors and exited out the back.

Dressed in a black jogging outfit with a baseball cap pulled down and dark glasses, he walked to the edge of the patio. Ignoring the railings, he ran down the meandering series of steps to the ocean. He paused halfway down at a bench and wooden tables where the rich and famous would have dinner or just drinks.

Resuming his descent, he reached the beach and slowed. It was low tide, and he stealthily moved to the rocks and shared the sun with the seals who were already claiming their territory. To Max, a reverence for animal life was not in conflict with his disregard for human life.

*　　*　　*　　*　　*

Max's left eye seemed pulled down on his cheek as if he were aiming down the sight of a sniper rifle. He was cocked and loaded. Jeremy's normally visually comatose colleague emanated toxic vibrations when he waited for a potential "kill" order. Occasionally, Jeremy would stretch out the decision so that he could amuse himself watching Max squirm.

"Who would win, Max?" Jeremy asked innocently. "In spite of your considerable talents, I believe that my little friends would get the best of you."

"We could both dive in and play survival of the fittest," countered Max.

Jeremy nodded as if he would consider it. The friends under discussion were the sole inhabitants of the coffin-sized aquarium in Jeremy's bedroom. Other guests had visited, but none seemed to stay too long.

Now living with Jeremy were only the most aggressive of the species—the red-bellied piranha. Jeremy's mother would have been proud of the little darlings because they would eat anything. Feeding time for his small school was delayed when Max was present. However, in Max's absence, the highest morsel so far on his pets' food chain had been an alley cat.

When Jeremy dropped food into the waist-high aquarium, the ensuing feeding frenzy made the water appear to boil and churn red with blood. The piranha attacked with such voracity that they would strip an animal of its flesh within minutes, often taking bites out of one another in the process. It was hard not to love nature's emotionless, efficient killing machines.

Jeremy and Max had just finished listening to the audio tape of Paul Parker's conversation with Mac McGregor. Max, Jeremy's personal piranha out of the water, was waiting patiently for his instructions.

Jeremy sighed. Killing for profit was always an acceptable risk. Tying up loose ends was necessary, but it was not like the Mafia, in which it was required to send a message that disobedience was punishable by death. Unfortunately for Jeremy, his killings had to be discreet.

The problem with the "loose lips equals termination" rule is that if a person told one other person, was that the only one? In spite of the efficiency of Jeremy's operation, suspicions could arise. Did the person who was told have enough knowledge to begin asking questions? It was imprecise, and that was repugnant to Jeremy.

Having made his decision, Jeremy spoke. "Lenny the bug, but not Parker.

Max raised an eyebrow.

"Parker tends to go in multiple directions and therefore has a short attention span," Jeremy went on. "When the Cramer news hits, it will not linger with him."

Max's face was impassive. When he received the go-ahead, Jeremy saw the tension drain instantly from his body. And knowing Max, he would also be hopeful about what they call in the trade a follow-on offering.

Jeremy tilted his head back and gazed at the ceiling. "Besides," he continued, "Parker is a bit too high profile to remove. It could get messy." He thought for another moment. "And then," he added with exaggerated sarcasm, "his friend Mac McGregor would lead a posse right to our door."

Jeremy nailed Jack Nicholson's smile from *The Shining* as he raised his arms in a flourish. He paused and gave Max a look of theatrical sadness. "Please say good-bye to Lenny for me."

CHAPTER 16

FORTUNATELY, SINCE I AM averse to travel, there was a direct flight from Reagan National to Sarasota, Florida. In order to ensure that we made the appointment with Margo Savino on time, R. J. and I flew in a day early.

Although I would never admit it to him, I was grateful that Sam had insisted that R. J. accompany me. In addition to his obviously superior organizational skills, R. J.'s intellect, insights, and empathy are invaluable to me. As an added bonus, under normal market conditions his verbal skills keep me honed for the required client abuse.

The Ritz-Carlton, Sarasota is located on eleven acres near the center of the city. Because we had been instructed to do so, we had ordered rooms with a view of the water. It is hard to think of a better use of the bailout money. Sam had told us to reserve rooms on the club level, which included the club concierge, but I had parried with, "I refuse to further balloon the deficit of my new president."

In fact, all I was willing to charge them for what I felt was most likely a wild goose chase was our airline and hotel accommodations. Admittedly, I have never had an expense account, but constitutionally I would not have been good at it.

The hotel was beautiful and sparkling clean, and Ritz employees tend to set the standard for service. The European décor and fine art were lost on me, but I loved the light and openness.

I am a frustrated beach bum, so as soon as we changed into swim trunks and T-shirts, we went to the lobby to get the shuttle to the hotel's private beach club. All spies are required to recon the area prior to a meet, so feeling no guilt for goofing off, we jumped into the van with books and shades.

It is hard for me to imagine a more upscale place than the beach club at the Ritz. Located about three miles from the hotel, this slice of heaven is in Lido Key, which claims to have one of the best white-sand beaches anywhere. No disagreement from these intrepid warriors. Others might be attracted to the Gulf-front heated pool and Jacuzzi, but for me, just get my behind on the sand.

If we had wanted to really spoil ourselves, we would have reserved a ten-feet-by-ten-feet pavilion, which advertised that it "offers a private retreat, assuring seclusion and tranquility with comfort and convenience." That felt over the top to me.

Normally, at our beach in Delaware, when we go down to the sand, we're schlepping chairs, water bottles, towels, footballs, and books. Here, we walked out onto the incredibly soft sand and sat on comfortable chaises. A large, soft towel was positioned at the top of each chaise.

If we even thought we wanted something, a waiter was there—a drink, a delicious lunch, more suntan lotion for R. J. the paleface, a cloth gag for R. J. Really, whatever I needed, they provided.

Although it was a gorgeous day, seventy-eight degrees and sunny, the pristine beach was semideserted. After lunch, we decided that serious reconnaissance required that we walk at least thirty minutes along the water's edge. R. J.'s BlackBerry was on vibrate in his pocket.

I had left my cell phone in my hotel room. To me, a cell phone is blasphemy at the beach, but R. J. has young kids, so I didn't press it. Also, we both have the grace to go far away from people when we check in with the office.

The journey began. For most of it we walked in silence. Toward the end of the walk, R. J. said gently, "It wouldn't be the end of the world if she didn't show tomorrow. I think we needed this."

I nodded silently in agreement. The ocean is always therapeutic for me. I'm partial to the Atlantic, with its crashing waves, but the Gulf could also become addictive. In the summer, I occasionally get up early enough to walk out and watch the sunrise at Bethany. It's a religious experience.

We walked back to our chairs, sat down, and got comfortable. As I lay back, the sun caressed my face like a gentle lover. The rhythmic lapping of the Gulf waters created a hypnotic effect, and I gave in and closed my eyes.

I allowed a slight but satisfied smile, and in minutes I felt a peace that had been too long absent.

I'm not sure how much time passed, but I do know that I was zoning out when R. J. broke the blissful silence. "Why didn't you warn me how hard it would be to have clients lose money?"

I cleared my head and then thought for a minute before responding. This could conceivably be the last thing that I wanted to discuss right then. Still, I could feel the pain in my friend's voice. I tilted my head and looked up at the cotton ball–dotted clear blue sky as if skywriting would appear with the answers.

"Money is the last taboo," I said quietly, as if my tone could preserve the tranquility. "People will talk about their sex lives before they will discuss their finances. Yet the one certification that the regulators don't require is that of a licensed therapist.

"Even in good times, our clients want to talk about things seemingly unrelated to their financial well-being. And we listen, and we learn. Instinctively we try to help them solve all of their problems because the better we know them, the better we can help them. So I believe that the bonds we form may be stronger than transactional relationships such as those with attorneys or accountants. Not always, but it seems that way with most of our clients. And maybe a Jeremy Lyons can be emotionless with his clients, but for us, dispassionate care is not possible."

I knew that R. J. would be patient, even though I had not yet answered his question. I turned toward him. "Bear markets are like bad colds. You hate them, but you know you'll feel better. In 1999, when stocks were soaring, the pundits all screamed, 'This time it's different!' It was an easy call. I knew that they were wrong. It was time to get defensive. Now I feel like the herd is getting to me, because it does feel so different.

"What is safe?" I asked. "It has all been redefined. Before, when people were scared, I had 80 to 90 percent confidence that my assurances were valid.

"History confirms that market timing is a joke. We did an excellent job of protecting our clients' lifestyles. Still, I feel impotent. Not only have our clients not called up and yelled at us, but it seems like every single one begins the conversation by asking us how we're doing."

R. J. nodded. We were both silent for a minute.

"Yet," I said softly, "we still feel guilty. In 1987, it was the same scenario, just quick pain. But the clients reacted the same way. My clients had 30 percent in cash. Their stock positions were all down, and yet they were concerned about *me* first. I felt like I needed to shrink. And the reason is, it's my job to take care of them, and when they hurt, I've failed!"

I took a long breath, closed my eyes, and rested my head on the chair. I felt spent. I knew that R. J. had to digest not only my words but also the unguarded emotion that accompanied them.

A few minutes later, he spoke in a tentative voice, "I would offer to give you a hug, but I know I'd get pummeled."

I gave his comment the silence it deserved. Then I said, "I've never doubted your instincts."

*   *   *   *   *

At exactly twelve o'clock, a woman in a light blue cover-up, wearing dark glasses and a Tampa Bay Rays baseball cap, approached us. Both of us started to stand instinctively, and I was amused to see R. J. having a tougher time getting out of his chaise. In fairness, I've had more practice.

"Who are you?" she asked, looking directly at R. J.

Before he could answer, I said, "Margo, this is R. J. Brooks, my partner."

She looked at him and then at me, and I was afraid she was going to bolt. Finally, she pointed at R.,J. like a master does to his dog and said, "Stay here." She swung around to me. "Walk with me." Realizing the fragility of the situation, we both did as instructed.

Margo and I walked along the water's edge, away from the Ritz property and away from the people. After about five minutes of silence, she spoke. "Why did you bring him?"

"While we were here, we decided to include client meetings and ... "

Her retort was like a viper strike. "If you fucking lie to me again, this interview is over. You arrived yesterday morning, spent the whole day on the beach, and ate dinner at Tommy Bahama's. You sat on the porch, probably shared piña coladas for all I know. Then you shopped, had ice cream, and went back to the hotel. You arrived here at ten this morning. There were no clients. No more bullshit."

It was rather humiliating to realize what an amateur I was. I'm uncomfortable lying, and I was embarrassed.

"Are you two lovers?" she asked, jolting me out of my self-indulgent reverie.

"No! Absolutely not! I'm married with four kids!" I protested loudly.

"Touch a nerve? It would make sense. You were the only swinging dick at Johnston Wellons who didn't try to screw me."

"I was married!" I exclaimed in a voice lacking my usual testosterone.

"Of course. I forgot. No married men have ever tried to get in my pants." Her smirk did nothing to restore my equilibrium.

One of the key factors in helping clients plan their investments is that a competent advisor needs to control the conversation. As important as listening skills, the advisor needs to be able to direct the flow of a meeting to avoid distractions and to agree on a strategy and direction. At this point, the only thing that I had control over was my bowels.

"I also know that the writing a book story is bullshit, so why do you really want to know about Jeremy?"

Having been previously hammered for prevarication, I considered my answer. Whatever I said would have her either walk away or start telling me why she agreed to meet me. An axiom from my father came to me, "When in doubt, tell the truth."

I stared down at my footprints in the sand as if they tracked the curious path that I had chosen and had now brought me here. I took a breath and turned to her. "An important friend believes that Jeremy is running a hedge fund and that some of his methods may border on illegality. He asked me to help him find Jeremy."

"Ha!" Margo snorted out a laugh. She stopped walking and looked at me. "No shit," she smirked. "Jeremy Lyons making his own rules, trying to accumulate all the money in the world. That's not fiction, pal; that's reality TV."

She turned serious again. "Why should I help you? What's in it for me?"

"I don't know why you should help me, but you called this meeting, so I know that you want to. And I can't promise that you'll receive any benefit other than helping put a bad guy away if he's guilty."

"*If* he's guilty? Are you freaking kidding me? Are you really that naïve?" She shook her head in obvious exasperation. Then she stared right through me. "If there is a reward, will you fight for me to get it?"

"Yes," I answered and unflinchingly met her gaze.

She continued looking at me, and then she grabbed my hand and pulled me into a secluded area. What must have been her beach towel and a pair of high-powered binoculars were on the sand. Standing by a beach chair was a short, fireplug-built man, deeply tanned. He had short black hair, and his chest and arms were covered with angry tattoos. He was obviously a body builder, and the glare he directed at me made my earlier assertion of bowel control questionable.

"Tony, he's good. Leave us."

"You sure?" he said in an almost unintelligible Italian accent.

She nodded, and he moved slowly toward me until his face was inches from mine. Every instinct screamed for me to back up or, better yet, run like hell. Yet, with forced passivity, I held his gaze.

"Tony!" she repeated, more sternly.

Like a pit bull loath to be called off of his prey, he reluctantly moved away. As he left us, his warning eyes stayed on me.

"That's my brother," Margo said. "He watches out for me. Sit." She motioned to the chair.

"I'm okay standing," I replied, still recovering from the hand grabbing and the fear of having my ass kicked and not knowing why it had happened.

Margo looked at me questioningly, as if she were debating whether to take the next step. Then she nodded and gave me an empty smile. "I'll show you why I'll talk to you," she said.

Margo took off her hat, and her still-dirty-blond hair spilled out. She removed her dark glasses, and except for some wrinkles and what seemed like a face that had known pain, the years had been relatively kind to her. She pulled the cover-up off over her head to reveal a dark blue bikini over a trim, tanned body.

With this expanded picture, I had to reassess that the years had been not just relatively good but very good to her. I had the frightening thought that I might have to extract myself from this situation, and bone crusher Tony might be hovering nearby.

While staring at me, she pulled down her bikini bottom. I literally recoiled at the awkwardness of the moment. Then she spun around and shoved what definitely did not look like a fifty-year-old ass in my face.

"Look," she commanded.

On her left cheek was a raised scar of a dollar bill.

"Oh, my God," I stammered.

She pulled up her bikini bottom and turned around to face me. "Now we'll sit," she said. "I've waited a long time to tell my story."

CHAPTER 17

WHEN MAX EMBARKED ON his cleanup missions, he never used one of the firm's airplanes. Instead, he used one of the many Marquis Jet accounts where they had purchased hours. Since 9/11, passengers were required to show their driver's licenses to one of the two pilots, but Max had more false IDs than the service had pilots.

The Citation V Ultra was an eight-seater, but Max and the two pilots were the only travelers. On this California trip, Max was Warren Ellison, a certified public accountant. Colored lenses lightened his eyes. He had on a blue blazer, a button-down blue shirt, khaki pants, and loafers. When he returned the next day, he would wear the same outfit, and the role of the overworked, disheveled accountant would have been played to perfection.

Although he had the requisite laptop to complete the picture, Max preferred to meticulously consider the options for execution in his head. After going over all of the possible scenarios, including reactions to any unforeseen impediments, Max began to relax.

Even though he needed no more than four hours of sleep a night, ironically he could fall asleep just by quieting his mind. Since he would get no sleep from the time of his landing until he boarded the plane for his return flight, he closed his eyes and folded his hands across his chest, and in minutes he was gone.

On Max's earlier sightseeing tour of Lenny Cramer's home, he had found a place where he could rent a motorcycle for the day with no ID. Cash was often convincing. When he arrived at the Monterey airport, he ducked into the men's room and waited until it was empty. He entered a stall, closed the door, and changed into black jeans and a fitted black T-shirt. His "work clothes" were stashed in a backpack.

Leaving the airport, he hailed a cab and asked the driver to drop him at a diner about a mile from the cycle shop. As the car disappeared from view, Max began walking toward the shop.

Then, riding the Harley down Highway 1, Max again reviewed the details of his mission. Audio surveillance confirmed that Lenny's wife would be playing bridge and would not return home until after eleven thirty that night. Lenny had told her that he would crash and watch TV, and she had left him lasagna and salad.

In case there was a glitch, Max carried a throwaway phone. As usual, when extreme measures were required, Jeremy would listen and watch on the surveillance equipment. In addition, if required, Jeremy could provide a warning for Max.

Arriving at the Highland Inn, Max pulled the bike over into an obscure spot. The woods behind the motel offered a perfect place for him to change into his third outfit—jogging clothes. A Lakers cap and dark glasses completed his facade as one more runner in the land of gym rats. It was about a twenty-minute walk to Lenny's house, but with his leisurely jog, Max made it in ten.

Max lingered outside of the house longer than was customary. The moonlight illuminated the foam as the waves broke softly over the rocks. Even in the dark, part of him wanted to go down to the ocean. If this had been a recon visit, he could have come up with a good reason if someone saw him. In this case, he thought with a twinge of regret, he had a limited window of opportunity, and he would never compromise a mission.

As he expected, the house alarm was still not engaged, and Max entered the side door easily. He listened until he heard the rattle of ice cubes in addition to the TV in the great room. Although there were four bedrooms upstairs, the master was conveniently located on the lower level. No contact from Jeremy meant that, as Max had anticipated, Lenny was alone.

In the master bathroom, Max's gloved hands found an almost full prescription bottle of Ambien. As he had noted during his earlier visit, Lenny's wife's dosage of the sleeping pill was ten milligrams. With his Swiss Army knife, he crumbled the tablets into a fine powder.

Walking into the great room, Max noted that Lenny was slumped in his chair. Not prepared for company, he had on pajama pants, a ratty looking T-shirt, and slippers that had also seen better days. About two swallows of Scotch were left in his glass. On the TV, Max was pleased that *Everybody Loves Raymond* was the chosen program. In Max's mind, Raymond's mother was an exceptional psychological assassin.

"Lenny, Lenny, Lenny," Max crooned.

With a start, Lenny jerked, and his drink spilled on the chair and his hand.

"Looks like you need another drink. Do you mind if I fix one for myself?"

"Nuh, no," Lenny stuttered.

"Please don't get up from the chair, Lenny, or I'll feel like company rather than family," Max ordered in a way that paralyzed his host. Keeping his eyes on Lenny, Max fixed an ice water for himself and a Scotch on the rocks for Lenny. Deftly, he obstructed Lenny's line of sight as he mixed the sleeping pills into his drink.

"After you finish your drink, I'm going to ask you a few questions," Max said as he handed Lenny the Scotch.

Lenny's hand was shaking as he tentatively reached for the glass.

"As you may remember, Lenny, I am a man who loves to give alternatives—not unlike the lady or the tiger. Do you remember that story, Lenny? Doesn't matter. Your choice is much simpler. Drink up, Lenny. We must be sociable. The choice is to tell the truth or take a flying leap." He smiled benignly at Lenny and watched as the man's red eyes widened in fear.

"Now, what I want is for you to answer my questions precisely and honestly," continued Max. "You've made us a lot of money, and Jeremy likes you. But even Jeremy can't control me when someone lies to me. And I'm afraid that we would have to walk to the end of your patio and see if you could jump all the way into the ocean."

Max hunched his shoulders and stretched his hands out in a pleading motion as if it would hurt him more than it would hurt Lenny to have to do that. Then he wagged his finger and warned, "Don't drop your drink, Lenny. I also am a neat freak, and that would piss me off."

Lenny was shaking, white, and in danger of losing his dinner and drinks while still rooted to his chair. He was too afraid to utter a word.

"You can wait until you finish your drink, Lenny, but please be careful with your answers." Lenny gulped down his drink like there was actual salvation at the bottom of the glass.

"Easy question—how many people did you talk to about our agreement, and how explicit were you? I'll need names, and if you lie, Lenny, I promise I will know. Work with me here. I would like to leave and just have this be a bad memory for you."

Max breathed in Lenny's fear. All the signs of a panic meltdown—the pasty white face, the left eye twitching, the unsightly sweat gathering under his armpits—all harmonized to form a perfect melody for Max Parnavich.

Lenny looked down at his drink again, the melting ice cubes symbolic of his melting hope. Then, because there was no alternative, Lenny took a halting breath and opened the vein of truth. He managed to find the table with his glass. "I, I screwed up, and I'm sorry. I had too much to drink and I just blabbed, but nothing specific," Lenny finished plaintively.

"How much have you had to drink tonight, my friend?" Max inquired sweetly.

"Three Scotches."

"And how much that night?"

"Uh, four, I think."

"Well," Max said as he walked over and picked up the glass, "let's see if we can re-create the situation." Max walked back, poured Lenny another Scotch—this time undoctored—and handed it to him. "They say liquor does loosen the tongue. Here's to your health."

Lenny tentatively took the glass in his trembling hand and sipped. Max sat and waited.

"I was with Paul Parker, a sports agent. All I said was that I was making $5 million a year."

"So you didn't mention that it was a 20 percent return?"

Lenny blinked, his eyes scattering furiously. "I probably did say that, but I did not mention you guys!" He raised his voice for emphasis.

"Anything else?" Max questioned menacingly.

"I made him swear not to say anything to anyone."

"Do you think that he honored his promise?"

"Yes, I ... "

"Wrong answer, Lenny," Max interrupted as he leaned forward. "Lawyers are curious, and curiosity—well, you know."

"I'm sorry! I'm really sorry! I swear that I'll never slip again! I'll stop drinking! If I tell anyone else, you can cut my tongue out!"

"Now that's a novel solution," Max mused, steepling his hands under his chin. "How about other transgressions?"

"There are no others!" Lenny shouted. "I swear on my children's lives, I haven't said anything to anybody else! You've got to believe me! Oh, God, you have to!"

Max studied him. Mucous was streaming from Lenny's nose, and his reddened eyes were wide in panic. "Last chance. You get one more free one. Are you positive?"

"Yes! Yes!" he wailed. "The fact that I talked to Parker has been eating me alive."

Again, Max measured the man. He smiled as if Lenny's tears and entreaties were soothing balm to him. Raymond's mom would have been proud. "Okay. I believe you. But Lenny, this is your last warning."

"Thank you! Thank you!" blubbered Lenny.

"Here's what we're going to do. You're going to finish your drink and take a nap in the chair. When you fall asleep, I'll let myself out, and I'm sure this will be the last time we meet."

Relief fell over Lenny like a warm blanket. "Can I take a piss first?"

"Of course, Lenny. We can't have you pissing in your pants."

Lenny struggled out of the chair and slowly wove his way to the bathroom. He put his hands on the side of the sink for balance and finished crying. He shuddered heavily and put his hand on his heart. He grabbed two pieces of toilet paper, blew his nose, and then tossed the paper into the trash. His eyes were heavier than they had been as he put his left hand on top of the toilet and pulled out his penis with his right.

As his stream was ending, Lenny felt a push from behind and pissed on the floor and on his pajama pants. Max's hand grabbed the back of Lenny's T-shirt and prevented him from falling into the toilet.

"Ah, sorry, Lenny. You had to suffer a little for your indiscretion." Max put his arm around the man. If he scared Lenny to death, that would be inconvenient. "Come with me. We're leaving this mess for the missus so that you'll catch a little hell when she comes home. Can I trust you not to clean this up?"

"Y-y-yes," Lenny managed to stutter out.

Max helped Lenny back to the chair. Improvising, making a better plan, always excited Max. Urine on the floor, tissues in the wastebasket, and urine on the pajama bottoms—he loved it when a plan came together.

Lenny looked up at Max with eyes that were desperately pleading and yet hopeful. Max knew that all he wanted was for this nightmare to end. Max leaned forward and gently patted Lenny's shoulder. "You've done well, my friend. Now close your eyes, and when you open them, I'll be gone."

After thirty minutes, Max checked Lenny's pulse. It was faint. If Max had to guess, in another hour or so, the booze and pills would do their job. However, guessing was for amateurs, not artists.

In 1829, an Irish criminal named William Burke got his victims drunk, smothered them, and then sold their bodies for dissection. Although he was convicted, his name lives on in infamy. In the dictionary, "burking" is defined as a form of murder that involves killing the victim by pressure or other means of suffocation so as to leave no mark of violence on the body.

To honor the originator, Max used his left knee and left hand to push on Lenny's diaphragm while his right hand covered his victim's nose and mouth. As if watching a scientific experiment that failed, Max was disappointed that there was no perceptible struggle. Both the fight and the life had gone out of Lenny. In a few minutes, he was dead.

Max walked back to his chair, picked up his water glass, and drained it. He walked to the sink, washed the glass thoroughly, and dried it with a paper towel that he then put in his pocket. He replaced the glass in the bar and exchanged places with a similar glass stacked behind. Finally, he removed the audio and video surveillance equipment and placed it in his backpack.

Max knew from past experience that his custom gloves and clothes left no fibers. Contrary to what TV crime shows portray, autopsies are not automatically done. He placed the empty pill bottle in Lenny's hand and let it fall on the chair. Then he walked again toward the glass windows. He had no concern that this mission would break his perfect record.

In spite of the fact that he had lingered longer than planned, Max gazed wistfully once more at the ocean below. As he turned to leave, the muted TV gave him another idea. A few minutes with the remote control uncovered a twenty-four-hour pay-per-view porn station. Mrs. Cramer would just want this to go away when she discovered that Lenny had committed suicide while watching porn.

"Improvising," Max mused, "is what distinguishes genius."

As he walked out of the house, Max was pleased that he had honored William Burke that night. Plan B, which was tossing Lenny off of his patio onto the rocks below, would have been aesthetically more pleasing. But if he hadn't died, it would be messy, and besides, Max had tossed garbage before.

During the planning phase of an execution, considered akin to foreplay by Max, the excitement built slowly, methodically. Administering torture, both physical and mental, made his body feel as if he were building to an explosive orgasm. The killing phase was climactic and cathartic, but, unfortunately, never long enough.

As a consummate professional, Max was required to effectively put a governor on his emotions during these operations. Lately, the temptation to be fully present and experience every sensation of the moment had been increasing. For it was only in the aftermath of the execution that Max allowed himself to feel.

The jog back began at a leisurely pace. When he was about a mile from the Highland Inn, Max broke into a sprint. Then, abdicating his coffin of discipline, he ran like a cheetah closing in on its prey.

Behind the Highland Inn, Max hurriedly stowed his jogging suit and pulled on his jeans and T-shirt. He climbed onto the bike and started the engine. As he sped into the darkness, his body began to rock from side to side, his face contorted, indecipherable between pain and pleasure. An unearthly animal scream rose above the loudness of the Harley and shattered the silence of the night. For while the aftermath of an execution comforted him with the satisfaction of accomplishment, it was inexorably joined with despair that it was over.

CHAPTER 18

MARGO PUT HER BATHING suit cover-up back on and sat cross-legged on the towel. She nodded toward the chair, and I took a seat.

"Shortly after Jeremy left Johnston Wellons, he began calling me," she began. "I loved working for Ron Judkins, but he wasn't really ambitious, and I had come from poverty. From the day Jeremy first saw me, he had rather clumsily hit on me. Not only was I not attracted to him, but I also wasn't going to sleep with anybody in the office. So he just went into the category of a loser, though admittedly a persistent one."

She leaned forward and continued, "Every woman is intrigued by the real-life bad boy, no matter what they tell you. So when I heard about his tough-guy exit, I was sort of turned on. But the clincher was that he sent me airline tickets and a cashier's check for ten grand. He said that I could keep both even if I never saw him again."

"That was a lot of money back then."

"No shit. I knew that I'd have to screw him if I went to see him, but he promised me that I would make $100,000 a year if I joined his firm. My parents were dead. Tony is fifteen years younger than me, and he was living with my grandmother. I never wanted to be poor again."

She paused to collect her thoughts.

"For the first six months, it actually wasn't bad. Sure, he was a twisted fuck, but the money was great. If you can believe it, I was the psycho's first, not counting hookers. "

I kept my face impassive. As much as I wanted to interrupt and ask her where she had gone to meet Jeremy, I was reluctant to break her rhythm.

"Then everything changed. He called me into his office, and that sadistic bastard Max was with him," she went on. "Jeremy told me, in a matter-of-fact manner, like you would tell someone what you had for dinner, that he was expanding his clientele. In order to attract super-rich influential clients, he needed a stable of irresistible women.

"I had two choices. One was that I could help recruit these women, train them, and supervise them. For this I would get a significant increase in compensation. If I hadn't known better than to ever interrupt Jeremy, I would have told the prick that I didn't sign on to become a madam in his whorehouse. My other option was that I could become one of his stable, and he would hire someone else for the madam job. He didn't call it that."

She looked directly at me with a challenging glare. "I know you're thinking that I could have just said that I was leaving. What you don't know is that he implemented a retirement plan.

"If you stayed one year and obeyed his rules, you would receive a pension of $10,000 a year for life. Two years equals $20,000, all the way to the maximum, which was ten years and $100,000 a year for life. I figured that I could do the time," she said with resignation. "I was only twenty-one."

Margo looked down, and I was afraid she would stop. She said nothing for about thirty seconds. I said softly, "So you chose to run his operation?"

"There was really no other option for me. If I'd chosen to be one of his high-class sluts, my first job would be to take care of Max. And he is the scariest son of a bitch that ever walked the earth.

"So I started hustling for Jeremy's 'perfect specimens.' Soon I had an assistant, and then he brought in a few young studs to also help me recruit. It really wasn't that difficult. The money, the clothes, the sex were all intoxicating to these women.

"Unless they liked it, there was never any rough stuff. Their one job was to subtly seduce rich and powerful men. Of course, there was role-playing and a lot of girl-on-girl threesomes. There were extra rewards for exceptional performances," she added.

With an instant change of demeanor, she turned and looked at me defiantly. Her accusing gaze made me feel as if she were blaming my gender instead of the responsible individual. I knew better than to comment.

"Except for the guillotine that hung over us," she said, "the whole thing might have been worth it. Only fools disobeyed the rules. Our instructor on the rules was none other than Max. Most of them were logical: no drugs, no alcohol abuse, no smoking. Because Jeremy liked everyone to look squeaky clean, no tattoos or body piercings were permitted.

"The last two rules proved more difficult to follow to the letter: absolutely no outside discussion of what you do, the organization, or who you do it with." She shrugged. "The girls were with some pretty famous men. Finally, no *unauthorized* sex."

The last rule was spoken with such contempt that I mentally took a step back.

"At random times, Max would call us together, and we would go over the rules. If one of the girls forgot a rule when he questioned her, he would put his hands on his hips and shake his head like he was disappointed. Then he would give the terrified girl a look like my parents gave me before a spanking. You know, the old 'this is going to hurt me more than you.' Then he would take her by the hand, lead her into a soundproof room, and debase her in every way imaginable."

Margo bit her lip and lowered her voice. Her tone became despondent. "If a girl disobeyed a rule, she was severely punished, or sometimes she would just disappear. There was always someone eager to take her place." She paused again and hung her head as if she were exhausted.

I waited in stunned silence. Finally, I asked, "How did you get the scar?"

She took a deep breath. "I fell in love," she said softly. "I was naïve, and I thought that after all I had done for the company, they would allow *me* a private life as long as I was discrete about it. Jeremy had long since moved past me to younger, more depraved receptacles."

I looked at her intently. "If it wasn't your job to seduce these centers of influence for Jeremy, why were you subject to what might be considered the random sex rule at all?" I asked.

She nodded ruefully and looked at me with half-lidded eyes. "Great question. You should have been my attorney. Here's another one. Why, after five years of my organizing the company, recruiting, and supervising women, did they still have hidden video cameras in my bedroom? Did they just like to watch me masturbate? Max didn't have to rape me; the cameras did." She spit out the words like venom shot from a snake.

She had grabbed the sides of her beach towel with both hands and scrunched it tightly as she talked. I watched her take a few more deep breaths and saw her force herself to relax.

"So Jeremy fired me. I had broken the rules. I begged him to reconsider. I reminded him how valuable I had been to him in the beginning," she continued woodenly.

She shook her head violently, as if trying to dislodge a foreign object. "I remember his comment as if he just said it yesterday. He looked at me and said, 'People are replaceable. Only genius is not.'"

Veins in her temples stood out prominently. Her words spilled out more quickly. "Then Jeremy gave me a choice: did I want to leave and forfeit my pension, or would I rather receive fifteen minutes of punishment and keep the money?"

Margo glared at me, which I took as a warning not to judge. "I knew it would be futile to ask him what the punishment was, but even though I had saved a lot of money over the five years, I couldn't pass up the pension."

Margo squeezed her eyes shut and started weeping softly. I was at a loss as to how to comfort her. She cried harder, with her head in her hands, and I hesitantly reached over and patted her arm. When she had cried herself out, she raised her head, opened her eyes wide, and said grimly, "Ready for the big finale?"

In a voice devoid of emotion or inflection, she recounted her ordeal. "As soon as I opted for the punishment, I felt a sharp prick in my arm, and Max was standing beside me with his eyes on fire. I passed out.

"When I regained consciousness, I felt dizzy and slightly nauseous. I was tethered to a piece of metal. I was naked. I screamed as I realized that what I was tied to was rotating slowly. Below me was a pit of red-hot coals. I was like a pig on a rotisserie.

"As my eyes began to focus, my fear escalated, because I had never seen the room I was in before. It had no windows and no doors. I screamed until I thought I had burst my vocal cords, and then Max came into my view. He was heating a branding iron. Jeremy was sitting calmly in a chair, watching. I begged, 'Let me go! I don't want the money! Please just let me go!'"

I had broken out in a sweat, and my eyes were tearing, but she recited her agony as though she were in a trance.

"My cries and screams not only fell on deaf ears, but they also seemed to inflame Max. He brought the smoldering iron to my face and then my eyes and whispered in my ear. 'No. You are going to want to see this.'

"I shrieked when he put the iron back on the coals. Suddenly the iron was inches away from my breasts, and the heat felt like it was burning through them. Like a demented frog from hell, he flicked his tongue over my nipples. 'So tasty; it would be a shame to waste,' was his fevered response."

Margo's head jerked from side to side as if she were trying to escape from the memory. She closed her eyes once again. "Still holding the metal so close to my breasts that I imagined I could feel them sizzling, he reached down and put his finger inside me. He told me that I was already burning there. His voice was barely audible, and my revulsion was indescribable.

"Then Max slowly turned the spit so that I was looking at the fiery coals. In a loud, singsong voice, he cried out, 'Money. That's all you care about. You're just like us. You need the money.' Viciously he seared the branding iron into my left buttock. The pain was excruciating."

She fell silent, and I wondered if she had any strength remaining.

After a moment she spoke again. "When I couldn't scream anymore, Max turned the spit so that I was looking right at Jeremy."

Margo suddenly shouted as if she wanted the whole world to know her pain, "The son of a bitch actually looked bored!" Her hand went to her forehead. She closed her eyes. After a few moments she raised her head and said wearily, "He looked at his watch and said, 'Only fourteen minutes. I must still have affection for you.' Then he left the room.

"Max cut through my bindings and took me off of the contraption. I crumpled to the floor, and he left. Shortly afterward, the in-house nurse came in and put salve and a bandage on the wound. I left that night." She went silent. Finally, in a child's voice, she said, "The checks still arrive like clockwork."

She collapsed onto the sand.

I could not speak. I was paralyzed. This was real; it was not a movie. My inadequacy humiliated me. I could not comfort her, console her, or help in any way. It took all my effort not to just empty my stomach onto the sand.

We both sat there, heads down, not looking at each other for maybe ten minutes. Yet as horrifying as her story was, I still had many unanswered questions. "I'm so sorry." I waited for another minute. "Where were you for those five years you worked for him?"

Her head rose slightly. "I can't tell you."

"The hell you can't," I blurted out in an angry tone that I instantly regretted. I took a breath.

Her eyes were still fixed on the sand.

"Sorry," I said gently, "but this is just an exercise in futility if we don't find and punish the men who did this to you."

She raised her head to look at me, eyes brimming with fresh tears, thrusting her lip out and daring me to judge. "I need the money he sends me to live." She paused. "And to remind me of what I did to get it."

I tried another way to overcome this obstacle. "How does Jeremy make his money?"

She thought for a moment. "Jeremy had money when I met him. It could have been from his family. I asked him about them once, and he said that both of his parents had departed to greener pastures. All he cared about was money. Why do you think I'm branded with a dollar bill?"

Margo didn't wait for an answer. "Even back then I think he made insider trading a new art form. I mean, I was in the business. It wasn't a coincidence that the girls ended up sleeping only with the heads of publicly traded companies. You have no idea how ruthless he was when it came to making money."

I considered her reply, and I noted that her anger had revitalized her. "Why am I the first person you've talked to?"

She looked at me, tears again appearing at the corners of her eyes. "I always thought that you were nice," she replied softly. "I trust you."

She lowered her head again and shrugged. "And you asked."

I felt like a detective who knows that he needs to unravel one more thread, but the witness is so fragile that a wrongly worded question could shatter her into a million pieces.

"Forgive me, Margo. I cannot imagine how difficult this conversation has been for you." I considered my next question and took the shortest route. "What else?" I asked softly.

Her head jerked as though I had struck her. It collapsed into her hands, and her sobs broke my heart. I closed my eyes, absorbed in her suffering. Finally, her head rose unsteadily, her eyes still filled with tears.

She looked at me like I was the ant trying to move the rubber tree plant and shook her head. Her eyes refused to let hope enter. "You just don't understand. When I left, he already had more surveillance shit than the CIA. Add that to a total lack of—lack of ..."

"Morality?"

"Exactly," she said and pointed at me. "Imagine the firepower he has. If they found out I was talking to you, I would be right back on the spit, but this time only an inch from the flame."

I waited in silence. As gently as I could, I asked her, "Please?"

Margo looked at me, and pain emanated from her eyes. I could barely hear her voice.

"Before my brand of shame, I was pregnant." Her lips trembled, and her eyes were blinded by the fountain of tears. "Fourteen minutes later, I was not."

CHAPTER 19

IT WAS A RESTLESS weekend. Unwelcomed replays of the brutality suffered by Margo Savino infiltrated my nights and whenever I let my guard down during the days. Her story had been like Drano, flushing all my intellectual curiosity down the drain. I was in *way* over my head.

After a few minutes of involuntary panicking, I decided that I couldn't just gracefully extricate myself. If Margo's story was accurate, and a dollar bill brand was pretty compelling evidence, then these animals had to be stopped. For over twenty years, she had blamed herself for losing her baby. If the men responsible were that cavalier about torturing her, what else had they done?

I needed to talk to Sam. But Sam's suggestion about our not communicating using normal channels had taken on a much higher level of urgency. Not only did Lyons and his sadistic playmate have access to the highest level of sophisticated surveillance, they were also not restrained by legalities.

So I did what I had done in the business for thirty years—make a list. Not concerned with prioritizing, I just wanted to outline my thoughts.

- Unanswered questions – Lyons
- Significance of dollar bill
- Rod's $30,000,000 loan
- Secrecy – examples of illegal acts
- How does partnership hide from the IRS?
- What evidence required to arrest?
- How far do tentacles reach?

- <u>Unanswered questions – George</u>
- Analyze accident report
- Analyze insurance – is there a pattern?
- Who benefits?

I studied my questions, knowing that I had missed some obvious ones. *It's a puzzle, just a different kind,* I told myself. Often when I'm stymied by a puzzle, my mind runs through possibilities, and then there's a click, like a remote that lights a gas fireplace. So why did it feel like I needed to change the battery in the remote?

I closed my eyes and rubbed my forehead. I had only one irrefutable conclusion: it was time to bring in the law.

*   *   *   *   *

Without close scrutiny of his badge, this barrel-chested, brown-eyed, flaming extrovert would never be identified as Special Agent Joe Sebastiano of the FBI. With silver hair swept back on the sides, a perpetual tan, and a mouth devoid of a mute button, he was just flat outrageous.

Joe was born in the Bronx, a product of a second-generation Italian-American family. Like his father, he worked construction for a while, but he became the first in his family to finish college. At six feet tall and 190 pounds, he was in superb physical condition. He was an expert not only with a pistol but also in hand-to-hand combat.

Even more frightening is his dead-on impression of the mountain man talking to Ned Beatty in *Deliverance*. It almost guarantees an involuntary tightening of the sphincter.

Grace has never been able to figure out how I can joke around if I'm angry, hurt, or upset. I attribute it to my defense mechanisms because I really don't know either. My friends are used to it, and keeping it light does seem to relieve pressure. Besides, if you were serious with Joe Sebastiano, he would likely stick a toe tag on you.

As expected, Joe had not been waiting by the phone for my call. About thirty e-mails and three calls later, one of my newer associates paged me with, "A Mr. Marlon Brando is on the phone." She looked at me like the name should mean something.

"How would you like a hot date Saturday afternoon?" I began.

"Do I get to play mountain man?"

"No. And you're making me nervous. You're going to a Maryland basketball game with me."

"That works. Barbie Doll will be happy to get rid of me. Are you picking me up?"

"Yes. I'll get there at two-thirty so I don't have to buy you a meal."

"No food, no Italian salami."

"Nice try, but I've already rejected R. J.'s offer of Hebrew National."

*   *   *   *   *

"Okay, Batman and Throbbin, follow me," Danny DeMarco barked as he walked toward my conference room. Danny is rarely politically correct and rarely agitated. In this case, his obvious agitation warranted intrigued compliance from R. J. and me. I grabbed my bottled water, and we took a seat.

Danny remained standing, again unusual. "I know this one knows," he said, pointing a finger at R. J., "because I've seen you two whispering." His eyes moved from one to the other, reminding me of a principal who has caught two boys misbehaving. "I've done what you told me to do. I've used *way* too many chits and too many *nonrevenue- producing hours*, but I've got your information."

I had asked Danny to use his insurance contacts and take a forensic look at the sale of George Grant's insurance policy. I wanted details. What company purchased it? How many such policies had this company purchased previously? How many of the insured were still living? I hadn't expected the process to be easy.

"Of course," Danny said, heating up, " there were a few *casualties* along the way. I asked my fifteen-year-old son, Chris, to do what none of our associates could do. Yes, he did uncover the website of the infamous Washington Group!" He looked at us, expecting a comment, but he was too worked up for us to do anything more than remain attentive and silent.

"They didn't like getting pinged," he said sarcastically, "so they let us know in a very *nonhostile* way. They took possession of my son's computer!"

R. J. and I exchanged puzzled and concerned looks. It was not inconceivable that Danny was trying to scam us. It seemed to make more sense to me than the story he had just told.

"How long were you on the site?" I asked, testing.

"Oh, let's see." Danny's hand went to his chin as he pantomimed computing. "About thirty fucking seconds!"

He is not that good of an actor. To envision anyone taking over a computer without legitimate access and doing it in thirty seconds is outside of my technological ZIP code.

"Did they stop with Chris's computer?" R. J. asked.

I looked at R. J. like he was smoking the same thing that Danny was.

"So glad you asked. No. In fact," he bent over the table so that his flushed face was inches from R. J., "these computer pirates displayed *my* browser history on my son's computer."

"Thank goodness you delete all of your porn-o-rama sites every morning," R. J. said automatically.

As serious as the matter was, the unwarranted images caused me to fight back a grin. Meanwhile, our normally impossible-to-offend partner found zero humor in the situation.

He was far from finished. He gave R. J. a glare of rebuke and stepped up the volume. "Who else but the government could pull something like that? Listen. This is more than just finding out if George Grant was scammed. There is some serious shit happening!" His flushed face and aggressive tone were totally out of character. His hands were gesticulating, emphasizing every word. "I want to know what the hell is going on!"

I waited, letting him calm to a simmer. I took a long breath, preparing for blowback. "No," I said quietly. "I can't discuss it."

"Give me a fucking break." He turned to walk out of the room.

"Danny," I said, my voice stopping him with his hand on the doorknob. I waited until he turned back toward me. "I'm sure that your information will be extremely helpful, and I appreciate all the work you did." I paused. "Both R. J. and I are over the wall on another matter. It may be related. This is something I'm discussing with the FBI."

He looked at me warily.

"I only had permission to bring him in. I need to keep this contained."

Danny turned and looked at both of us. We are all close friends with a long history of trusting each other. Still, I knew he felt hurt and excluded. I sensed the possibility of an impasse. I believed that every fiber of his being wanted to get past this; he just needed an exit row.

"Danny, when we finish analyzing the information, I'll call your lovely wife."

He gave me a confused look.

"I'll tell her that I've put you under considerable stress, and I would be deeply indebted to her if she gave you a little 'sumpin, sumpin' tonight."

In one continuous motion, his eyebrows raised, the contagious DeMarco smile appeared, his notes hit the table, and he scooted into the chair between us. Included in this synchronized metamorphosis, Danny muttered something that sounded suspiciously like, "Will work for sex."

CHAPTER 20

PONZI SCHEME! THE FLAT screen on the wall to the left of my desk screamed the words. The chattering magpies of CNBC tripped all over themselves sorting out the details of what was, this time, truly breaking news.

Everything stopped, not only in our office, but probably in every brokerage firm in the country. All eyes not on the phones were riveted to the screen. Certain words and phrases demand the attention of financial advisors: *crash, terrorist attack, assassination*, and *Ponzi scheme*.

A Ponzi scheme is a blight on the financial industry. Investors were conned, defrauded, fleeced, and cheated. In our world, it is the classic twenty-car pileup on the freeway, complete with rubbernecking. Every advisor instantly fears, "Were any of my clients involved through outside investments? Anyone I know?"

Everyone gathered around my desk, mouths agape, staring in horror. As details unfolded, it appeared that the largest, longest-running scam in history had been uncovered. The alleged perpetrator was a man named Barney Farb. He was a well-known philanthropist, socialite, and bastion of the Jewish community.

As I surveyed the stupefied looks of my team, I recalled a conversation from five years ago with a young man who had received a $10 million inheritance from his father. A long-time client had referred him to me. He told me that he appreciated my offer to help, but he had an opportunity to invest with the legendary Barney Farb. The only way to participate was to be referred, and then perhaps the master would accept your money.

The theory behind this allegedly fail-safe methodology was that Farb was a market maker and, therefore, could automatically profit from markups (commissions) as long as there was trading. Being a natural skeptic, I said to the young man, "If the man consistently makes 10 to 12 percent in any market environment, he then must make a profit on your investment. Let's assume that he makes from 2 to 3 percent on your money. Why wouldn't he just use all of his money and keep *all* of the profit?"

Fortunately, I was 50 percent convincing. He agreed to give us half of the assets to invest and also to take the distributions from Farb and pay off his home mortgage rather than reinvest what turned out to be phantom returns. I glanced at R. J., who I know was sharing my thoughts. He nodded and left to call our only investor with Barney Farb.

A second thought then crossed my mind. *Was this charlatan somehow working with Jeremy Lyons?*

*   *   *   *   *

As a child, Jeremy's only sanctuary had been his mind. Protective layers of psychological barriers were formed that insulated him from hurt and rejection. Resentment built strength, resolve. Numbness turned to calculation and, ultimately, to a sense of invulnerability. No one was allowed to enter. If an intruder forced his way in, the consequences would be terminal.

As a man, he collected sanctuaries like a boy collects baseball cards. His favorite was naturally his bedroom. Soundproof, secure access—no man had ever penetrated this world.

Silver satin sheets, changed daily, covered his massive bed. Women visited but never stayed. In his most private sanctuary, Jeremy Lyons slept alone.

Classical music played with the clarity of an orchestra in residence. In rhythm, Jeremy flicked his right hand, and his cat-o'-nine-tails pierced the left buttock of the exquisite Sabine. As she had predicted when she gave Jeremy the engraved whip, inflicting pain served as an aphrodisiac to him.

The whip cut through the air again, lacerating her right buttock and spraying tears of blood onto the sheets. Jeremy reached down, caressed her thigh, and brought his bloodstained hand back to his hairless chest. He absently massaged and finger painted his chest as his eyes glazed.

The ebony goddess moaned and stretched languidly, like a leopard in the sun, turning her head toward him. Her pupils filled her eyes. She parted and moistened her lips as desire seemed to emanate from every pore. As he whipped her again, her head moved from side to side and her body writhed in passion.

Sabine, who sometimes seemed to have an instinctive insight into Jeremy's mind, had cautioned him that although moderate lashes heal with no scars, severe lashing causes scarring that does not disappear, and savage lashing kills. However, even the intuitive Sabine could not know that with Jeremy, violence begat violence. Punishment served as retaliation for everyone who had underestimated him, ignored him, or discarded him.

Suddenly, her eyes widened in fear, but he gazed right through her. It was as if a switch had been flipped. Like a scene from a horror movie, Jeremy's eyes changed from a look of lustful curiosity to the eyes of a ravenous wolf. The incarnate evil of his soul rose like bile in his throat, screaming for release.

In the tortured theater of his mind, he conjured up a graphic preview of relentless, brutal strikes with the whip. The whip appeared attached like a mighty snake to his arm. The piston-like strikes accelerated until unearthly cries of anguish faded in a sea of blood, gore, and skinless bones.

Jeremy's face had reddened dangerously, ribbons of veins protruded from his neck, and his muscles tensed hideously. Sabine shouted, "Stop!" and threw her arms and hands out like a traffic cop. Although her trembling body betrayed her fear, her dark eyes were locked defiantly on his. Bodies froze as if waiting for a camera.

Jeremy's head jerked toward an unfamiliar sound. An emergency intercom that had never been used squawked. "I'm sorry to disturb you, sir." Frank Griffin's tentative voice pierced Jeremy's psyche. "I believe that we have a business situation that you may want to attend to as soon as possible."

Jeremy threw his head back and roared a primal scream. His sanctuary had been violated. In one motion he grabbed his black running shorts, stepped roughly into them, and bolted out of the room. The cat-o'-nine-tails had never left his hand.

*   *   *   *   *

Waiting in the situation room with Frank Griffin were Jeremy's computer gurus, Richard Hwang and Milton Peterman, and, of course, Max. For five years, Frank had been in charge of the recruiters. He was thirty-five years old and movie-star handsome, with wavy brown hair and brown doe-like eyes. A born salesman, he was charismatic, trustworthy, and shrewd.

The situation room's door burst open as if a battering ram from a SWAT team had forced it. Frank's eyes widened in obvious horror at he gazed at the rage-consumed face of Jeremy Lyons. Clad only in running shorts, Jeremy's hairless body was grotesquely painted with sweat and blood. Every muscle of his body was flexed in anger. His eyes were executioner's eyes.

As Frank opened his mouth to try to explain, Jeremy moved quickly and savagely brought the whip down with enough force to almost rip the shirt off of Frank's back.

"No!" cried Frank with an inhuman scream of terror as he stumbled backward, throwing his hands up to shield his face.

The accompanying gasps of terrified protest from Milton and Richard served only as gasoline to Jeremy's fire. Two purposeful steps forward—*crack*! The whip came down on Frank's back and buttocks. Blood spurted from the lashes as Frank's bladder gave way.

Jeremy raised his arm again. A shrill, high-pitched, involuntary scream of "Stop!" escaped from the lips of Richard Hwang. Milton tried to climb inside of him as he slammed his hand over Richard's mouth to silence him.

Reacting, Jeremy whirled toward them. His eyes blazed as his arm quivered in the strike position.

Then, as if the switch were turned off, Jeremy dropped his arm, bent down to his interlocked employees, and quietly said, "Okay." In one motion, he straightened and casually tossed the whip to Max, who snatched it out of the air effortlessly.

As Frank crumpled to the floor, his agonizing screams resounded throughout the room. Jeremy knelt over him and observed him with scientific dispatch. When Frank's misery became tiresome, Jeremy yelled, "Quiet!" The sounds were reduced to sobs as Frank's blood- and urine-stained body writhed on the floor.

Jeremy took a seat and continued studying the disgusting remnants of Frank Griffin. No remorse. The execution of a minion does not require justifiable provocation. Jeremy leaned forward and addressed the room. "Why was I disturbed?"

Richard and Milton, who still had their mouths open in horror, remained huddled together for protection. Frank was traumatized to the point of almost being comatose, so Max, after letting the drama build a bit, filled the void. "CNBC just reported the discovery of a multibillion-dollar Ponzi scheme. Frank thought that the magnitude and duration of the fraud might have raised some serious questions from your clients."

Jeremy nodded. The misguided reasoning was not really relevant. "And did Frank ask anyone about the wisdom of interrupting me?" His eyes swept the room, but Jeremy directed the question only to Max.

Max waited a long beat and then responded. "He asked me, and I said that it was his call." With this, Max's mouth twitched, confirming to Jeremy that Max had enjoyed the show.

Jeremy studied Max, considering to what degree he should be annoyed over Max's instigation. Jeremy endorsed corporal punishment for stupidity or betrayal. It had a powerful impact on the employees present, and its psychological reverberations served as a continuing deterrent to the rest of the company. However, Jeremy preferred to orchestrate the violence, and even Max was not allowed to manipulate him.

Jeremy's gaze turned to Milton, Richard, and what used to be Frank Griffin. He pursed his lips in disgust as he thought of their worthlessness in combat.

"Take him!" Jeremy barked. "Clean him up and be prepared to discuss the situation in thirty minutes. I will have Manuel bring us some refreshments."

Richard and Milton both jumped up as if poked with a cattle prod and helped the still-weeping Frank out of the room. Jeremy mused that he did not need Sabine's assessment to know that Frank's scars would not disappear.

Jeremy walked purposely to his shower, stepped in, and turned it on. The temperature was instantly eighty-five degrees. Repulsed and feeling dirty, he rigorously scrubbed his body with soap and then took a steadying breath as the blood disappeared down the drain. He felt a tingle in his semi-erect penis, which seemed to still twitch from the blood lust of the beating. Jeremy hated to waste opportunity. He called Sabine on the intercom.

*　　　*　　　*　　　*　　　*

Thirty minutes later, Jeremy reentered the situation room dressed in a clean black kimono. Max leaned against the wall with his arms crossed casually. Milton and Richard sat close together on one of the couches. Frank sat on the other couch with his head in his hands, afraid to look up. Drinks, ice, mixed nuts, fruit, coconut shrimp, and stone-crab claws had been delivered.

"We will drink and eat to gather ourselves before we strategize. Frank, you will notice that I included stone-crab claws, which I know are your favorites. I insist that you eat. All great warriors require nourishment before battle." Jeremy watched with amusement as the men hesitantly filled their plates.

Jeremy realized that Frank respected his boss's superior intellect and his business prowess, if not always his methodology, and it was a pity, but before today Frank had probably felt safe.

Jeremy watched Frank eat haltingly, more than likely struggling to control his nausea. It was time to begin. "Assessment of the potential damage," Jeremy commanded. There was a nervous quiet.

Unsteadily, Frank rose and walked over to his PowerPoint presentation. Looking at the screen, eyes half-open, he spoke as if he had to pull the words out. "Barney Farb seems to have run a gigantic Ponzi scheme, which defrauded investors out of $40 billion."

The effort it took Frank to make this statement showed in every pore of his ashen face. Milton and Richard watched with horrid fascination because it seemed inevitable that Frank would vomit before completing the thought. On the other hand, both Max's and Jeremy's countenances reflected only annoyance at the delay.

Frank began again. "The victims were primarily Jewish charities and Jewish investors. About a year ago, the SEC finished an investigation of his firm and found no improprieties."

Jeremy's eyes narrowed. In the past, the inefficiencies and lack of staff in the enforcement area of the SEC had worked to his advantage. Yet when they failed to catch someone who could harm his business, it infuriated him. Frank had paused to collect himself, so Jeremy spoke impatiently. "Continue!"

"Here's why we care," said Frank, straining to focus on the screen. "One, people had to be invited to invest. Two, no due diligence was permitted. Three, investors could withdraw all their money, but then they would not be able to participate again. Four, Farb represented double-digit profits every year for the investor, regardless of the market. Five, manager compensation was not discussed.

"The differences in our model are the letter of credit backing, higher returns, communication requirements, and penalties for violation of privacy. However, the similarities will cause anxiety among some of our clients. How will that manifest?" Frank sat down, plainly exhausted.

Milton, who had minored in behavioral psychology, spoke hesitantly. "They will contact their recruiters for assurance, break the privacy pledge and speak to advisors, or exercise the letter of credit."

Jeremy scanned the room. The conclusions were accurate, and if he were not so furious about the situation, he would have been pleased at the thought process. After a few minutes of silence, he spoke. "Have the contacts call each client."

Jeremy was amused to see Frank wince at his suggestion. There were still lessons to be learned.

"Frank, you will prepare the script for my approval," added Jeremy. "The purpose of the call is only to determine if the client had any exposure to Mr. Farb. Our call is a simple courtesy, and we will allege that if they do have exposure, we may be able to use our connections to increase their chances for potential recovery of their losses.

"The victims were predominantly Jewish. It is important to assert that we are calling clients regardless of their religious affiliations."

Jeremy looked again at Frank, this time noting a glimpse of the boyish wonder returning. Even in his depleted state, Frank would realize that if their clients did have money with Farb, they would be so grateful for help in the recovery of their assets that all questions would disappear. On the other hand, if the clients did not have money with Farb yet asked about the difference in the two models, the caller would simply point out that if the Farb investors had had 100 percent principal protection, they would have lost nothing.

"All contacts should be made within twenty-four hours of my approval of the script," said Jeremy. "All recorded conversations should be put on a disk, and within forty-eight hours, Milton and I will listen for nuance. Additions?" he asked.

Everyone shook his head, acknowledging the dismissal, except Max. The computer gurus helped Frank up and walked on either side of him. From a distance, the victim resembled a wizened old man.

Neither Jeremy nor Max had had anything to eat or drink with the others. For Jeremy, it was another inflection point of psychological control. Max just knew the drill: masters must allow slaves to eat.

They ate leisurely and in silence. After savoring his last stone-crab claw dipped in mustard sauce, Jeremy spoke, but mostly to himself. "In a rising market, I profit by knowing which companies will beat earnings expectations or which companies will be acquired. We analyze probabilities, eliminate variables, and therefore control the outcomes. What cannot be eliminated or controlled are event risks like this fucking Farb asshole."

Max remained respectfully quiet.

"Volatility in the markets to me is like blood to a vampire. If companies go out of business, I profit. Often, I am a major contributor to their demise.

"And now we discover that the amazing Alegria has allowed me to literally pillage markets in free fall. Yet to my personal embarrassment," he laughed, "her gains are totally legitimate!" He leaned forward. "Perhaps even *I* am replaceable, Max."

CHAPTER 21

FOR THE SECOND DAY in a row, the CNBC breaking news feature caused me to execute an *Exorcist*-type head turn. "The former head of bankrupt Bay Savings and Loan, Leonard Cramer, was found dead this morning in his palatial California home. Officers at the scene indicated that the cause of death appeared to be suicide, but the investigation is ongoing."

Another talking head chimed in. "It's not like he was the *only* head of a financial institution to take his company into bankruptcy."

After exchanging a knowing glance with his fellow reporter, the original commentator volleyed back. "My guess is that Lenny Cramer is one of the first casualties of Barney Farb."

It felt a bit too convenient, but I nodded absently in agreement. R. J. was looking over my shoulder, still staring at the screen when he remarked, "That's a hell of a coincidence."

I nodded again; that was exactly what I was thinking. R. J. and I had previously discussed Paul Parker's conversation with Cramer, but I had not had the chance to show him my list of unanswered questions. I retrieved the list from the middle drawer of my desk, and he joined me in the conference room.

R. J. read the list in silence. When he finished, I reached over and pulled it back. Under the column "Unanswered Questions – Lyons," I added "Cramer –scared. Was 20 percent real?"

"Any thoughts?" I asked, passing the list back to him.

He glanced up quickly and then dropped the paper like it was radioactive.

"I think it's a concise list, very thought–provoking. There are definitely connect-the-dots possibilities, and we need help now!"

Looking at his flushed, earnest face, I managed to suppress a smile. I waited a few seconds. "I'm a step ahead."

*   *   *   *   *

The blessed relief of a weekend was slightly tainted, as I was either engaging in an instinctively clever clandestine operation or absurdly overreacting. As I had assumed, Sam Golden had been able to get us good seats for the Maryland basketball game, and surprisingly, he had no issue with my paranoia.

The e-mail that I had received from Larry Pusey increased my overall apprehension. There were no skid marks from George Grant's accident. Larry's hypothesis was that if someone had been asleep at the wheel, after hitting George, the car would have continued on and at least run up over the curb. If it was just a drunk driver, would the car have clipped George, straightened out, and just kept going? Neither the police chief nor Larry had any logical answers. Consequently, the hole in my stomach became more inflamed.

Joe Sebastiano lives in a quaint community in Gaithersburg, Maryland, called the Kentlands. It is about fifteen minutes from my house, and Grace and I are frequent visitors to the adjacent shopping center on movie nights.

One of the advantages of hanging with "GI Joe" was that I would be safe with him as my wingman. He was watching for me when I pulled up in my Lexus convertible. It was fifty degrees and clear, but it needs to be at least sixty-five for me to put the top down. Joe's wife, Barbara, waved enthusiastically at me from the door.

As Joe approached the car, he motioned silently for me to get out. When I complied, he took what looked like a TV remote with a small antenna on it from his jacket pocket and waved it over the car.

I watched with increasing apprehension. Apparently, he took my precautions seriously. Then he motioned for me to turn around and put my hands on the car. I looked at him like he was nuts but proceeded to do it. Big mistake!

Even before the device was pressed against my butt cheeks, I knew that I had been had. "Who's your daddy? Who's your daddy?" came the guttural cry from one of America's finest. I pulled away and started smacking his shaking body.

On the porch, Barbara was also laughing hysterically. I looked at him and then at her. Take instant action, or accept total defeat? I bounded up the driveway, grabbed her in a Hollywood embrace, and planted one on her. I shouted, "Honey, I'm afraid he's catching on!"

Joe was literally on the ground as Barbara, playing her part perfectly, said in an excellent Mae West imitation, "Come back and see me some time, big boy." The line would have had more impact if she had not still been laughing.

I walked proudly to the car, got in, and said, "Get your big behind in the car."

He stumbled in, still laughing. I waited until he collected himself and then offered, "I'm trying to solve the crimes of the century, and you're humping me in full view of all your neighbors. What is wrong with this picture?" For the record, my theory of being safe in his presence was not well thought out.

Unfortunately, that just restarted the giggle machine. I made another attempt. "What was that thing you just gleefully shoved up my ass? And don't say your dick because this I could actually feel."

He wiped the tears away and said, "Cowboy, you were just violated with the advanced Pro Bug Detector."

"I'll cowboy you, you *Brokeback* reject. So I assume that what's said in my car stays in my car?"

"Sure."

"Good! Kiss my ass!"

"Do you think we have time?" he asked, still laughing and simultaneously wiping tears from his eyes.

I shook my head with bemused exasperation as I watched the clown laugh himself out. Remember, folks, we're talking about the Federal Bureau of Investigation. Not expecting a reply to his inane banter, he changed to at least a semiprofessional mode. "So what's the scoop?" he asked, trying to sound businesslike. "Tell me all about this guy who's going to be number one on our most wanted list."

"Do you have the tape recorder I told you to bring?"

From another jacket pocket, he produced a mini recorder and hit **Play**, and I was once again treated to "Who's your daddy?"

"Perfect," I told him. "I can't wait until you submit that as evidence. And because of your boorish behavior, you'll have to wait for the main event like everyone else."

We drove in silence for a few minutes, which is unusual when you're riding with an Italian. Joe probably thought that my paranoia in the staging of this meeting was over the top, and I agreed, but I don't carry a gun.

"What sort of visual surveillance gizmos could people have that would be hard to detect?" I asked.

Joe thought a minute. "A standard laundry list would include a pen video camera system. They go for about two grand. Video glasses where the camera is built into the nose frame cost about $3,500. Finally, there is even a Dick Tracy wristwatch camera."

"I suppose that someone could also just have binoculars and read lips at a basketball game."

"Sure, if they cared enough."

It was about twenty minutes before tip-off when we pulled into parking lot 4B. This was my first experience in the premier parking lot. Hanging with the VIPs is always fun. We parked, walked up some concrete steps, and were inside the Comcast Center.

In Cole Field House, the predecessor to the University of Maryland's current basketball home, the rich folks and the important people had the floor seats. In Comcast, as in archrival Duke University's Cameron Indoor Stadium, the students are the VIPs. There is no entrepreneurial option because the students cannot scalp their floor seats. Those who have them have to present a student ID.

By the time we got to our seats, which were low enough to offer great viewing but high enough to see over the Maryland bench when the players stood up, Sam was already seated. Since he had the aisle seat, we had to step over him.

As predetermined, Joe had the far seat and I sat next to Sam's date, who looked like Michelle Phillips. Straight blond hair touched her shoulders. She wore granny glasses made popular in the sixties, and she had pale skin with apparently no makeup. She was dressed in a light green sweater dress that matched her eyes.

Note that these observations were made in the five seconds it took to walk in front of her, but she did look like she had stepped off of an album cover of The Mamas and The Papas.

After Joe and I had taken our seats, she spoke while staring straight ahead. "Mr. McGregor, I'm Kay Murrey. You set the parameters for this meeting, and we will adhere to your instructions. Mr. Golden asked me to attend because I have a photographic memory for anything that I read. I also have total recall for anything that I hear."

I cleverly pointed to my left and said, "That's quite impressive. However, if you are required to practice these talents for Mr. Golden's dissertations, you must also be immune to boredom." Attempted levity can relax a person or serve as a gauge as to their sense of humor.

I got zero reaction, so I waited a beat and tried again. "In addition, your boss needs to reread Spy 101 because you are way too attractive to be his date. And please call me Mac."

Her eyes went to half-lid.

She canted her head slightly right toward Sam. With machinelike efficiency, she said, "Mr. Golden said this was a serious matter. May we hear your conclusions now, Mr. McGregor, before the crowd noise makes hearing more difficult?"

Was it possible that Joe had stuck the bug detector up *her* rear end? I said nothing and waited. I am a master at petulance.

After about two minutes of silence, Kay asked in a louder voice, "Mr. McGregor, may we proceed?"

I continued to stare at the basketball court. She looked helplessly at Sam, who whispered to her. With a small but exasperated sigh, she said, "Mac, may we proceed?"

"Of course, Ms. Murrey," I said. "R. J. Brooks and I went to Sarasota, Florida, where I spent some time with a woman named Margo, who used to be Jeremy Lyons's lover. He coerced her into being his madam. Her job was to find perfect female specimens who would slowly seduce CEOs of public companies. The objective was to get these fine, upstanding gentlemen to divulge inside information about their companies."

"Any collaboration?" asked Joe.

"No. That will be your job, but Margo did have convincing evidence of her veracity." I paused for emphasis and to make sure that everyone was paying attention.

"Max Parnavich is Jeremy's right-hand man," I said. "On Jeremy's instructions and while Jeremy watched, Max branded Margo on her left butt cheek. This was after they stripped off her clothes and rotated her over burning coals for fifteen minutes. After more than twenty years, the brand of a one-dollar bill is still quite clear."

I snuck a glance at Kay, whose pale skin had turned two shades whiter. The poor kid clearly had not been prepared for this. I spoke quickly. "Jeremy spies on his employees. Margo broke one of his rules. She had to be punished."

Kay's eyes were now closed, either in concentration or perhaps in retreat.

I would tell Joe later, but I decided not to share that Margo had lost her baby because of this atrocity.

"Max Parnavich is another story," I continued. "Although she has no evidence, Margo was certain that Max was Jeremy's personal assassin. Too many of the girls just disappeared mysteriously. She also knew that Max used to rape girls who forgot a rule."

I temporarily ended my report, knowing that both Kay and Sam would need to absorb what I had said.

The game had started, so we watched for a while. No one talks through an entire basketball game. At the first time-out, Sam asked. "Where is his base of operations?"

"That goes in the 'what we don't know' category."

Sam did not hide his look of exasperation.

"But—" I paused. "Margo knows where he is." I took a few minutes to outline why Margo had not revealed the location and then offered what I felt was a logical solution to the problem.

Out of the corner of my eye, I could see Sam fidgeting. I knew that he was uncomfortable that a payment would be required. More than likely, he was also uncomfortable that people not normally in the need-to-know category would be aware of the transaction.

Joe remained respectfully silent, although he probably would have preferred snatching Margo and sweating it out of her.

While Sam mulled over his decision, I focused on the game. Although I understood the awkwardness of his position, it was as if Margo Savino were a client. I needed to protect her. Finally, Sam nodded. Not good enough. "Use your words, please." If it were possible, I did not say it unkindly. Still, I got a sideways glare.

"We'll take the deal."

I changed the subject quickly.

"Here's where I start looking over my shoulder," I said. "A client of mine had dinner a few weeks ago with Lenny Cramer, former CEO of Bay Savings, who recently was thought to have committed suicide. He tells me that Lenny had a secret deal with a clandestine organization. For the past five years, they had paid him a 20 percent annual return."

I turned to look at Joe. "Can the FBI look a little deeper and make sure this really was a suicide?"

"Yeah. I'll check out the locals, and we'll trace the money."

"Great, because I have a large client who recently made what may be a similar financial transaction."

"Who's your friend?" asked Joe.

I paused again. "Unless you tell me that it's absolutely unavoidable, I would like to keep him under the radar. Cramer talked about his deal, and now he's dead. If it's the same company, then you need to find a way to protect my friend. Joe, I want to find out where Lenny wired the funds. If it's the same place that my friend wired *his* funds, I'm really concerned."

*　　　*　　　*　　　*　　　*

On the way back to Joe's home, he was all business. "From here on, you're out of the picture, pal," he said, as if it were an acknowledged fact.

"Wow! Does that mean that I'm officially employed by the Bureau now?" He looked at me strangely. "Sorry, Joe, but I'm going to be in the loop every step of the way. I've spent a lot of time on this, and I've seen this asshole's handiwork," I added bitterly.

"Margo will only talk to me, I have a unique perspective on Jeremy's activities, and I've earned the right. And because of my sniffing around, I don't have 100 percent confidence that I'm not in danger."

Joe was quiet, and I suspected that he was wrestling with his response. He knew me well enough to know that I felt totally justified in remaining involved. He let out a loud sigh and looked over at me. "I can remember when the authority of my voice commanded instant obedience. I must be losing my touch."

I knew that Joe didn't want to add to my concern, but I didn't respond because my position was nonnegotiable. Joe changed the subject.

"You do know that the deal with Savino will somehow escape Ms. Murrey's infallible memory and never make the notes."

I nodded.

"And you are going to check on the possible connection with your client and Cramer's deal?"

I nodded again. I appreciated the fact that Joe did not press me about the identity of my client. "It's not going to be easy," I said as I turned to look at him. "A straightjacket of secrecy surrounds the transaction. Lenny Cramer talks about his deal. He's scared shitless …" He knew the rest of the story.

"We'll find it."

"Obviously, if my friend is receiving money from the same source, then it is conceivable that he is in danger."

"Will he tell you?"

I looked over at him again. "I sure as hell hope so."

We drove in silence. After a few minutes had passed, Joe asked, "Anything else I should know?"

I flashed back to Danny DeMarco's research. "I may need help on another situation."

Joe's eyebrows went up in surprise.

"Are you familiar with the life settlement business?" I asked.

"Nope."

"It's the practice of selling life insurance policies to corporations or partnerships that do not have insurable interests. An individual sells his policy and gets money in excess of the cash value, and the agent gets a big commission."

"Why would somebody do that?" Joe asked.

I shrugged. "Money, or if they have no further need for death protection."

"And the buyer?"

"Actuarially, whoever buys the policy expects about a 10 to 12 percent return on their investment. You can see where it can be attractive to a buyer."

Joe thought for a minute. "It sounds ghoulish."

I nodded. "If you're an investor, you want the insured to 'hurry up and die.' Assume that I paid you $5 million to be the beneficiary of your $25 million policy. Now assume that as soon as the ink is dry, you die."

"You make $20 million!" Joe interjected. His face was scrunched up like we had run over a skunk.

"On the other hand, if I, the investor, have to continue making premium payments of $2 million a year until you die and you last ten years, I make nothing."

"Got it."

"The Washington Group bought my friend George Grant's $50 million policy for $15 million. Two years later, he dies in a suspicious hit-and-run." I paused to let that sink in.

I continued in a pedantic tone. "Within a two-hundred-mile radius of Washington, DC, the same investors bought five other policies that we could uncover. It would take considerably more research capabilities than we have at our disposal to do a nationwide survey of the policies purchased by this Washington Group."

I had arrived in front of Joe's house and stopped the car. I turned toward him. "I need your help."

"What happened to the other five individuals?" Joe asked, anticipating my answer.

I could feel my anger rising. "Four of them were dead within three years of selling their policies."

CHAPTER 22

"ROD, I NEED TO talk to you."

"Why?"

"I need to talk to you, and it needs to be in person. Would you like to helicopter into DC, or would you rather I schlep down 95 and meet you in Richmond?"

He waited a moment. "Definitely not door number one. And as much as I normally like to torture you, I won't choose door number two. It would cost you a whole day. So, my technological neophyte, I choose door number three. Go buy a prepaid cell. I will get one, too, and we'll chat. Can I assume that it's not necessary for you to see the whites of my eyes when we have this important discussion?"

I let him feel the silence. "That is correct. Good idea. I already have a prepaid cell, so why don't you just e-mail me when you get yours?"

Silence—a very satisfying silence, even acknowledging the seriousness of the situation. "You're full of shit."

I sighed loudly but did not respond.

More silence. He was trying to figure out if I was bluffing. Finally, he spoke, "I'll e-mail."

*   *   *   *   *

I couldn't decide whether the FBI's untraceable cell phone made me feel like a drug dealer or a philandering husband. Either choice would have been hazardous to my health, the latter probably terminal. Still, there was a certain feeling of power. I called Margo's brother's cell. "Tony, Mac McGregor. I need Margo."

I was greeted with a grunt and then nothing. I assumed that she would have to call me back. However, after a few minutes of waiting, she answered. "Hello?"

I got right to the point. "Margo, in the event that you lose your pension, you will receive a tax-free lump sum of $1 million. If you would like, I could invest it for you to ensure that you get a minimum of $50,000 a year for life."

Contemplative quiet. "You're sure?"

"Yes."

"What if something happens to you?"

Now I was quiet. This was a thought I had pushed aside. "This agreement was guaranteed way above my pay grade. I will have a binding letter sent to you if you give me a preferred address."

She gave me the address she wanted, and then she gave me the address I wanted, in Naples Florida.

*   *   *   *   *

Sweat ran down Jeremy Lyons's forearms as he pushed through his third rep. Two hundred and fifty pounds bench-pressed in perfect form, as if a machine were lowering the bar and raising it with robotic precision to a perfect extension of the arms.

"I'd like to take a closer look at McGregor."

Max's intrusion into his concentration caused Jeremy to narrow his eyes and clench his jaw. He did not respond. He completed the last of fifteen perfect repetitions and laid the bar on the brackets. Slowly he rose, grabbed a towel, and wiped the perspiration from his body. Under no circumstances would Jeremy engage in conversation when he was lying down and the other person was standing up.

Raising himself to full height, Jeremy stood close to Max, looking down. "Max," he asked evenly, "have you ever been to the Sistine Chapel in Rome?"

Standing toe to toe with his hands on his hips, Max Parnavich's eyes locked on Jeremy's. After a few moments, he moved his head slightly to the left and then to the right.

"Pity. Imagine if you had been with the great Michelangelo as he painted his masterpiece from a position similar to mine just moments ago. Would you have dared to interrupt him?" The question was accentuated with a raised eyebrow as Jeremy awaited an answer.

Max's face was flaccid, exuding no emotion whatsoever.

Jeremy watched in disguised amusement as Max worked to maintain control. Then, as if brushing away a fly, Jeremy back-waved his hand. "I think not!"

He turned and walked to the glass water container. With his back to Max, he poured the ice water into a cup and slowly drank it. He tossed the empty cup into the wastebasket. Turning theatrically, he said in a mocking tone, "Come, come, Max, enlighten me. Why do you perceive the affable Boy Scout Mac McGregor as a threat to our empire?"

Max, remaining rooted to his spot, continued to glare at Jeremy before responding. Not breaking eye contact, he replied, "Intuition." He waited a beat and then added, "It has served you well in the past."

Jeremy was growing tired of the man's petulance. Max was bored, and when he was bored, he invariably became tedious. Jeremy threw him a bone. "That it has, Max. Your preservation skills are unequaled. What else?"

"McGregor's smart, has an insider's knowledge of the business, and is probably well connected. Remember, he was good enough to be number two to you while you were at his firm."

A subtle dig. Jeremy smiled. "As are you now, Max."

CHAPTER 23

LIKE MANY NATURALLY CHARMING males, Frank Griffin was an actor. At Northwestern University, where he graduated with honors, he had a major role in every significant drama production put on by the school during his tenure. His directors, critics, and audiences all had him targeted for a career in Hollywood.

Movie-star looks, bedroom eyes, and an undeniable charm promised easy success. And like a perfectly cut diamond, a box of Godiva chocolates, or that first glass of wine after a hard day, Frank Griffin was irresistible to women.

Halfway through his third bourbon and water, in his underwear, staring bleakly at the TV, Frank was playing the part of the alcoholic loser to perfection. His two-bedroom luxury apartment looked like it was inhabited by college kids on Spring Break.

Dirty dishes were piled in the sink, clothes were strewn all over the bedroom, the door to the medicine cabinet in the bathroom was ajar, and his hairbrush held up the uncapped toothpaste tube. He would not have been able to find his uncased Gibson guitar if his life depended on it. It was collecting dust behind the open closet door.

Frank's trance was partially broken as he moved off the couch toward the bathroom. He stumbled over a discarded pizza box that was still half full of day-old remains.

If he had turned on the semiambient light and looked in the mirror, he would not have recognized himself. The once immaculate man now looked through bleary eyes. Greasy, filthy hair and an unshaven, dirty face completed the image. It had taken God seven days to create the world, but it had taken only seven seconds for Frank's world to end.

After that fateful day, Jeremy had decreed that Frank would take a week off to get himself together. So for the next seven days, the man with the perfect apartment, the man who took enormous pride in his appearance, had vegetated. When hunger became too uncomfortable, either pizza or Chinese was delivered. Too listless or too drunk to shower or shave, he merely existed.

After relieving himself, instead of returning to the safety of his couch, Frank opened the glass doors to his balcony. He walked slowly to the balcony's edge and gripped the railing with both hands. As he leaned over the rail, tears streamed down his face.

A few minutes later, he hesitantly staggered away from the railing and sat heavily in the chair overlooking the Gulf for the first time in a week. Gradually, the combination of the sun on his face and the smell and feel of the ocean caused a flicker of life in his comatose demeanor.

Frank became conscious of his breathing. He looked at his dirty fingernails and then clenched his fists until his nails dug into the palms of his hands. Anger swelled in him as he reflected again on the perfidy inflicted upon him and the toll it had taken.

The instant the whip carved into his body, the shock and injustice had almost caused his heart to stop. He had idolized Jeremy for his intellect, ruthless cunning, and decisiveness. More importantly, he had felt that Jeremy appreciated him, valued him, and even liked him. With two vicious strokes, Frank had been indelibly scarred—physically and emotionally.

All week Frank had worn the same wretched undershirt. If he never examined the destruction, perhaps it had never happened. He had always slept in the nude—never again. How many women had gasped at the magnificence of his well-tuned body? If a woman saw his naked body now, she would be repulsed or overcome with pity.

The humiliation of being beaten like a slave would never end. How do you spin "I was curled on the floor in a fetal position crying and screaming for mercy"?

Frank closed his eyes and took a deep breath. As the sun caressed his face, he began to reminisce about happier times. He had been the quarterback of his high school football team, which went to the state finals, and he remembered his coach's favorite message. "I am a God-fearing man, and I believe in the Bible, but I don't believe that Jesus meant to turn the other cheek in football. If they hit you hard, hit them harder. Otherwise, they will never respect you. They will run right over your sissy ass."

Frank actually managed a slight smile, a recent stranger to his countenance. A week ago his goals were to become indispensable to Jeremy, keep the money machine rolling, and bed beautiful women. *Change in plans*, he thought ruefully.

Taking a deep breath, Frank put a hand on each side of the chair and pushed himself upright. He gazed a final time at the azure Gulf waters, turned around, and walked back into the apartment. On the way to the kitchen telephone, he bent down to pick up trash. He called his cleaning service and promised to pay them double if they arrived within an hour. He hung up the phone and walked into the bathroom.

Stripping off his fetid underwear, he walked to the clothes hamper, paused, and then tossed everything into the nearby trash instead. He turned the shower on full blast and started to get in, but then he stopped. With fury, he slammed the light switch on and glared at his angry wounds in the mirror. He fought against the urge to turn his head in disgust and humiliation. When steam finally clouded the mirror, he stepped into the shower and let the scalding water sear his body.

CHAPTER 24

WITH THE REVERENCE IN which a Christian might hold a favorite biblical passage or the pride that a father feels when his child scores the winning goal in the championship game, Jeremy Lyons silently read the words that served as *his* Apostles' Creed:

> *Awake to the truth,*
> *the meaning of life;*
> *platitudes, hypocrisy aside,*
> *my reason for being*
> *is victory.*
> *Painful to accept,*
> *yet disregard at your risk;*
> *obstacles are obliterated*
> *in the pursuit*
> *of victory.*
> *All methods*
> *and all strategies*
> *should be applauded;*
> *judgment is irrelevant*
> *to victory.*
> *Embraced by our culture,*
> *we search for something more*
> *while we celebrate winners*

and collectively praise
each victory.
Marvel at my results
for success determines genius;
I manifest all desire,
for I have achieved
my victory.

The ritual never changed. Each time before Jeremy entered a thought, incident, accomplishment, or chapter into his literary masterpiece, he reread the opening poem. Succinct, deadly accurate, and profound, he considered it his greatest literary work. It stood to reason that his own words would serve as his inspiration.

Not even Max knew about the small room that could be entered only through Jeremy's bedroom closet. Construction had been done at night, between two o'clock and four o'clock, by a specialty builder of hidden rooms and panic rooms. The entire project had been off the books.

Jeremy had paid an exorbitant fee in cash, and he assumed that the builder's widow was enjoying it. He felt as if he had cheated on Max by tying up this loose end himself, but an artist needs to practice his craft. Jeremy also appreciated the historical link; it was not dissimilar to the pharaohs, who, after their tombs were built, killed their architects. Finally, a promise of discretion always increases in value when there are six feet of dirt over the promisor.

The room was a square, ten feet by ten feet, with white walls. It contained a desk, an office chair, a computer, and a tiny refrigerator filled with bottled water. The small attached bathroom had only a sink and a toilet. The weathered desk showed its age, and only the chair looked like it was this decade's vintage.

There were no windows and no television, radio, or telephone. Although Jeremy had an emergency flashlight, the only illumination in the room was a chrome desk lamp. Jeremy loved being there. It was like playing hide and seek and knowing that you could never be found.

At an early age, Jeremy had learned the art of disappearing and displacement. His father, a brilliant mathematician and renowned scholar, was an emotionless, walking cadaver. His unique form of abuse was withering, disdainful silence. From his first conscious memory, Jeremy knew that the pleading cries and upraised arms of a child would not be rewarded with a father's touch.

Jeremy was a mistake. His father never forgave his mother for hiding her pregnancy and for not aborting the unwanted fetus. Undoubtedly, her only rebellion had caused him to turn what had surely been the cold water of his emotions into a constant, arctic IV drip.

When he was old enough to understand, Jeremy watched as the continuing cancer of his father's coldness destroyed his mother. Instead of wanting to rush to her, love her enough for both of them, he observed with morbid fascination as this weakling who had borne him disintegrated before his eyes.

On his twelfth birthday, she mercifully died in her sleep, an empty shell dried up like a pile of dead leaves without family, friends, or comfort.

The next day his father had her cremated without ceremony or words. Afterward, he placed her ashes in Jeremy's room to validate that her demise was a result of his birth.

The following day, Jeremy's father brought in a brochure for the Fork Union Military Academy. He dropped the brochure along with a bus ticket on Jeremy's bed. For the first time in Jeremy's memory, his father actually put four sentences together when addressing him. "Pack your clothes. You will leave Monday. My secretary will send you a monthly stipend for your expenses. If there is to be value in your existence, the military will find it."

He did not respond to his father or cry for compassion. Instead, Jeremy returned the coldness of his father's words with a look of competing disgust. Then the naked hatred and intensity of the boy's stare forced his father to divert his eyes. After a moment's pause, Jeremy's father turned and walked out of his room and out of his life.

Outside of Jeremy's private room, he never had a thought about his pathetic mother or his reluctant, sperm-donating father. Nor did he ever envy those who achieved success and credited their perfect parents or some omniscient, omnipresent deity.

The essential lesson of his sterile upbringing was self-reliance: Greatness can be achieved without support, faith, or financial advantages. And only when it is will the victory be pure.

Jeremy's eyes lingered on the last stanza of his poem. To him it was not strange that he wrote his manifesto in the nude. About a year ago, after a strenuous workout, he had taken a photo of himself behind the desk. Rippling muscles and a slight sheen of moisture on his body completed the picture of intensity and intellect that was apparent in his penetrating gaze at the camera. Even though he had made the concession of sitting behind the desk so that only his upper body was visible, the required author's picture would nevertheless be compelling.

As the opening poem indicated, this book would not be just another nonfiction instruction manual. Due to Jeremy's natural insights into people, it would read like pulp fiction. It would be impossible for the reader not to be riveted to every page. To ensure acceptance by the masses, he included necessary acts of violence and, of course, his sexual exploits.

Each chapter outlined Jeremy's updated net worth and described in minute detail how he manipulated the markets and the system. Phrases such as "the ends justify the means" and "it's just collateral damage" were coined not by Jeremy but by his predecessors. Nevertheless, those popularly held views added justification to Jeremy's methodology.

Everybody cheats, everybody lies, and with the right motivation, everybody would kill. Is not killing justified if we are protecting our family or defending ourselves? Throughout the ages, men have killed for their religions and often been labeled heroes.

Jeremy smiled. He killed only when necessary or expedient. In a world in which the only real rule was survival of the fittest, his objective was simply to be the fittest.

The temperature in Jeremy's sanctuary was kept at a consistent sixty-nine degrees. Still, he felt an unaccustomed chill. He turned the computer off. He rubbed his eyes and considered once again his conundrum.

Secure arrangements had been made to distribute his work posthumously if Jeremy were to die unexpectedly. When his heart stopped beating, the designated lawyer would have the manuscript, sufficient funds for the self-publication, and the motivation to follow Jeremy's instructions to the letter. If the attorney deviated, evidence against him would be revealed, and that evidence would lead to his certain incarceration.

On the other hand, if the regulators became so intrusive that they examined every trade, Jeremy would ride off into the sunset. In this environment, that was no longer just a remote possibility. The other risk, albeit slight, was that his operation could be exposed. Intimidation, compromising information, and lack of financial incentive were all factors that should safeguard his companies. Still, Jeremy thought, with resignation, that stupidity can never be underestimated.

Contingency plans were as much a part of Jeremy's DNA as guilt is to that of a Jewish mother. Thus, in the unlikely event of his risks becoming reality, he was more than prepared. It would require leaving the country, but his desire to never leave US soil had diminished with the increasing cowardliness and loser mentality of the so-called "leaders of the free world."

And it would be quite a consolation prize to be able to publish his masterpiece and witness the outrage, the prurient interest, the acknowledgement, and inevitably, the acclaim.

CHAPTER 25

OUR QUAINT CHURCH, WHITE with dark red doors, is like something you would expect to see on a picture postcard. Surrounded by an immaculate three-hundred-year-old cemetery, it is nestled in the heart of Potomac, Maryland.

I would like to say that the strength of my faith matches my church attendance, but God knows better. Still, Grace and I relish the time we spend in this warm, loving atmosphere.

At least for us, they might as well have assigned seats in our church. Grace and I, and family when possible, always sit on the right side about eight rows from the front. I am sure that our other three offspring have some extraordinarily creative excuses for not attending this morning, but we were pleased to have our oldest daughter, the lovely Frannie McGregor, with us.

After the sermon, the minister always asks visitors to stand up. I noted a full-bird Army colonel almost directly behind me as he rose. I smiled and nodded acknowledgement. He nodded back at me and then sat down.

Next on the agenda, the congregation rose and passed the peace. I made a point of shaking the officer's hand first. "Peace be with you, Colonel. Thanks for all you do."

"Thank you, sir. I appreciate your kind words."

We both moved on to shake hands with other well-wishers and then sat back down as the service continued. After the service ended and the choir had walked down the aisle, I noticed that the colonel remained standing. He just stared at the cross on the altar as the other parishioners made their way out of the church.

Before I spoke, I took in his appearance. He wore a perfectly pressed uniform adorned with a chest full of combat medals. His short, cropped, salt-and-pepper hair framed a tanned, weathered face. *Warrior* was written all over him. I speculated whether he had recently returned from Iraq or Afghanistan.

"Colonel Jackson," I said, after reading his name tag, "welcome to our church. I'm Mac McGregor. This is my wife, Grace, and our daughter Frannie."

"So nice to meet you, Grace," he said as he took her hand. His intense black eyes seemed to dance out and meet hers. Then he turned to Frannie. He surrounded her hand with his hands, and his eyes lingered on her face.

Slightly disconcerted, I asked, "Colonel, where are you stationed?"

"Please call me Mark, sir. My last assignment was Afghanistan." He looked at me when he spoke and then turned his eyes to Grace and finally to Frannie. It was like he wanted to be sure that everyone felt included.

"Was it as bad as we hear?" I asked softly.

"In some respects, yes. The conditions for battle are not favorable. Becoming involved in something that is really not your business can be hazardous to your health."

The colonel stopped and made the eye circuit again, as if he were programmed. His eyes stopped at Frannie, and he fixed her with a strange smile for a few moments. He then added, "But there were many acts of heroism."

Frannie was blinking nervously at the attention, so I interjected quickly, "What do you do for the Army, Mark?"

He gave us an exaggerated shocked look. "Why, McGregors, if I told you, I would have to kill you."

His accompanying half-chuckle did little to alleviate my feeling that I was really sorry I had started this conversation. I was at a loss for words with no ability to extricate us from what had become an awkward situation.

After a few more moments of uncomfortable silence, he smiled and said, "You were so nice to introduce yourselves. I won't forget your kindness, but I do need to leave. Peace be with you." With that he executed a precise about-face and walked quickly out of our church.

We stood there and looked at one another, trying to figure out what had just happened. "My guess is that he recently returned from combat and his behavior reflects combat fatigue," I offered.

Frannie looked dubious but nodded. "At the end, he actually sounded almost charming," I added, hoping to quell her concerns.

Grace looked at me, raised an eyebrow, and whispered, "I think I need another shower."

As he walked, "Mark Jackson" surreptitiously took in all of his surroundings. He did this not out of concern; it was simply an ingrained habit. If he had been asked the purpose of the episode in the church, he would have shrugged. He had not analyzed it himself. Although he had determined that McGregor had no knowledge of Jeremy's operation, the self-appointed colonel was messing with him, leaving remote clues as to his connection with Jeremy, and in short, trying to rattle the man. If he had examined his motives, he might have discovered that he was just frustrated that McGregor was clean.

He stopped at a tombstone. He had absently walked through the cemetery on a seemingly purposeless wander only to read the inscription of this particular one. "Angus McGregor, 1920–1999." *Like father, like son*, he mused. With satisfaction, he noted the adjacent reserved plots.

*   *   *   *   *

If an idle mind is the devil's workshop, a twisted mind is the devil's playground. Which is why, even though Max Parnavich had completed his mission, he was considering extending his stay.

With a minimum of effort, Max had been able to tap McGregor's office's phone. He had learned who his clients were, how he interacted with them, and what his family's plans were for the weekend. There was nothing to indicate that Jeremy was on his radar. The face-to-face had been arranged primarily because McGregor's older daughter had sounded interesting. Also, because McGregor had a history with Jeremy, Max thought it would be fun to fuck with him.

Max's beige Ford Taurus cruised onto the George Washington Parkway toward DC. He was staying at the Ritz-Carlton. The hotel's fitness center and proximity to Georgetown had overridden Max's normal desire for anonymity. As he weaved through the lights in the afternoon traffic, he examined his thought process. By the time he pulled into the hotel and turned the car over to the valet, he had concluded that there was nothing more to do here.

As Max entered his hotel room, he glanced at the full-length mirror. He had decided on the Army uniform because it made him invisible. People's eyes were drawn to the uniform and chest of medals, not to the chameleon inside. Reluctantly, he took off the uniform and hung it carefully in the closet.

Stripping off his underwear, he tossed it on the floor of the closet. He glanced again at the mirror, appraising his enviable muscle tone, highlighted by the myriad of scars. Max jerked back from the image. He turned and grabbed his jock strap and running shorts from the drawer. Discipline—the price of self-absorption was an added number of punishments in the gym.

Max quickly laced his athletic shoes and snatched a T-shirt. He put his hand on the door. He paused and froze, not lifting a muscle. Then he walked back over to his suitcase, removed the prepaid cell from the inside zipper pocket, and made a call.

*   *   *   *   *

Checking the number on her portable phone, she saw that the caller was unknown. *If you can't tell who's calling, why pay for the service?* she thought. Nevertheless, she held the phone to her ear. "Hello?" The huskiness of her voice was genetic, not artificially induced.

"Is this Frannie McGregor?" asked the confident voice.

"To whom am I speaking?" came the cautious reply.

"Ah, a careful woman, generally a sign of keen intellect. Frannie, this is Mark Jackson, Colonel Jackson. We met this morning at your church."

Frannie blinked. By family consensus, this was a strange man. Why on earth was he calling her? "Uh, sure, I remember," she responded hesitantly.

"I realize after our brief conversation, you're probably wondering why I might be calling."

The lightness of his tone felt unnatural to Frannie. She wondered not only why he was calling but how he had gotten her number. It was unlisted.

"I find myself staying in Washington for a few more nights. I'm afraid I'm a novice in your city. So that I don't have to wander around Georgetown by myself, I hoped that I could entice you to join me for dinner."

A chill went up her spine. She wanted to shout, "No! You're weird!" and "You're old!" Frannie felt like her tongue was frozen, and she couldn't speak. Her mind had gone blank. It took her thirty long seconds to finally respond.

"I'm flattered," she said, "but I'm seeing someone."

145

"Really? Tell me about him," Max challenged in a voice now sounding reptilian.

Her chill morphed into genuine fear as Frannie felt physically assaulted by his tone. She was dumbstruck, unable to utter a sound.

"Frannie, Frannie, my sweet Frannie," Max cooed. "Life is all about making choices. Your first choice was to have a lovely dinner with a distinguished soldier, one of America's best." He sighed deeply into the phone. "Regrettably, you took the second fork in the road."

CHAPTER 26

I ANSWERED THE PHONE and listened. Her words poured out like water over a broken levee—borderline panic. Pushing my surging anxiety and fury into my hiding place, I responded, "I'll pick you up. Pack a suitcase. I'll be there before you close it." It was understood that Frannie was coming home.

No arguments, no debate. My fiercely independent daughter was, for the moment, my baby again. Grace, standing next to me, grabbed my arm and looked at me with wide-eyed concern. In the same measured voice, I told her that Frannie had received a harassing phone call. I hugged her and softly assured her that Frannie was upset but fine. I was having her stay with us for a few days.

I backed the Lexus out of the garage, drove down my street, and turned right onto River Road. I mashed the accelerator to the floor. Careering around corners, I half hoped that cops would stop me so that I could have a police escort. Frannie is not an alarmist.

Gliding through the stop sign on Muddy Branch Road, I punched it again. As I barreled past the school zone sentries, their traffic camera flashed indignantly. Fumbling with my cell phone, I hit the speed dial for Joe. His answering machine picked up. "Joe, call me now!"

Turning too wide with one hand, I was halfway into the other lane when I heard a screech of brakes and an angry horn. The approaching car swerved and went roughly into the dirt. Adrenaline ripped through my body as I pumped the brakes and stared into the rearview mirror. I prayed that no one was hurt.

A man emerged from the car and shook a fist at me. The relief that I felt momentarily assuaged my guilt. I hit the gas again, screaming obscenities at myself for my stupidity. The fear of hurting an innocent person was fortunately sufficient to restore a semblance of sanity to my driving.

As my car screeched to a stop in front of her house, Frannie threw the door open, ran down the walk, and fell into my arms. I hugged her tightly. I could no longer expect the blind faith of a six-year-old who knows that her daddy can protect her from anything. Yet I felt her seeking that comfort, giving in to the familiar smells, the reassuring heartbeat, the strength and steadfastness that are somehow indigenous to fathers.

Still holding on, she leaned her head back and looked at me with teary eyes. "How ... how did you get ..."

"I rode on the wings of angels," I interrupted as I smiled into those trusting eyes. I pulled her closer so that she wouldn't focus on the fact that a fifteen-minute trip had somehow been shortened to ten.

*   *   *   *   *

I had just turned Frannie over to Grace when Joe called me back. "Sorry, Mac. We were at the movies."

Without a breath, I detailed Frannie's conversation with Colonel Jackson. Then I asked for his help. "Joe, this is your area of expertise, but I've had more time to grind on this. Do you have any connections with the Army to get a read on this bastard? His name is Colonel Mark Jackson. Full bird colonel, Infantry. around Five feet ten inches tall, solid, military-cut salt-and-pepper hair, black eyes, scar. When he smiles, his eyes don't sync up."

"Mac, how do you know what he looks like?"

"Sorry. We saw him at church this morning." I brought Joe up to speed.

"If your description is accurate, it shouldn't be too hard to find him. It may be tough to get into his jacket, but I do have a few friends. Do you think he was stalking you?"

"Why would ... " It was like a fist punched me right in the gut.

I staggered and sat heavily on the couch. I rubbed my free hand over my eyes, trying to wipe away the image.

"Mac, are you there?"

"Yeah," I said unsteadily. I swiveled my head to look back at Grace and

Frannie. Then I stared out into the black night. "I'm afraid that the Army will not have a record on our Colonel Jackson, Joe."

"Why not?"

I paused, begging not to be right. "Pull a twenty out of your wallet."

He was silent.

"I'll call Margo Savino tomorrow," I said woodenly. "I believe that our descriptions will match. Max Parnavich just tried to get a date with my daughter."

*　　*　　*　　*　　*

When Margo answered the phone, I wasted no time with preliminaries. "Margo, I need your help. Max Parnavich showed up at my church posing as an Army colonel named Mark Jackson. He chatted with my wife, my daughter, and me. Obviously, at the time I had not indentified him. Somehow the sick bastard got my daughter's phone number, called her, and asked her out." I took a few breaths to lower my blood pressure.

"Are you sure that it was him?"

I gave her a description. She sighed. "How can I help?"

"Is there anything you can tell me about his tendencies, eccentricities, or mode of operation? I've got to narrow down the horrific possibilities."

Margo spoke softly. "I'm sorry, Mac. He's a nightmare. You were just trying to do the right thing, and now you're scared shitless for your daughter."

Her summation was right on point. Joe had referred a retired Special Forces guy who would be Frannie's bodyguard for a while. But there was no longer-term solution as long as Max Parnavich was running free.

"Did you ever talk about Jeremy or Max on a traceable phone?" she asked.

I furiously thought back. I knew that any tactical discussions had taken place over the cell phone Joe gave me. Shit—calls to Judkins and Mosberg. Plus, we asked Sam about Sal Seminara over R. J.'s cell. "Yeah," I said with resignation. "If he was able to tap into my office phone, he might have found out that I was looking for him. I can't imagine that he could do that, and I have no idea what would trigger their interest in the first place."

Margo certainly had no answer for this. I was just asking myself. She spoke into the silence. "It really doesn't matter how he found out. I've obviously had no contact with the animal for over two decades, but I'll give you some thoughts."

"I'd really appreciate it, Margo. I'm grasping at straws."

"I don't believe that this leopard changes his spots. Max loves to play, to toy with people. He would have derived no pleasure out of kidnapping your daughter. Maybe you were better than Jeremy when you worked at Johnston Wellons. It may have been curiosity on Max's part. He used to love road trips."

She paused and then continued. "I do think that Max wanted you to know that it was him, or he would have chosen a name not associated with money. Even if he doesn't know that you're snooping around in their business, he wants you to know who he is." She stopped to think for a minute. "How would he get the maximum reaction out of you?"

I had been holding my breath. I let it out slowly. Everything about Margo's thought process made sense, maybe because I needed it to. "Frighten my daughter."

"Of course. If he threatened you, you'd probably just get pissed and start carrying."

"I would have a fight at home, but you're right."

"I know," she said gently. "The macho response is extremely predictable."

I forced a soft chuckle. "Any other thoughts, Margo? You have been extremely helpful."

"Nope. Just get the bastard, and then we can both sleep at night."

CHAPTER 27

IT HAD BEEN TWO weeks since Frank Griffin had literally had his ass whipped. For the first week, surveillance had been a walk in the park. The putz never left his apartment. Max had watched his disintegration with morbid fascination. When Frank walked out on his balcony on the last day, Max had thought that a swan dive might have been in order.

Frank did finally manage to pull himself together and get in to work. Max had mixed feelings about Frank's return. On one hand, witnessing Frank's body hurtling over the rail would have been visually exhilarating. On the other hand, it would have eliminated the ongoing pleasure of torturing him. On the surface it was business as usual for pretty boy, except that the smugness, the confident walk, and the obligatory flirting were replaced by a deer-in-the-headlights look. *Maybe Jeremy whipped his balls off*, thought Max.

Overall, Max had little regard for humanity, and he had no regard for cowards. He would take a bullet for Jeremy or follow him into hell. But if Jeremy had brought that whip down on Max, the whip would have to have been extracted from Jeremy's throat. In Max's mind, any sign of courage from Frank might have prevented a second strike—a look of defiance, a shout of indignation. Even remaining upright would have demonstrated a hint of manhood.

The shrieking, wailing, shivering coward who pissed himself should consider himself lucky. If Max had held the whip, he would not have stopped until he had flayed every inch of skin from that poor excuse for a man. To Max, there was no reason for cowards to take up space on the planet.

Apparently, Frank was still able to do his job, but one specific thing that had changed was that he was afraid to look at Max. Although he would make eye contact with Jeremy when required, his head would whip around like a cobra's whenever Max walked into his field of vision. As a result, Max was not concerned that Frank would spot Max following him.

Thursday night was the first night since the beating that Frank had ventured outside of his apartment, and he went early. He took the last barstool on the right at Handsome Harry's bar. A relatively new restaurant in Naples, Florida, it was located on 3rd Street, right across from another establishment belonging to its owner, Tommy Bahama's.

During the tourist season, Thursday nights were the most crowded of the week because Thursdays on 3rd meant that live music played in at least four different locations, all within a block of each other. The right side of Handsome Harry's bar was the perfect spot to be swallowed up by the crowds.

The glistening light-wood bar was packed three deep. Max stood behind two short, plain, middle-aged women who had little hope of conversing with anyone other than each other. Because he was positioned directly across from Frank, it would not have been difficult for Frank to spot him. Had that been the case, Max was sure that Frank's pussy ass would have hightailed out of the bar.

But Frankie boy stayed in his cocoon. He spoke to no one. His eyes were either focused on his drink or staring absently at the flat screen above him.

As Max sipped his Grey Goose on the rocks, he gazed around at his surroundings. He was in a surprisingly good mood. Earlier he had been obliged to discipline a forgetful young lady. To him, that was like a sip from the fountain of youth.

The high sheen on the bar, the sparkling glasses, and the efficient bartenders gave a sense of clean precision. At Handsome Harry's, about half the tables were outside, and that was the preferred seating. The music was not loud enough to discourage conversation, and the diners could either watch the dancers or join them.

As Max watched the dancers, he concluded that dancing was merely an excuse for men to try to look younger and for women to try to look sexy. One woman, dancing alone, looked hopefully at Max. She was short, weighed probably 120 pounds, and had streaky blond hair. She had a face that might remind someone of their next-door neighbor when they were growing up or some great-aunt that they hadn't seen in forever.

Her nondescript attire made the chance that she would receive a second glance a remote one. Certainly not from Max, who chilled her with a "not in this lifetime, bitch" look that reddened her cheeks and caused her to turn away in embarrassment. She hurriedly walked off the dance floor.

By this time, Max had secured a seat at the bar, in plain sight of Frank but still undetected. He noted two blond women who were dancing together and succeeding in looking sexy. He motioned for them to come over. As they approached, Max spoke to the huddled bodies at the bar in a low growl. "These ladies are with me. Make room for them." Bodies parted like they were the Red Sea and Max was Moses.

The two blondes, both trying to look like Jessica Simpson, with tanned skin and beckoning cleavage, were also high. Otherwise, they might have been more reluctant to join a man who was twice their age. Max put an arm around each woman and pulled their heads close to his. "You ladies look like you might be up for a challenge," he whispered.

"Did you bring a paramedic with you?" asked Jessica number one as she looked at her friend and they giggled in unison.

Max looked at her evenly. He held his hand palm up as an open invitation. Still speaking softly, but ominously, he said, "If you want to give me your hand, I will give you nine reasons why it might be you who would need resuscitation." Her eyes widened. She shrank back. With a soft laugh, the chameleon changed colors. "But alas, this is not about me. See that man at the end of the bar?"

In spite of their anxiety over Max's demeanor, the women both looked reflexively at Frank Griffin. "The man's name is Frank," Max said, so pleasantly that they felt that they had been mistaken about his earlier tone. "He is single and rich, and last week his heart was broken. If he knew that I was putting you up to this, he would kill me."

"What do you want us to do?" asked the obviously alpha blonde, who was now respectful and intrigued.

Max took out a roll of hundred dollar bills big enough to choke a horse. "One hundred dollars if he dances with one of you, five hundred if he kisses you, and five thousand if one or both of you have sex with him. Pick your poison." He gestured toward the prey.

Their eyes lit up as if he had offered them lines of high-grade cocaine. They looked at each other gleefully, and then the quiet one asked in a whiny voice, "Wait a minute. Is he gay?"

Max peeled off two hundred-dollar bills and handed one to each of them. "Absolutely not, but these are yours to keep even if you do not get him to accept the challenge." They grabbed the money greedily, and Max watched intently as they threaded their way around the semicircular bar. In the process, a few drinks were jostled, but allowances are made for beautiful women dressed provocatively.

As the women approached Frank from both sides, he momentarily looked up and then back down in an attempt to be dismissive. The aggressive one worked her way between Frank and the man to his left so that her ass was almost in the stranger's lap.

She then pushed her well-constructed right breast into Frank's left arm. Frank jerked his arm away. However, the man seated next to him did not even move a muscle as he looked on in astonishment. Meanwhile, the other woman was trying to crowd Frank from the right, so soon his arms were pulled in like he was receiving a volleyball serve.

Max was enjoying every second of Frank's agony as the women cajoled, pleaded, promised, and mauled him. Max couldn't remember ever laughing enough to cause tears, but this couldn't have been any better if Frank *had* been gay.

Finally, Frank shook them off like a golden retriever after a bath, threw cash on the bar, and pushed patrons aside as he hurried out. He moved like he was escaping a swarm of bees. Max was glad that he had not wired the women. If he had the audio as well as the video, it might have been Max who peed in his pants.

CHAPTER 28

ON MARCH 9, 2009, Citigroup mentioned that it had actually made money for the first two months of the year. Immediately, the other former major banks chimed in with, "Me, too." This would not be particularly newsworthy except for two things. First, companies generally do not disclose their earnings before a completed quarter. Second, the stock market rallied.

This was a good thing not only for the country, which alternated between panic and more panic, but also for the psyche of the artist formerly known as "The Wizard." A little less economic anxiety meant that I could possibly lower the client alert level from blazing red. Now all I had to do was to figure out a way to lower my personal alert level.

*   *   *   *   *

"Are you okay?"

"What?"

"I asked if you're okay, Mac."

"Of course," I answered dismissively. R. J. stood in the entryway of my conference room wearing an annoying concerned look. "Is there something in my demeanor or my behavior that compelled you to ask about my welfare?" I added with an edge. Otherwise, he would continue to stand there.

"It seems like you have been acting strangely. May I come in?"

"Are you trying to piss me off? No, dipstick, just stand there and continue to look at me like I'm a mental patient."

So, of course, he remained rooted to the spot, the only change being that his face now took on the sympathetic martyr look. I wished that I had something to throw at him, but all I had were the remnants of a partially eaten lunch. "Out of curiosity, when have you ever had to ask me to sit down when I'm in here, alone, and the door is open?"

"When you're acting strangely,"

I popped out of my chair so quickly that it toppled backward, startling R. J. He jumped back reflexively, and I smothered an evil smile. "Please, R. J., come in and have a seat and shed some light on my abnormal behavior." The artificial sweetness of my tone was the equivalent to about a hundred pounds of Splenda.

He took a seat and gave me the look that a lawyer gives when he believes that the verdict will be in his favor. He began ticking off points on his fingers because he knows that is a habit of mine. "The prosecution's first exhibit is the half-eaten salad resting despondently by your side."

"You're definitely prosecuting me."

"I took that side because you tend to be defensive when I'm right."

I nodded. "So being defensive once every decade is bad form?"

His raised eyebrow indicated that he felt no rebuttal was necessary. "Exhibit two is that you had been staring into space for twenty minutes before my initial query."

"Do you have a nanny cam?" I asked irritably.

"Would you at least admit that wasting time is not in your DNA?" Frustration was beginning to show in his voice.

Beaten, I replied, "Did I request this journey into introspection?"

This time I got the look of the ever-patient parent. "As you know, there is no off position on the caring switch."

"I thought it was no off position on the genius switch."

He shrugged his shoulders, raised his hands with palms up, and gave me a look to let me know that I was stating the obvious. I would deny it under oath, but both statements about him were closer to truth than fiction.

"You seem to have blocked it out, but you have to be upset about the incident with Max and Frannie?"

I got up from my chair, gathered the lunch trash, took it out of the room, dumped it in the trash can under my desk, came back in, shut the door, and sat back down at the table. I folded my hands on top of the table and said, not unkindly, "Are you my shrink now? I thought I was the only one allowed to practice unlicensed therapy."

"You're deflecting. Answer the question."

I took a breath and thought for a few moments. Then I unloaded. "I've been scared every second since I realized who the bastard was. We have security at the house now, but it's just temporary. Even if Grace and I wanted to make it permanent, Frannie wouldn't put up with it."

I shrugged. "So I'm in a quandary. When our kids were growing up and were afraid to try out for a team, or give a presentation at school, or swim in the ocean, I told them that they should 'face the fears; embrace the fears.' And no matter how busy I am, no matter how intense my focus, my mind wanders to this alleged ninja maniac, and I am paralyzed with fear. How do I protect my family? Every instinct shouts for me to head to witness protection, although the evidence isn't sufficient to even add up to circumstantial. I have no idea whether there is a real threat or this lunatic is just playing with me." I lowered my head and my hand rubbed my eyes closed.

"Are you getting help?"

I squinted at him like I could make him or me see more clearly.

"From whom, grasshopper? There is no help until they catch this bastard. I've been over it with Joe, thought about buying a weapon, which, translated, means the whole family freaks, and now I've shared it with you. Do you have any answers? "

R. J. shook his head.

"About 95 percent of the time, I can act like everything is normal," I said. "In the past, depression has visited but never stayed the night. Anxiety tries to possess us in every severe bear market, and we acknowledge the introduction but pass it on to the pundits. The real danger to our equilibrium is abject fear. So, I will fake it. I would have been a great hot young woman for a rich old guy because I can fake it all day long."

He gave me a brief smile. "So what will you do?"

"I will get past this because I have no choice. If I let the fear consume me, he wins."

*   *   *   *   *

My prepaid cell phone had not rung once. Only two explanations for this silence could be considered. Either my liaison, GI Joe, had nothing at all to report, or Joe had played me, and I was, in reality, out of the loop.

I had kept the letter from Sam Golden that had been hand delivered to me two weeks ago. As expected, he had sent both Joe and me an eerily accurate regurgitation of our group discussion, compliments of the amazing Kay Murrey. What was not expected was the touching, heartfelt note that my friend of almost forty years had included.

Dear Mac,

When I first approached you, I felt uncomfortable because I know how involved you are with your clients. I am embarrassed that I used our friendship to persuade you to help. What I anticipated was a few phone calls by you. What I received was due diligence and analysis that far exceeded my expectations.

When R. J. called and described your scenario for the passing of the information, my first thought was that your security measures were a bit loony. After your extraordinarily insightful analysis, I understood, and I marveled at your creativity. Please believe that if I had had any idea of the danger associated with this frightening individual, I would never have asked for your help.

Mac, the real purpose of my letter is to tell you how much the administration and I appreciate all your efforts. If we are successful, we may destroy someone who appears to be the poster boy for the cancer affecting our stock markets.

Although I know that you are deservedly blessed with many friends, I consider you my best friend. Thank you.

Warmest regards,

Sam

In this age of e-mails, texts, cell phones, and BlackBerries, the handwritten note trumps them all.

The ringing of my Batphone snapped me out of my reverie. I picked it up and walked into my small conference room. "I'm feeling unloved."

"How could you feel unloved after the tender moment we had with you leaning against your car?" came the mellifluous tones of Joe Sebastiano.

"The only way I can continue to perform with Grace is to believe that was an antibug device rather than 'little Joe.'"

He laughed and then got serious. "By the way, you are aware that I'm breaking all sorts of rules by discussing this operation with you. You're a civilian and therefore not authorized to be apprised of any aspects of a criminal investigation."

That FBI by-the-book tactic would probably work on most civilians. "I do realize that, and I appreciate the fact that you're breaking rules in order to honor a commitment. My lips are sealed, not only about this, but about your unauthorized backdoor assault."

Another chuckle, and if it were possible to have a chuckle sound like a surrender, this one did. "Okay. Here's where we are. We have five agents, including me, working this. After your clever extortion play, which gave us the location, it wasn't difficult to determine the recluse's hideout."

"Is it protected?"

"Fort Knox could use their expertise."

"How about when he leaves the office?"

"We're not sure he ever does."

I was quiet, out of questions. Joe's tone told me that he had something going, so I waited for him to enlighten me. It wasn't a long wait.

"Right now, it looks like our best shot is a guy named Frank Griffin. I've got no solid intel, but he dresses like he is important, and he seems to be an angry loner."

"Interpret."

"If I had this guy's mug and my charm ... ," he said wistfully. "Yet he eats dinner at bars alone, like, four nights a week. Then he goes back to his fancy apartment. Any broads get near him, he brushes them off."

"How do you know it's a fancy apartment?"

"Uh, he left the door open once."

"You're the freaking FBI!" I almost shouted.

"Relax, *paisan*. We were investigating. By the way, your girl Margo was right. The place is bugged."

"Video, too?" I asked with alarm.

"Yep, the whole shootin' match—real high-tech stuff. But we had the super go in, not us, and he acted like he was checking shit. He got a kick out of it, a real patriot."

"What's the plan?"

"We've got a secret weapon. Agent Ellen Williams will do her magic. Wait till you see her, Mac. You look at this face and your heart stops. A runner with olive skin, blazing green eyes, dark hair, a tight body, and a razor-sharp mind."

"So what will she do if this guy rebuffs her? Maybe he's gay."

"Nope. We checked his checkered past. Used to be happy-go-lucky, nailing every hottie that walked. All of a sudden, he wants no human contact. I've got a feeling that this is the one and that Ellen will turn him."

"What happens to her when this Griffin guy gets his computer experts to prove that she's FBI?"

"She's fully backstopped."

"What does that mean?"

"You know that sign in your office? 'Nobody gets in to see the Wizard, not nobody, not no how'? Well, being fully backstopped means that no one breaks her cover—not no way, not no how!"

*   *   *   *   *

At this particular moment, Agent Ellen Williams really liked her job. Working for the FBI always sounds glamorous and exciting, but most of the time it's just tedious. Yet when your job is to shadow a testosterone-laden hunk like Frank Griffin, you grin and try not to bare it. And please don't throw her in that briar patch, but her real job was to get close to him. *And I'm getting paid for this*, she thought.

Since Ellen had made no move to communicate with Frank, it was possible that he could be as uninteresting as two-day-old toast, but she doubted it. The subject worked during the day. In order to be sure that she had the stamina for night duty, she spent her days relaxing on the beach. Well, somebody had to do it.

Night duty alternated among Handsome Harry's, Campiello's, and Tommy Bahama's, three spectacular restaurants in downtown Naples. Eat your heart out, Sebastiano.

At least four nights a week, Frank planted himself on one of those restaurants' barstools. He had no more than two drinks, and he ate dinner while he watched the flat-screen TV above. To the untrained eye, Ellen thought ruefully, he had the makings of a couch potato. But from her perspective, the wall of silence that seemed to surround him did not appear as if it were his standard operating procedure. In addition, his quiet dismissals of all attempts at conversation also did not fit. If he were antisocial by nature, Ellen mused, then she was Auntie Mame.

Each night that Frank ate out, Ellen had a one-in-three chance of picking the right spot. Actually, her odds were a little better than that because he never ate at the same place twice in a row. His arrival time varied only slightly, and the fact that the three restaurants were all in the same block and all served excellent food made Ellen's preliminary work easy and enjoyable. On the other hand, getting him to talk to her would take considerably more effort and creativity.

Ellen thought it was interesting that her supervisor, Joe Sebastiano, had not asked her how she was going to compromise the subject. Her long, graceful fingers stroked her cheek. *I wonder if Joe expects me to knock boots with Frank to accomplish the mission,* she pondered. *Maybe that's why he just said, "Get 'er done."* No, the plausible-deniability coat wouldn't fit on GI Joe. She nodded her head in acknowledgement. He trusted her.

Two nights before, Ellen had taken a seat at Tommy Bahama's and guessed right. Frank preferred the end seat at the left of the bar because the right side faced the outside seating. She had left him that seat, but she was in the next one.

When he entered, he paused, and his face took on a pained expression. It was as if it would make him uncomfortable to sit next to a strikingly beautiful woman, but the bar was filled.

Frank had subtly planted his body to the left upon seating. Ellen mirrored his actions by shifting to the right, thereby assuring that they were back to back. He was not aware that until she had spotted him, her purse had occupied the empty seat.

Even if the opportunity had presented itself, Ellen would not have struck up a conversation at Tommy Bahama's. Although the bar seats were not exposed, they were in the paths of the restrooms and the clothing annex. With the live music playing, meaningful dialogue would have been almost impossible.

She had been pleased that while she ate her spinach salad with shrimp and drank her pinot grigio, three men had tried to initiate a conversation with her. Only one woman had approached Frank.

Ellen liked winning, even if the other contestants didn't know they were playing. On one other occasion, also at Tommy's, she had made casual eye contact with Frank, and she saw a flicker of interest before his face went void of expression. First step, get him to recognize you.

The previous night, Ellen had taken herself off duty. Too much familiarity looks suspicious, so another agent, Joey "Skinny" McLister, stayed on Frank. If the intra-agency fraternization rules were more lenient, Ellen would be hanging with McLister. A former golf pro who enlisted after 9/11, he equaled her competitive zeal and added a quick wit that always made her smile. In her opinion, if he were not an FBI agent, he would be a stand-up comedian.

Later that evening, McLister called her and reported in. "I believe that this is what hell must be like. In a city filled with young lovelies who could help heal a war veteran, I'm watching a guy straight-arm said lovelies. I have no pride; I would even pick up his rejects. And the final indignity of this torture—it's my job to help my fantasy woman hook up with this ungrateful robot."

Ellen had laughed over the phone and said in her most seductive voice, "Oh, Joey, can you imagine what I'm going to do with him when I get him alone? You've seen me work out; you know that I pride myself on my endurance. I'm going to tie him up and with my hair, my fingertips, my breasts, my tongue … "

"Let the record show," he shouted, "that I'm in my hotel room using the hotel phone, and I'm not holding the phone in my hands!"

"Good night, Skinny," she said, giggling as she disconnected the phone.

CHAPTER 29

IN THE EVENT THAT Ellen guessed wrong tonight, she would mosey over to one of the other restaurants and at least observe. It was Thursday, and Frank's proclivity had been to eat at Handsome Harry's. She thought that was because the music was less raucous, and people were coming and going to listen to the other bands.

For no logical reason, Ellen's intuition told her that tonight just might be show time. She had no script and no designated plan on how to break Frank Griffin's wall of indifference. That was just the way she liked it.

In order to increase her odds of success, Ellen had thrown on a fitted, burnt orange, spaghetti-strapped sundress that fell to midthigh length and emphasized her shapely legs. In the lighted mirror in her bathroom, her tousled curls had shone like ebony.

She applied a minimal amount of makeup, with just a shimmer of Silver City Pink lipstick adorning her full lips. At five feet seven, she did not need heels and opted instead for gold Grecian sandals. The look that she was going for was unintentional hot. Her gold clutch purse held only her lipstick, her keys, some cash, and, of course, her false IDs and credit cards.

Ellen was pleased to see that the two seats on the right end of the bar were vacant. Even on a Thursday in season, a five-fifteen arrival time allowed sufficient choices at the bar. She placed her purse on the empty seat beside her, hopefully reserving it for her target.

By far the toughest part of this assignment for Ellen had been to stifle her normal sociability. All her life, she had been able to walk into a room and light it up with her smile, laugh, and quick wit. Now she had to mimic Greta Garbo's "I vant to be alone" attitude so that Frank would think she was a kindred spirit.

It's a hell of a thing to do to the original party animal, Ellen thought with a measure of resentment. *I may have to punish the boy for putting this butterfly back into its cocoon.*

From her vantage point, she saw Frank arrive at about five forty. Less than thirty seconds earlier, she had shooed away a young hopeful who had asked if the end seat was taken. Almost simultaneously, she had seen Frank. Forsaking the normal response of "I'm sorry, but this seat is taken," she snarled, "Yes. Please leave."

The chagrined male moved quickly enough that Frank did not see the aftermath of the incident. In one swift motion, Ellen had snatched her purse and turned so that she was looking straight ahead. As Frank took his seat, he started momentarily with a flash of recognition.

In one casual motion, Ellen placed her right elbow on the bar, used her hand to support her chin, and canted her head to the left.

Anthony, not Tony, the bartender, smiled at Frank, who returned the pleasantry with a half-smile and a nod. "I'll have a dirty martini, extra dirty," Frank said softly. Anthony had previously served him and just nodded in affirmation.

After about thirty minutes, all the bar seats were full, and patrons were two deep in the center section. With adrenaline pumping, Ellen turned toward Frank and poked his shoulder. He turned to her with a surprised look. She spoke in a low voice while rising from her seat. "Pretty boy, I'm going to the little girl's room. Save this seat, or I'll cut your balls off."

Frank's head tucked into his neck like a turtle's.

As she walked away, Ellen wished she had a partner with her tonight who could have snapped a picture of the poor sap's face. Raised eyebrows, mouth in the classic "O," Frank had no time to respond. When she returned a few minutes later, she was sure that he had been at least mentally shaking his head.

Ellen pulled out her barstool, and Frank instinctively turned her way. "It's all right. You did good; you can keep them," she said. He looked at her as if he were trying to determine the planet of her birth. "Sorry, pal, but you're not my type," she said with a shake of her head and a partial eye roll.

"Do—do I know you?" Frank stammered incredulously.

"Hey! He speaks," Ellen said appraisingly. "What's next? Do you want to know my sign?"

"No," he said, as he shrugged his shoulders and opened his palms. "Listen, I'll just leave you alone and you leave me alone." He started to turn away.

"Giving up that easy? Oh," she said with a look of understanding and in a slightly louder voice, "I get it. You play for your own team."

Frank whipped back to face her as if he had been hit with a cattle prod. "Are you from the firm?" he whispered malevolently. "Did Max send you?"

She gave him a look of mock fright. "Was that voice supposed to be intimidating?" She laughed softly again. "Does the world really revolve around you? I've been in town three weeks. Right now I'm unemployed because Hollywood hasn't figured out that I'm Angelina and Jennifer rolled into one. I don't know anyone named Max, and I don't want to because he sounds like a turd."

Frank laughed, and Ellen thought that he looked surprised by the sound. She knew that she could sound like a little girl who would hold her breath until she got what she wanted.

Frank shook his head and started to shift his back to her.

"Whoa, sport! I'm not done with you yet," she said, poking his shoulder. "We're into show-and-tell now."

"I—I don't think so," said Frank, turning toward her with obvious reluctance.

Ellen rolled her eyes; he got a full one this time. "Do I look like someone who asks for permission or takes no for an answer?" She bent toward him, and her sundress gaped open, revealing two perfect, milky white breasts in stark contrast to her bronze skin. "I'm bored. I don't want to go back to eating and counting the number of guys who are trying to hit on me.

"So here's the deal, Roger Recluse. Either we chat it up a bit, or I yell and break away, screaming that you grabbed my boob."

She remained bent over, and Frank was paralyzed. The "make my day" look in her eyes assured him that she would carry out her threat.

Frank sighed with resignation. "Why the hell did you choose me to harass if I'm not your type?" he asked warily.

She leaned forward again, and he nervously grabbed his drink with both hands. In a low voice she answered, "You sat here, so you drew the short straw.

I'm not looking to hook up with a guy. I'm gay." She paused to let it sink in, and after digesting her news flash, Frank seemed, curiously, to relax.

"Look around. You're definitely not Chatty Charlie, but at least you're not a cretin. I'm a pissed-off drama queen who is looking to start fresh after being chewed up and spit out in Hollywood." She smiled a wry smile. "Tag, you're it."

Frank looked like a man trying to decipher a Rubik's Cube. "Are you looking for work?" he asked.

"Sure, if you're a movie producer on vacation."

"Not quite," he chuckled. As the bartender approached, he nodded and motioned toward the lady.

"I'll have another," she said, "but keep the checks separate, please."

"I would be happy to—" Frank interjected automatically.

Ellen fixed a seductive and mesmerizing gaze on the bartender. "Why do guys think they can buy you a drink and then you'll jump in the sack with them?" she asked sweetly.

"Okay," Frank said hastily. "Separate checks will be fine."

Ellen winked at the bartender as he left, and Frank said, "I surrender. I'm Frank Griffin." He held out his hand.

"And I'm Tracy Lane, Mr. Griffin. So nice to meet you." She shook his hand with a firm, confident grip. The same woman who not so long ago was threatening to castrate him was now playing the part of a debutante at her sweet sixteen coming-out party. Ellen hoped the boy could keep up.

He smiled at her. "In order to preserve what little shred of masculinity that's remaining, I defer to you, Ms. Lane. In a battle of wits with you, I am afraid that I have arrived embarrassingly unarmed."

"Good decision. We're gonna have fun getting to know each other. We'll have a good time. Neither one of us wants to mess with these barflies, and we'll be a good cover for each other. Now, where can a California girl find a hot, young lesbian?"

Frank laughed, and Ellen noted with satisfaction that this time he seemed more comfortable letting his smile linger.

*   *   *   *   *

"I need your undivided attention. I need you to have an open mind," I said to Rod Stanton. He and I were on our prepaid cell phones. In circumstances not so serious, I would have let it slip that mine was FBI issued and encrypted.

I took his silence as consent and continued. "Out of concern, not out of curiosity, I need to know the details of the investment you made when you withdrew $30 million from me."

A protracted silence—I felt that in my chest. I couldn't debate the silence, so I moved on. "After meeting with the government and the FBI, I have reason to believe that you're in business with dangerous people. I don't know whether it's a Ponzi scheme or some other questionable strategy. I need to find out if there are similarities between your arrangement and the late Lenny Cramer's."

I paused, this time prepared to wait him out. Rod filled the gap.

"It's not a Ponzi."

"How do you know?"

It took a few moments for him to say, "I need something concrete."

Heat rose inside me like gasoline on a fire. "How about thirty years of your trusting my instincts and it working? I don't give a damn about your return on the $30 million. I only care about the return of you!"

Rod wasn't used to angry outbursts from me, and I could almost hear him thinking. Hell would freeze over before I spoke another word. He either gave it up or this call was ended.

I heard an exasperated sigh. "It's a loan, backed with a letter of credit by Morgan." Awareness dragged over me like the hot flush of a first kiss.

"That's how he does it," I said softly.

"Does what?" Rod responded with annoyance.

CHAPTER 30

AFTER THEIR SECOND "BUDDY date," Ellen Williams had suggested that she and Frank Griffin change the pace and meet at the Outback Steakhouse on Route 41. With the fear of expected intimacy removed, Frank had readily agreed. She had broken through his shell and discovered a lively conversationalist with a growing sense of humor.

In a perfect world, she would have had the time to coax him out of whatever was haunting him. But baby steps don't work with a subject in an operation where the information was needed yesterday. Ellen knew that she had to blast through his protective walls to reach the lonely guy inside. Inevitably, she would have to puncture his balloon of trust and reveal her true intentions, but not tonight.

Ellen had arrived first and secured a booth in the perpetually busy restaurant. From her vantage point, she could see the door. Skinny McLister was sitting at the bar, and she had resisted the temptation to walk by and pinch his ass when she entered. He would leave before Frank and Ellen finished dining. His job was to see if Frank was being followed. Later, Joe Sebastiano would come into the bar, and he would leave after Frank and Ellen had left. Two women at the bar turned their heads toward the door, and that was Ellen's cue that Frank had arrived.

Dressed in jeans and a powder blue, button-down, long-sleeved, starched shirt, Frank was even more attractive than he was in his business attire. His face had gained color since she first saw him, and his easy smile and perfect white teeth did make it seem like Hollywood had missed out. "Hey, gal pal," he said by way of greeting and gave her a kiss on the cheek.

"Just don't lay one on the lips, pretty boy. I might never go back."

He laughed as he sat down across from her. "If you weren't such a pushy broad, I would still be a happy hermit."

Frank's only possible reaction to her instant pout was to back off from his facetious remark. He raised his hands in a placating manner. "No. That's not right. I really am having fun with you."

She gave him a begrudging smile that told him he had dug his way out. "Are you sure you don't want me to introduce you to a beautiful lesbian?" he asked. "I can become awfully boring."

"*Become* boring?" Ellen asked with raised eyebrows. He laughed again. "And no thanks," she continued. "I'm giving up women for Lent. They are entirely too needy."

Frank shook his head, still chuckling. "I've never eaten at an Outback Steakhouse. What would madam recommend? Must I eat a Bloomin' Onion?"

"First, I recommend a drink because we are early enough to get two for the price of one," she said eagerly. "Then I will order for you because your tastes are entirely too plebeian for these culinary delights. And no Bloomin' Onion. Our bodies are our temples."

When their drinks arrived, they toasted to new adventures. Ellen put her elbows on the table and her head in her hands. With a teasing lilt, she asked, "So, if you hadn't ended up being a prissy old businessman, what would you be doing?"

Frank could not suppress a smile. Their salads arrived, and he purposely took a languid bite of his and chewed meticulously.

Having no sense of humor with being ignored, Ellen sat back indignantly. "Did I stutter? What's your passion? What's your hot button, you recalcitrant twit?" she asked, taking the teasing up another notch.

He looked at her like an annoyed parent looks at a child who has asked for the same thing a dozen times. "Forgive me. It takes a while to digest the 'prissy old businessman' crack. Yet now that I am also a recalcitrant twit, I had better respond before you decide to say something insulting."

Ellen nodded approvingly, so he continued. "I wanted to be an actor. I was in plays in high school and college, summer stock. You know the drill."

"Wow! We could've been Brangelina!" came the wide-eyed excited cry.

"You're hotter than Angelina, and I've been told that I'm way too uncoordinated to be Brad," Frank replied with a grin.

"You're working your way back," said Ellen thoughtfully. "I will graciously retract the 'twit' part. What plays were you in, and what were your roles?"

"Let's see," said Frank as he leaned his head back, gazing upward. After a moment of contemplation, he continued. "I'll stick with the musicals because I liked those the best. Every one was *way* before your time because our drama instructor loved what he considered the classics. Let's see, I was Pharaoh in *Joseph and the Amazing Technicolor Dreamcoat.*"

Ellen smiled and starting humming "The Amazing Coat of Many Colors."

Frank gave her an acknowledging nod of respect. "I was also Conrad Birdie in *Bye, Bye, Birdie.*"

"You've got the Elvis thing going," she said, nodding back with approval.

"Oh, and I was Mr. Applegate in *Damn Yankees.*"

Ellen pushed back from the table and started slinking toward him. In a seductive voice that could peel the frock off a monk, she sang softly, "Whatever Lola wants, Lola gets ... "

Frank almost laughed himself off the chair. Ellen knew that he was smart enough to realize that if he did not give her another role quickly, what was a small scene could end up out of control. Putting his hands up in protective surrender, he said, "I'll give you one more if you sit down."

She did a backward slink to her chair, primly sat, and looked at him expectantly.

He blinked rapidly, and Ellen watched him. The pained expression on his face made her think of the look people get with a slow computer. Finally, he said, "I was Will Parker in *Oklahoma.*"

She was out of her chair like a jack-in-the-box. Her hands shot up in the air, and she began waving them excitedly. "I was Ado Annie!" she cried with absolute delight.

In one movement, Frank's arms folded on the table, and his head dropped to them. His soft laughter was just another log added to her roaring fire.

"We sing till our food arrives," declared Ellen triumphantly, her eyes alive with excitement. As she began the chorus of the Will Parker and Ado Annie duet, "All Er Nuthin," Frank closed his eyes, and his head slowly tilted down toward the table.

With his shoulders hunched and his head about six inches off the table, Frank softly sang the duet with his irrepressible date. At the conclusion of the song, the applause from nearby tables evoked a bow and a curtsy from Ellen, while Frank folded his arms on the table and rested his head on his arms.

Ellen smiled. He looked like a little kid taking a nap at recess. If she hadn't broken through, it sure wasn't for lack of trying. "That was fun," she said brightly as she sat and folded her hands like she was in church. Frank's head rose hesitantly. "Thanks for joining in," she said, grinning from ear to ear.

"Like I had a choice?"

After their identical dinners of blue cheese chopped salad and shrimp grillers, Frank expressed his surprise at the quality and deliciousness of the meal. Ellen smiled and then took a deep breath. She was going to take him to the final stage. "Are you ready for the next big step in our relationship?" she asked in her little girl voice.

"Uh-oh. Do I have to meet the parents?"

"Of course, Sherlock, that's it," Ellen replied sarcastically, giving him a look like he had just broken wind. "That's all my mother needs is to think I've switched teams and she now gets to have her grandbaby!"

Frank laughed and held his white napkin above his head. "I give up! What's the next step?"

"Follow me," replied Ellen sweetly as she moved out of the booth. She handed him a card with her address. "Be there tomorrow night at seven and bring a present because I'm making dinner."

As he walked her toward the door, Frank added, "Perhaps Dear Abby will tell me what gift is appropriate for my loony lesbian gal pal."

*   *   *   *   *

As the attractive couple walked toward the door, a solitary figure moved toward the waitress who was heading to their table. Just as she reached for the first glass to put it on her tray, she was jostled from behind. She fell into the table, dropped her tray, and was headed for the floor when a strong hand grabbed her.

"I'm so sorry," spoke a low voice in her ear. She turned to see a man in jeans with a Miami Heat sweatshirt and matching cap. His dark eyes seemed to try and show sympathy but were incapable of doing so. The heads of the restaurant's customers had turned instantly in response to the clatter of the tray, but the fact that the waitress was upright and talking to a rather nondescript man made most of them turn back to their own business.

"The only way I will be able to forgive myself is if you accept this token," the man told the waitress. He pressed two bills into her palm, closed her hand over the money, nodded, and walked out through the crowd.

The waitress watched him go, still not sure what had happened. Her side hurt where she had hit the table, and it would bruise for sure. When she opened her hand and saw two one-hundred-dollar bills, she was ready for a bruise on the other side. Smiling and shaking her head as she bent to clear the table, she reflected only momentarily on the oddity of just one glass remaining.

CHAPTER 31

RECENT EVENTS HAD CAUSED Grace McGregor to ease her restrictions on phone interruptions during dinnertime, and although fear had turned to anger and she was ready to return to normalcy, Frannie McGregor was still in residence.

I gave a forlorn glance at my half-eaten filet, fumbled my cell phone out of my pocket, and went into my office. "Do FBI agents have this special sense to know when a man is halfway through his perfectly cooked steak?"

"I'm on the job, eating nothing but MREs, and you expect sympathy?"

I sighed audibly. "If only I believed that you were suffering. So what's up, Joe?"

"I'm simply bringing you up to speed, like the conscientious agent and friend that I am."

There was no need to reply to that nonsense.

"Our task force has expanded. We brought the Naples chief of police, Jed Tully, into the loop. This is very unusual because we normally bring in a local operative, but certainly not the chief.

"In this case we don't know how far Lyons's tentacles go, so we vetted the chief. He is a good ol' boy, as straight as an arrow. We'll bring him with us for the takedown so that we can get backup in case it's needed."

"Who else is on the task force?"

"Skinny McLister, a real stud who has been with me for six years. He has Ellen's back but would love to have the rest of her, also. Dean Segrum, who would remind you of 'Face' on *The A-Team* but could shoot the wings off a fly.

"Last, and probably least, is Henry Major. He can't shoot worth shit, but he's as big as a house and one intimidating son of a bitch. Tully and Ellen Williams will be in a backup role.

"We also have two IRS guys back in DC on the task force. They've made some tentative connections. They've uncovered other shell companies that may be linked. Coincidentally, one is called Hamilton and Hamilton, and the other is Grant Enterprises."

"A currency freak," I shuddered. "Colonel Jackson" continued to hang over me like an angry cloud.

"No shit. It may take months to interlock, but it's like Lyons left us a road map. He's too smart to avoid paying taxes, but his income from the Franklin Corporation alone could cover the bailout."

It sounded like an interesting, and obviously capable, cast of characters. At least in my mind, both Jeremy and Max were guilty as sin. Still, unless Joe had more, probable cause seemed like a stretch. "Please tell me you have more."

"We have circumstantial evidence coming out of our ying yang. Let me go over the holes in the Lenny Cramer so-called suicide first. I had to bring Mrs. Cramer slightly into the loop because she's fit to be tied about the cause of death."

"Wasn't that risky?" I asked.

"She's on hold until we wrap this up," Joe continued, "but this sure smells like homicide. After his dinner with Parker, Lenny came home, and he was terrified. They didn't talk. She just held him and they went to bed. The next morning Lenny said that he had just felt sick. He swore that he would never again have more than two drinks outside of the house."

"Go on."

"The weekend before his death, Mrs. Cramer had walked down to the ocean with Lenny. He told her to book a trip to New Zealand and plan to stay for a few months. He had her make the reservations from a friend's house and told her they could only discuss the trip when they were down at the ocean. He insisted on no paperwork being at the house."

"Didn't this sort of behavior raise her antenna?"

"You would have to meet this woman, Mac. She worshipped her husband unconditionally and would do anything he asked her to do without questioning it. Now let me give you the more sordid evidence.

"It seems that the killer got a little too cute. All-night skin flicks were on the tube. Mrs. Cramer was adamant that her husband would never let that happen. Her contention is that Lenny was too cheap to pay for porn and that he made fun of people who paid for it when they could see real people on youporn.com for free. Finally, he needed Viagra to get it up, and she had his stash in her purse because they were going away."

"I'm not sure I had a need to know that," I interjected, grimacing.

After a few moments of silence, Joe continued. "Also, neighbors of Lenny Cramer said that they saw a man in a jogging suit and a baseball cap gliding down Lenny's path to the ocean. He climbed on the rocks, sat with the seals, and then disappeared. That was weeks before Lenny died. The neighbor asked the missus if there had been guests at their house, and she said no."

I considered Joe's information. It seemed like there were a dozen flashing one-way signs all pointing at Jeremy's hit man. I took a deep breath and asked, "What about George Grant? Were you able to follow up with local law enforcement?"

"Let me give you our insurance analysis first. Nationally, there were way too many deaths for the insureds whose policies were owned by the Washington Group. It's about as close to statistically impossible as you can get.

"In George's case, as your friend indicated, an examination of the scene revealed no skid marks from the car that hit him. That early in the morning, the odds were that there was minimal traffic on the road. Who wouldn't stop? They could have blamed George, or the dog, for that matter. The only other excuse would have been a drunk or a panicked underage driver. Not conclusive, but damn suspicious."

The silence between us lingered until Joe cleared his throat.

"Suspicious?" I said in a voice that seemed to come from someone else. "Max Parnavich is guilty as hell. Find him. Shoot him in the balls."

CHAPTER 32

THE DESCENDING SUN WAS bisected by the gleaming white balcony rail. Above the sun, dark clouds furrowed in a scowl, foretelling not the coming of night but an inevitable storm. Powerful, sporadic gusts of wind from the Gulf sent fine, intermittent sprays of salt water onto the balcony.

Max Parnavich, languidly lounging in a nondescript white plastic chair, was oblivious as he reread the report on Tracy Lane. His bare feet shared the small white table with the remnants of his drink. His right hand went inside his navy blue running shorts, and he adjusted himself. Then, with the same hand, he reached forward and picked up one of the few remaining cashew nuts that were scattered on the table. Still sitting, the report in his left hand, he tossed the cashew high in the air. He watched its flight and at the last instant moved his head imperceptibly to the left, opened his mouth, and, lizardlike, caught his prize.

At some point, he had unfinished business to tend to with McGregor's lying slut daughter. If Jeremy didn't have some hard-on for McGregor, Max would have already revisited the situation, but she could wait. Revenge *is* better served cold, and Tracy Lane could only be served hot.

Leaving the enclosed pictures on the table, Max reviewed the report highlights while beginning to form a plan.

Graduated from UCLA 2002, magna cum laude, with a double major in journalism and drama. Debate team, swim team.

Hobbies: works with humane society; second-degree black belt in karate.

After college lived in California, worked as a fitness instructor, tried unsuccessfully to be an actress.

Tracy Lane. Could she be the real deal? Could she be sufficiently interesting to be more than chattel? Could she actually be a challenge, a worthy adversary, or even a mate?

Max's first reaction had been that Tracy couldn't be as perfect as she appeared or she would not be wasting time with that coward Frank. On second thought, beautiful women loved to have gay friends, the drama connection was there, and Frank had been effectively neutered.

Frank obviously could not handle her. In the restaurant, she had been dancing and singing while Frank was hiding his head in the sand. Her exhibitionism should have turned Max off. Instead, he watched every move with fascination.

Tracy's lack of inhibition, her disregard for what anyone thought, her confidence, and her sheer animal magnetism had captivated the entire restaurant. Yet to Max, it was if he and Tracy were the only ones in the room. Her performance was just for him.

Max closed his eyes and relaxed. The hypnotic lapping sounds of the Gulf took him back to a place he had repressed for a long, long time—senior year in high school, first love. She understood him. Very early in the relationship, he was consumed by her. He could not believe his luck. As the two of them were walking home from school one afternoon, two college football players screeched their blue Chevy Impala convertible to a halt in front of them.

Max tried to push the memories back, but like an avalanche of evil the vivid image advanced ferociously. Out of the car, the two jocks were cajoling his girl to join them and go to a party. Although she appeared reluctant, her eyes indicated that she was flattered and perhaps even tempted by the sense of adventure. Yet she looked at Max, imploring him to take charge.

At seventeen, Max was undersized, and he had never been in a fight. But when they started to drag his girl to the car, he shouted for them to stop and pulled one of their arms. The two collegians stopped, looked at each other, smiled maliciously, and then grabbed Max.

Within seconds, in broad daylight, they stripped off all his clothes. Laughing at his ineffective resistance, one held the naked boy's hands while the other held his feet. Swinging him like he was a hammock, genitalia exposed to his girl, they screamed that he was too small to keep. On the count of three, they threw him into the bushes. They then tossed his clothes into the back of the convertible and jumped in. As they drove away with his blushing girl, they parceled his clothes out into the air.

Max never went back to another day of school, nor did he ever speak to or see his first love again. He took the money he had saved from his paper route and invested it in creating physical dominance.

For the next twelve months, Max went six days a week to martial arts classes. Seven days a week, he hit the gym. His sensei remarked that he had never seen a more gifted or driven student.

On the anniversary of his humiliation, he ambushed the first culprit outside of his dorm. As the man got out of his car, a perfectly placed strike with a baseball bat at the back of his skull made him crumple to the asphalt. Max turned him over and, with a scalpel, cut open his pants. He reached in, pulled out the man's genitals, and expertly sliced off both testicles. Max squeezed the bloody sacs in his gloved hand and then dropped the remains on the butchered man's face. He jammed a sixteen-ounce ice bag into the man's groin and left him there.

Exactly one year later, in an alley behind a bar, the second culprit suffered the same fate. The next day, Max joined the Navy to see the world.

Max breathed deeply and forced himself to come back to the present. He meditated, and soon his mind found nothingness. When he finished meditating, he kept his eyes closed and stilled his body.

Then Max brought his knees back to his chest and, with an explosive thrust, hit the edge of the table and simultaneously let out a piercing scream. The table hit the balcony rail, fell back, and crashed to the floor. His drink glass flew over the rail. The eight-by-ten prints of Tracy Lane scattered, except for one that caught the breeze and fell into Max's lap. His maniacal laugh matched the insanity of his eyes. "Fate!" he cried triumphantly.

CHAPTER 33

AS FRANK DROVE TOWARD the Dunes condo in Vanderbilt Beach, he felt like a kid going out on his first date. He tapped his hand on the steering wheel and added vocals at the top of his lungs to Sir Mix-a-Lot's often repeated phrase, "I like big butts," on his satellite radio. Not that this woman had a big butt. On the contrary, her caboose was damn near perfect. Imagine if his college friends could see him all up and excited about having the hottest-looking woman he had ever seen cooking him dinner at her condo. And check this out—he had zero chance of getting laid!

Traffic on Vanderbilt Drive was minimal. The sun was still shining, although a light drizzle misted his window. Frank glanced casually to his right at the large cemetery. Normally superstitious, tonight he not only didn't hold his breath as he passed it but he cranked up the volume on the radio.

"Tracy" had left his name at the gate, so he passed through easily. Frank parked his black BMW in a visitor's spot, picked up two bottles of moderately expensive wine from the passenger seat, and got out of his car. *Girl's got herself a pretty fancy gated community*, he thought.

The lobby in the high-rise was elegant contemporary with attractive metal sculptures. A light-wood interior made the elevator feel even more spacious. Frank had a touch of claustrophobia, so he noted things like that. When the bell dinged, signifying his arrival on the sixth floor, he exited. He noted that the elevator serviced only two condominiums.

Tracy answered the door in a pale yellow sundress and barefoot. Her smile made him feel like he had been in a tunnel and emerged to a glorious sunrise.

"Oh, goody, presents! You do listen well." She greeted him with her infectious charm. She gave him a kiss on the cheek, took the wine bottles, and with a sweeping motion, stepped aside and said, "Come on in."

As he had been instructed, Frank had dressed casually. His jeans and sockless loafers were accessorized by a bright pink, long-sleeved, starched shirt. Questions of his masculinity would not be an issue with his lesbian pal. "Damn," he said and added a look of surprise. "Something smells good."

"Dial soap and Herbal Essence. Works every time."

Frank laughed, "I mean the food, Comedy Central."

"In that case, 'tis my fabulous hors d'oeuvres. You may sample my wares after a quick tour and I fix you a drink." She took his hand, and the warmth from it seemed to traverse all through his body. He brought his mind back to the harsh reality: *She likes girls, and I am a hideous wretch.*

As if she had read his thoughts, she started bouncing around like she was on a mini trampoline. Her eyebrows went up and down as she pointed and cried, "Three, count 'em, three bedrooms. Can you imagine the slumber party I could have?"

Her excitement and childlike enthusiasm made Frank smile and resolve just to go with the flow. When you're in Disneyland, you don't think about how much it costs. "What next? What next?" he asked, mimicking her enthusiasm as if he were also a six-year-old.

"Ta da!" she said as she gestured magician-like to the lanai. "Sit down. I'll bring you a drink and then some yummies, and we'll watch the sunset. Do you want a mixed drink or some of that delicious Ripple you brought?"

"A glass of the white Ripple will be fine," he said through laughter.

Frank sat down in an all-weather wicker chair with a natural finish as Tracy hustled to the kitchen. The pale green cushions were quite comfortable, and the glass table had a matching wicker base. *Very tastefully done*, he mused. And, of course, any time you face the Gulf of Mexico, it's hard to mess up the atmosphere. *Currently unemployed, yet she can afford this place?* Frank didn't want to pry, but he was curious.

Tracy came back to the lanai holding two glasses of white wine and a third wine glass filled with ice. "I admit it," she said as she put the glasses on the table. "I like my wine really cold. I'm not a purist."

"I knew there was a dark side to you," he responded. She grimaced for an instant and then stuck her tongue out at him as she walked back to the kitchen to get the hors d'oeuvres.

*   *   *   *   *

Frank had scarfed down the baked parmesan stuffed mushrooms appetizer, but a sea fog had made the sunset less than spectacular. Dinner consisted of a light, but delicious, salad, to-die-for scalloped potatoes, and crab cakes that were so light and fluffy it was a miracle that they held together. She had gone all out and had even managed to secure genuine Maryland crab instead of the Florida version.

The boy had eaten like a man coming off a hunger strike. By previous agreement, she had promised to not provide dessert. "Unbelievable," Frank praised for the fifth time. "What other secrets are you hiding from me?"

As the evening progressed, Ellen felt her anxiety level rising. Even though she was confident she could do this, she was afraid of Frank's reaction. Violence might be preferable to devastating hurt. She liked him. His kidding had opened the door, so she took a deep breath and walked in.

"Please come sit on the couch with me." Her soft tone had a touch of sadness, and Frank looked at her quizzically as he got up from the dining room table and walked over to the couch. She motioned for him to sit, and then she sat facing him. She had made sure to have only one glass of wine so that she could be at her best.

"I want to ask you what will seem like strange and uncomfortable questions," she began. "Please think before you answer each question, and above all, answer honestly. If you believe nothing else, believe that your answers are literally a matter of life or death."

"How about if I plead the fifth?" asked Frank, sounding confused but trying to make light of her mood change.

"That is not an option," said Ellen as her eyes began to tear. She straightened up. "Although your initial reactions will be anger and distrust, I pray that you will conclude ultimately that I have been your friend."

"Shoot," said Frank, folding his arms across his chest.

"Have you ever been involved in a homicide, either directly or as an accessory?"

"No! Are you kidding?" he answered immediately. His emphatic "no" was matched with a look of incredulity as he unfolded his arms and leaned toward her. "Do I look like Jack the Ripper to you?"

"No," she said softly, as she leaned toward him. "Please consider your answers. Are you aware of the homicides perpetrated by your business associates?"

"Who the hell are you?" Frank shouted as he jumped up from the couch. His face reddened in anger, his body was rigid, and his hands were balled into fists and held at his sides.

Ellen's face remained passive. She walked over and opened the kitchen drawer. She walked back to him, stood about two feet away, and held out her ID badge. "I'm Ellen Williams, and I'm with the FBI."

"And I'm fucking out of here, you lying bitch!" he snarled as he pushed by her and headed angrily for the door. Ellen raised her voice and spoke with authority. "If you open the door, Frank, Agent McLister, who is waiting outside, is prepared to arrest you on suspicion of insider trading."

With his hand on the door and his face a mask of fury and hurt, Frank snarled, "You have no idea what you've done! You've signed my death warrant!"

Ellen took two steps closer to him and said defiantly, "I have every idea of what I've done. We know that your apartment and your car, by the way, are bugged. Are you aware that your friend Max was watching us at Outback? How about the fact that he created a diversion after we left and copped my glass from our table?" With this Frank turned white, and his knees buckled.

"Don't worry," she added quickly. "I'm fully backstopped. Not even your computer gurus can come up with anything other than Tracy Lane." Ellen paused to let it sink in. "The government is paying for this place, but when your computer gurus check, they will see that Daddy has a trust fund for me. Now, do we keep standing and shouting at each other, or can I tell Agent McLister to go home, and you and I can have a conversation?"

"You lied to me!" This time hurt was the overwhelming emotion in his tone.

She waited a beat and then said softly, "I know, Frank." She continued looking into his eyes as tears started running down her face.

Frank shook his head violently from side to side as though he was trying to wake up from a nightmare.

"And it's the hardest thing I've ever had to do," Ellen continued. If you will listen to me, I promise that you'll see that I've acted in your best interest." She held out her arms, not for an embrace, but as a plea.

Frank stood motionless, looking back at her with waning defiance. Finally, he shrugged his shoulders in defeat. "I'm not sure that I can ever believe you," he said with resignation, "but you've given me no choice except to listen."

"Please have a seat," instructed Ellen as she motioned to the couch. He walked over and sat at the far end. She walked to the door, opened it, and said to the man outside, "I'm good. You can go."

McLister gave her a questioning look, shrugged, and walked away.

When she returned, she sat across from him again and began talking. "When I first met you, you thought that I was a pro sent by Max, and the venom in your look told me you hated him. Why?"

Frank closed his eyes and recoiled as if struck by a blow. When he opened them, he looked at her with undisguised hostility. "You wanna know why, little Miss Tracy-slash-Ellen?" he spat out as he again bounded up from the couch. "Why do I despise my boss, Jeremy, and his sick puppet, Max?" he shouted. "Here's why!" With a violent motion he ripped off his shirt, tearing buttons and fabric, and threw it on the floor. He continued looking at her combatively, but tears of shame were running down his face.

Ellen rose and walked slowly over to him. She reached her hands gently toward his chest. He started to pull away, but she whispered, "Don't," and the tears streaming down her face stopped him. Her fingers gently caressed each mark. Then she leaned forward and kissed them. He stood transfixed.

She took his hand and led him back to the couch. As he sat down, she continued. "Our task force was commissioned to bring Jeremy Lyons and Max Parnavich to justice. At this time we may have sufficient evidence to arrest them."

Frank's eyes widened in response.

"You are not a flunky in the organization, regardless of how you've been treated. Obviously, you have the ability to give us evidence that can increase the scope of the charges and, we hope, assure their convictions."

Frank raised his hands palms up in frustration. He said wearily, "Do you have any idea how powerful they are? How rich? How connected?" Regardless of the futility of his tone, it still reminded Ellen of listening to her father tell her how dangerous drugs could be.

She paused to give his concern weight. "We have an idea, but we need chapter and verse from you, Frank. We also want you to advise us on the best way to capture them. Normally, we would march into the office and arrest them, but my boss thinks that at least Lyons could find a way to escape."

Frank gave her an incredulous look. "You can bet your ass on that. Your only hope of catching Jeremy is with an ambush." He threw his arms up in frustration. "Why the hell would I help you? I recruit the politicians who recruit the CEOs who spill their secrets. I sure didn't have sex with the marks or coerce them into giving up inside information. But you guys will say I knew about it, aided and abetted, so I'm as guilty as they are."

She nodded and shrugged, acknowledging his logic. Then she honed in on him. "The only way I would go along with this deception was if they gave you immunity."

"Immunity?"

"Yes." She looked into his eyes. "Rarely does it happen, but I have an immunity agreement from the US District Attorney. You will not be prosecuted for insider trading crimes. But you must tell us everything."

Ellen paused again to let it sink in. Then she said, "May I get a tape recorder?"

He looked at her for a long minute. "Yes, if you answer one question for me. Are you really a lesbian?"

Ellen leaned over, placed her hands on each side of his face, and kissed him full on the lips.

As Frank began speaking into the recorder, tension seemed to seep out of his pores.

CHAPTER 34

A TELEPHONE RINGING AT eleven thirty on a Tuesday night cannot be a good thing. Saint Grace is nice enough to have the phone on her side of the bed, so she reached over, fumbled with the receiver, and picked it up. She got a dial tone. The fact that the ringing continued allowed my rapier-like mind to conclude that indeed it was another phone waking us up. Our cell phones were downstairs, so I further deduced that it was the Batphone. A picky person might add that Grace's, "It's your Batphone! It's your freaking Batphone!" was helpful in my analysis.

I moved gazelle-like to my closet and picked up the offending intruder. All parents know that if you get a late-night call and it does not involve your children, then all is right with the world. Nevertheless, after Joe identified himself, I gave an intimidating "Hold on" into the phone and tiptoed down to my office.

My nervousness spilled out in lame humor. "You're calling to tell me that the case has been solved and that *The Washington Post* and *The New York Times* want to come over and interview me and take pictures for the front page." If Joe failed to take the bait, things were not good.

"Most men dream about women when they fantasize," he said, amused.

"Whereas I can only dream that I am being sodomized by the short arm of the law."

"A good one," he laughed. "I'll use that one at the office."

"Ellen Williams came through like a champ," Joe said proudly. "On the record, Frank Griffin was explicit about the insider trading charges. His job was to recruit and control the politicians and centers of influence who would then convince the prominent CEOs to become clients."

"Compromise the mark and then you own him? Isn't that page one of *How to Be a Spy*? I guess there really is nothing new under the sun. I sort of thought that Lyons might be more innovative in his criminal activities."

"Go figure. Anyway, Griffin confirmed that Lenny Cramer was a client. He also said that everything is compartmentalized and that only Jeremy and Max have a need to know. Without a doubt, he believes that Max is a killer, but he has no evidence. He did say that Max was definitely out of town when Cramer died, and get this, Max is a freak for the ocean."

He paused, so I asked, "Does this solidify the arrest?"

"Definitely, and we have a strategy for the arrest."

"What is it?" Any remaining remnants of sleep had disappeared.

"Griffin agreed that a takedown in Jeremy's office would be impossible. It's a myriad of secret doors, hidden rooms, and secret passageways. But the good news is that Griffin is privy to their schedule.

"Thursday night, Jeremy and Max will go to Jeremy's private club, Someplace Else. In the past, Griffin went to the club a lot. Lately, he has stayed away; I'll get to that later. He said that this club is the epitome of over the top. No expense was spared, and it's a visual masterpiece."

I laid my head on my hand as I continued to listen.

"Griffin never saw Jeremy or Max when he was at the club. Out of curiosity, Griffin had sniffed around before, looking for them when he knew they were there, but never a sighting.

"Obviously, this limits our options for arrest. Even if we covered all the exits and forced entry, we probably couldn't find the schmucks.

"Griffin also thinks that these guys have a secret floor where they play pit bosses at Vegas. He swears that there is audio and video surveillance everywhere. As these CEOs are getting hustled by drop-dead gorgeous women, those two perverts are watching and recording every move.

"They usually get to the club at about ten o'clock and stay until one thirty or two. There is a private entrance at the back of the club, and they park in a motel lot about a hundred yards from the back door. The motel is currently being renovated, so it's empty.

"Griffin knows all this because he was banging some broad in a car parked in the same lot. To let you know how good Ellen is, he became embarrassed when he told us that in Ellen's presence. I guess he figured out that she's not gay."

"Not gay?" I asked, my attention increasing and dimming like a faulty light bulb. I had been insistent that Joe call me anytime. It had sounded like a good idea when I said it.

"Long story. I'll brief you on my prize pupil's Academy Award performance after this is over."

"It may be due to my sleep-deprived state, but this plot is becoming complicated. You never told me why Frank Griffin no longer goes to the club."

Joe waited a moment and then answered, "Because Jeremy de Sade brutally whipped and scarred him for life with a cat-o'-nine tails."

I recoiled from the phone as if it were somehow connected to this brutality. Adrenaline shot through me like battery acid, and I grabbed the phone in a stranglehold. "How can these monsters exist?" I shouted. "Why doesn't Griffin grab an AK-47, hide in the bushes, and blow them to hell?"

Joe waited a few minutes to speak, letting me calm down. Rather than answering my question, he continued as though my outburst had not happened. "It's a top priority for the agency, Mac. The plan is that after Jeremy and Max enter the club, we position ourselves outside of the back entrance. Jed Tully, the Naples guy, and Ellen will be hidden behind Lyons's vehicle.

"By the way, Lyons is one cautious cockroach. Not only is he never out of his office building except to go to his club, but the Lincoln they drive is bulletproof. Also, it appears as if there are some newfangled security cameras or lights that are directed on the area between the club and where they park their car, which means we have to hug the building to set up and then stand there and wait for maybe four hours."

"Wouldn't neighbors or passersby see you? Is the back area always illuminated?"

"It wasn't tonight, nor was it when Griffin was doing boom-boom in the car. The location of the club doesn't lend itself to traffic in the back. It's rather foreboding back there. Besides, there's really nothing to see. Any gawkers would hang around the front of the club. Unfortunately, this plan is not without potential glitches." He paused. "But I believe it's our only option."

I yawned. "I think I'm on information overload. It's midnight, and I'm going to climb back into bed. Joe, please get them so that I can concentrate my worrying on my normal plethora of anxieties."

"I'm on it," he replied. "Have a good night."

CHAPTER 35

THE NEXT MORNING, I went out on a limb. I didn't mention to Joe what I was going to do because he would have gone ballistic. Also, he might have been able to prevent me from doing it. I am sometimes a believer that instead of asking for permission, it's better to act first and then beg for forgiveness.

It took until the fifth ring for Rod Stanton to answer his unregistered cell phone. "What!"

He was annoyed either because I was bothering him or because I was calling too freaking early.

"I haven't figured out whether I'll be guilty of aiding and abetting, obstruction of justice, or just plain screwing up an arrest, but here's what I need you to do." My tone assured that I would not be interrupted.

"On Thursday evening, the FBI will arrest Jeremy Lyons. The Franklin Corporation is his company. I think that your money will still be safe, but a criminal investigation could freeze your assets for quite a while, in my opinion. I read your letter of credit and did some research on what would happen if you presented it. Are you familiar with the process?"

He stayed quiet momentarily and then answered, "Not entirely."

"I need to go through it quickly. When the letter of credit is presented, the bank is not obligated to notify the Franklin Corporation. Fax the letter to the bank. No e-mails, no written communications.

"I want you to receive your wire transfer as late as you can on Thursday. But I need a stone-cold bank CEO's testicles on the line that there will be no notification to the Franklin Corporation until Monday.

"Use the phone you're on now to call the CEO so that the call can't be traced. Please, please be extra careful," I added. "If somehow Lyons gets word that you're pulling your money out and gets suspicious, and that screws up the arrest, I couldn't live with myself. This bastard has to go down."

He gave me a long pause, took in my rapid-fire instructions, and said, "So your friend Joe hasn't authorized this call?"

"Not in this lifetime, pal."

Rod was silent for about ten seconds. "Tough call. I understand the severity of the situation. There will be no leaks. You have my word." He paused again. "Thank you."

*   *   *   *   *

The rain-challenged traffic acted like a balm instead of an annoyance as I slowly made my way in to work. I tell myself that if I have more time to think and sort out my thoughts, clarity will break through the clouds. Often this theory is disproved.

When I pulled into the parking garage, I still had anxieties about my anxieties. Is my family safe? Will the arrest go as planned? What are the chances that my interference will jeopardize the arrest?

As I walked into the office, I momentarily tabled my ruminations and motioned R. J. into my conference room. My demeanor indicated that banter would be inappropriate, so R. J. took a seat and leaned forward, prepared to listen intently.

I told him what was supposed to happen that night at Jeremy's club. Although I had wrestled with whether R. J. truly had a need to know, I decided to brief him on my call to Rod Stanton. His eyes widened. He knew that I had crossed the line, and I don't do that. Yet he also knew that our moral obligation to our clients is sacrosanct.

When I had finished, he responded. "The question that I don't want to ask you, but my mouth is ahead of my brain, is if telling Rod screws up the arrest ... "

"How can I live with myself?" I shrugged helplessly and then responded like a lawyer giving a summation. "I attempted to determine objectively the probability of a leak or of Rod's not having sufficient influence to ensure silence. I do believe that there is an extremely low probability of it blowing up because of me. Nevertheless, I'm making a big conscience bet."

He studied me and maintained a respectful silence. Then he said, "You're a hell of a friend, Mac."

Sometimes in our business, we say just the right thing.

CHAPTER 36

MAX PASSED FRANK GRIFFIN as he left the situation room. Instead of turning his eyes like a frightened rabbit, Frank actually held the other man's gaze for a moment before moving on. Max considered the slight change in demeanor. If Frank had screwed Tracy and grown some balls, Max would be forced to cut them off.

In some respects, it made Max uncomfortable that one woman had begun to occupy more and more of his thoughts. Although Sabine had become exclusive to Jeremy, Max had never cared enough about a woman to give a shit whether she was passed around. He didn't think that Jeremy really cared about Sabine; Jeremy just did what he wanted to do. The disturbing thought to Max was that if his boss saw Tracy, he would definitely want a piece of the action.

Throughout their relationship, Max had rarely had conflicting thoughts about Jeremy. He had few secrets from him, but this would be one. He had concluded that he could stash Tracy Lane on nearby Marco Island and keep her all to himself. As soon as Max made decisions, conflicts tended to disappear.

That night, he planned to shadow Frank and find out where Tracy was staying. He knew that she had not been to Frank's place, but Max had been doing some reconnaissance on a possible future mission, so he didn't know if they had hooked up since Outback.

His preferred method would have been to shake down Frank for the information, but he didn't want Frank to think that Tracy was personal. *Plus,*

Max thought with a smile, *the little pissant might tell her some unflattering things about me.*

*   *   *   *   *

Max's mind wandered as he was finishing dinner with Jeremy. Most of these dinners took place in Jeremy's suite, and for the first time, that made him a little agitated. In Jeremy's company, Max self-consciously concentrated on his table manners.

Although Jeremy had never pointed it out, the fact that his own table manners were impeccable meant that even on his best behavior, Max could not compete. But the real source of the agitation was that for the last forty-eight hours, Max had not been able to locate Tracy.

Frank was a dry lead. He had not called her or seen her. Max liked to think that she had gotten smart and just dumped him. Finally, after too long of a search, he had gotten the address of her condo and the phone number. He called a few random times to see if she was home, but all he got was that butter-melting voice on the answering machine.

Earlier that day, he had sent one of the girls over to ask one of the gate guards where Tracy had gone. A little flirting, a little cajoling, and the guard said that he didn't know where she had gone, but when she drove away, she waved good-bye and said that she would be back Sunday night. Even with this knowledge, Max's patience seemed to be wearing thin.

"Do you agree, Max?" Jeremy asked evenly.

"What? Uh, sorry. My mind was wandering," Max said, masking his resentment at being called out.

"I gathered," said Jeremy, raising an eyebrow. "And that is so unlike you."

"Yeah. I know," said Max, inwardly recoiling from Jeremy's mocking tone.

As Jeremy watched him, Max's mind took a more purposeful wander. He wondered how Jeremy would feel if Max mentioned that he had had a chance to interview Mac McGregor up close and personal. He could tell him that McGregor seemed pretty sharp. It was no wonder that he had been chosen to lead over Jeremy. Or he could just tell him that McGregor remembered him as an arrogant asshole. Then Jeremy would kill McGregor, and Max could watch for a change.

"Are we drifting again?" Jeremy asked with increased annoyance.

No. We *aren't doing anything*, thought Max as he worked to control his temper. He bit the inside of his lip. He glared at Jeremy but did not reply.

Jeremy gave him an exasperated eye roll and changed the subject. "Do you ever have premonitions, Max? Or perhaps an extra sense that warns you of danger? When all the data in your brain computes and all logic dictates a certain course of action, does a tingle, or an instinct, or even a vision ever cause you to override?"

Jeremy sat back and studied Max. When Jeremy got all professorial on Max, it took every bit of Max's self-restraint to either not cut the class or not cut the fucking teacher.

"I've got combat instincts. Every elite soldier does. You need them to survive," Max replied defensively. "Do I have Spidey senses, supernatural powers? Hell, no," he said in a tone that required forced passivity.

Jeremy leaned forward, eyes blazing. "Well, I do, Max. I do." He paused for dramatic effect. "Does winning lose its flavor when there is no challenge? Is victory sweet without an element of uncertainty or danger?"

Max knew that when Jeremy pontificated, his role was to be an interested listener. For some reason, that was harder than ever tonight.

"Would Michael Jordan have enjoyed playing against high schoolers when he was in his prime?" Jeremy continued. "How about you, Max? If you sparred every day with your boy toy, Frank Griffin, wouldn't it become tedious, boring?"

Max acted like he actually thought about it. Then he shook his head and said, "Nope," adding a wry smile.

"How silly of me," said Jeremy with amusement and exaggerated hand gestures, "to forget your incredible endurance when it comes to administering torture."

Max looked at him again, not sure if he was the butt of a joke.

"If you do not share my beliefs, Max," Jeremy offered tauntingly, "it may be more prudent not to be so predictable. Perhaps we should cancel tonight's visit to the club. What do you think?"

Max looked at Jeremy and breathed deeply to control and hide his mounting anger. A telltale vein began to emerge on his forehead. He wanted to go to the club tonight. He needed to go and to be distracted. "I think that we should go as planned," he said mechanically.

"Why?" Jeremy challenged.

Max met his gaze and was silent for a long moment. Then he spoke. "Because there is nothing other than a force of nature that can take us down when we're together." He threw the gauntlet back at Jeremy.

As he sat back in his chair, Jeremy steepled his hands under his chin. He was purposely silent for about two minutes, as if he were calculating all the permutations of the universe. Max continued to hold his gaze. Finally, Jeremy said, "Perhaps you're right, my friend. Perhaps you're right."

*   *   *   *   *

Even though he had worked out vigorously the day before, Max was back in the gym. Until recently, emotions such as stress and anxiety had been foreign to him. He controlled his life, his actions, and his environment. Even his temper had been under control since he first met Jeremy.

With sweat streaming down his muscular, scarred chest, he continued ruthlessly attacking the heavy weight bag as if he could destroy his demons through unrelenting aggression. Finally, when his mind could no longer ignore his leaden arms, he stopped, pulled off his gloves, and threw them to the floor.

Later, as the shower spray pelted his body, he considered whether Tracy Lane was the antidote for these disturbing emotions. Since he had first seen her, he had not had sex. It was obviously not for lack of opportunity; it was for lack of interest.

Max smiled at the thought: he was saving himself. In the end, he concluded that she would be the solution. The other alternative, that something might be irreversibly wrong with him, was unacceptable.

*   *   *   *   *

At ten o'clock, Jeremy met Max in the small, private basement garage. If anyone actually saw them together, the similarities in attire might have invited speculation that they were more than just friends or business associates. Jeremy wore triple-pleated black linen trousers and a black silk mock turtle. Around his waist was a three-hundred-dollar black alligator belt, and on his feet were five-hundred-dollar custom Italian loafers. The only curious addition was the unusual pair of glasses tucked into the top of his mock turtle.

Because he wore a lightweight brown and black houndstooth sport coat, at a distance Max might have appeared more sartorially splendored. Yet his black silk mock turtle was accompanied by a faux black leather belt, black jeans, and black Mephisto tennis shoes. Max clicked open the doors of the armor-plated black Lincoln.

Max always drove, and Jeremy occupied the front passenger seat. Before opening the reinforced steel garage door, Max opened the lid of the ashtray and pushed his index finger on the scanner. Immediately, the center panel moved forward and opened, revealing an UZI and a .357 Magnum hanging on either side. "We can keep it open if you feel we need extra insurance," said Max as he looked blankly at Jeremy.

Jeremy smiled. "Ever the Boy Scout. I do tend to forget how quickly we can become an army."

The customizing of the car had been Max's design. The trunk was finished so that the forward part was not visible when the trunk lid was raised.

The folding center armrest in the rear seat had been replaced by a spring-loaded sliding panel containing the weapons. Finally, the panel was held in place by an electronic latch that was controlled by fingerprint scanners hidden underneath the ashtray lids.

Even though the odds of this arsenal ever being used in Naples, Florida, were infinitesimal, Max and, of course, Jeremy were extremely cautious men.

CHAPTER 37

THE SIX PEOPLE ALTERNATELY watching through night-vision glasses as the car pulled into the parking space were not visible from the street. Only the glasses peered out from the window of the abandoned motel room. They watched in silence as the two men exited the car and walked toward the rear entrance to the club. One of the men, presumably Lyons, placed his hand on a sensor, and the door opened. Quickly they entered the building, and the door closed quietly behind them.

Watching with critical eyes, the task force members had studied every movement. "They may be old, but those guys are warriors," Skinny McLister offered with grudging respect. Joe Sebastiano noted that McLister had positioned himself protectively next to Ellen Williams.

"Max was a SEAL, and Jeremy is a martial arts fanatic. This is not your typical white-collar roust," said Joe.

"How could these men have been terrorizing my city without my ever having seen or heard of them?" They were standing now in the darkened room, but the full moon gave sufficient illumination to see the bewildered look on the face of Naples Chief of Police Jed Tully.

It was a weathered face, damaged by the years and the persistence of the Florida sun. Yet it was a kind face, and his light gray eyes seemed to acknowledge that he was over his head in this high-risk mission. On the other hand, the fact that every few minutes he just started grinning indicated that Jed Tully wouldn't have missed this for anything in the world.

"I was told that this place was owned by foreign nationals. Admittance is by invitation only. Ever since it's been open, we've had absolutely no trouble, no complaints, so I've stayed away. I guess I should have checked it out, but I hate to stick my nose in business where there's no trouble." He shook his head in obvious regret. "I feel like the biggest fool in the state of Florida." Tully offered these observations with feeble hopes of absolution.

"It's in their interest to be invisible. Even the government had no idea where they were," Joe offered, commiserating.

"I still think that we should have gotten Jed to get us all tasers like his," said Dean Segrum, pointing at Jed's toy and shaking his head like an excited child. "We could have jumped out and zapped the suckers when they got outta the car."

Joe knew that innovative takedowns were Dean's fantasy. This suggestion was tame compared to previous offers.

"Or I could just hide on the roof and drop down on them and squish 'em like bugs," said the 280-pound Henry Major.

Dean nodded, smiling his approval. "My guess is that the roof has pressure sensors. I know that you're light on your feet, big guy, but that might not have worked."

Joe shook his head. He knew that humor before an operation was positive. "This isn't a perfect plan by any stretch," he continued. "These guys haven't stayed invisible because they're stupid."

"What if they spend the whole night in there?" asked Ellen.

"Then I will personally tuck you in and tell you bedtime stories," McLister volunteered, flashing his pearly whites for emphasis. Ellen smiled back as if considering the idea.

Joe spoke. "That's not their usual MO, but however long, we wait." He looked around at his team. From a competency standpoint, this was as good as it gets. Still, he could not get over this unusual level of apprehension. Takedowns of white-collar criminals are supposed to be easy. He once again went over his thought process. If, somehow, the subjects were warned of the FBI's presence, they would simply leave by the front entrance, and his team would be left sitting on their thumbs. He could not envision a scenario where they would exit out the rear of the club brandishing weapons.

The customary FBI weapons on an arrest such as this would include his beloved Remington Model 870 12-gauge shotgun and either a Colt M4 rifle or an H&K MP-5 10mm submachine gun. However, because of the area and the possibility that terrified spectators would call the club or the police if they saw the usual arsenal, the agents carried only the standard Glock Model 23 40-caliber handguns.

Although his supervisor had readily approved his plan for the arrest, Joe could not shake the queasy feeling that he was still missing something. He sighed, rubbed his neck, and ran his hands to the back of his hair. The next part was not going to be easy. Unlike most task force commanders, Joe allowed discussion. It was about to bite him in the ass.

He began in his most authoritative voice. "McLister, you and I will approach from the south. You're skinnier, so you will lead. From the north, Dean leads Henry, same reason."

"I'm the skinniest of the lot," challenged Ellen.

"Yes, but I need you and the chief behind their vehicle," said Joe quickly.

"Behind their vehicle?" Ellen's raised voice was instantly filled with hurt and anger.

"Shh. We use our quiet voices on an operation," quipped an instigating Dean.

Even in the dimly lit room, Ellen's glare was enough to cause Dean to hide behind Henry. "The reason we're here is because of me. I'm the one who had to lie, deceive, and then intimidate to get the information. And then you put my ass on the bench?" To Joe, Ellen's quiet but barely controlled fury was more painful than shouts would have been.

Joe waited, looking at her and hoping that her anger would dissipate. He quickly saw that was not going to happen. "Listen, kiddo."

"No 'kiddo' bullshit, Joe," she interrupted. "I'm a trained agent, and I can outshoot any of these bozos except Dean." Skinny McLister's eyebrows shot up, but discretion seemed to prevent him from stepping in front of a runaway train.

Joe took a breath because he could feel his heat rising. It was partly because her reasoning made sense and partly because he was admittedly protective with Ellen. Nevertheless, he had gone through this before he decided on it, and the decision had been made.

"Someone has to stay with Chief Tully," he said evenly. "He has to stay back so that he can call for backup if we need it. All of the other agents have experience in high-risk takedowns. You have none."

"And how do I get experience?"

His silent glare shouted that he was her superior and she had been given an order.

In spite of that, she spit the words out. "What do I do if they get by you, boss?" she asked with bitter sarcasm. Joe could tell that she wanted to say more.

He looked at her stonily, keeping the look for at least a minute. She matched his gaze. Then he spoke. "Shoot 'em."

Ellen turned away, perhaps realizing that she had crossed the line. Joe stared at her for another minute, turned his head, and then said, "Let's roll."

As they left the building, McLister reached over to touch Ellen's shoulder. She smacked his hand away.

CHAPTER 38

THE NAPLES NIGHT WAS quiet, with temperatures in the comfortable range, low seventies. Joe hugged the building as he passed by Skinny McLister, who was moving forward to take the position closest to the door.

When he arrived at the corner of the building, Joe sat down and pressed his back to the wall. His neck ached and his back hurt. He'd stood in the ready position for the last two hours. He was too old for this shit.

As Joe gazed at the beautiful Florida moon, he rubbed the back of his neck. He came back to the same conclusion as before. Usually, when they knew the whereabouts of the suspects, the takedown was considerably less complicated than this operation. In this phase, Joe normally got a little anxious, although he hid it from his team. His anxiety tonight had escalated to flat-out fear. He kept telling himself that his fear was irrational, but his gut ignored him.

Meanwhile, Ellen was crouching behind the hood of the armor-plated Lincoln. Using her flashlight, she had peeked into the car, but she had seen nothing unusual. Tully had taken his turn on guard and was now sitting cross-legged on the ground with his back to the stakeout. "How many of these type operations have you been on?" Ellen whispered.

"You mean counting this one?" asked Tully.

"Yes."

"One."

"Ah, local humor. Humiliate the poor city rube."

Tully laughed. "Ma'am, I don't believe anybody could humiliate you, and you sure ain't no rube."

"Don't try to butter me up after you were just playing me."

Tully laughed again. "I know when I'm outmatched. I admire you, though, standing up to your boss like that."

"Thanks," she replied. "Fat lot of good it does when the All-Boys Club is led by Don Joseph Sebastiano."

"We may see some action yet. Wake me if the shootin' starts," the chief said with a yawn.

Ellen leaned over and whispered, "No way! I'm going to swipe your taser, zap the perps, and then zap all of my guys for leaving me behind."

"Ol' Jed is safe, ain't he?"

"Absolutely, cutie," Ellen replied, nodding her head. "You're my witness that it was all self-defense."

Tully laughed once more, dropped his head to his chest, and closed his eyes.

*   *   *   *   *

Max was glad to be leaving the club. Four hours of watching assholes get manipulated by women and peeking in on random sexual acts and occasional brief shots of bathroom self-abuse had not provided any distraction. He would have been better off in the gym. He had no idea where Tracy was, and he had nobody to hurt. He followed Jeremy out the door.

"Don't move," came the calm but demanding voice of a professional.

"Wow! Who do we have here?" asked Jeremy in an excited tone. In the light of the moon, his eyes seemed to dance.

"On the ground! Do it now!" shouted Joe as he put his hand firmly on Jeremy's right shoulder. Jeremy's right hand came up with the palm facing Joe in a childish, half hands-up surrender pose. His left hand remained in his pants pocket. Max did not move. His eyes scanned only the two agents who had their Glocks drawn and trained on him.

Jeremy's body moved down about two inches under the pressure of Joe's hand, but to Joe it was like pushing a statue to the ground. "I have my glasses on," Jeremy said in a high-pitched voice. "Even in this light I should be able to determine the authenticity of you gentlemen's credentials."

Max shifted his body imperceptibly. Henry Major grabbed Max's arm with a fury. "On the ground now, asshole!" Henry growled with spittle flying into Max's face.

At that precise moment, an unbelievably intense light shot from roof-mounted fixtures. The agents were instantly blinded. As in a choreographed ballet, Jeremy spun away from the grasp of the disoriented senior agent and headed toward his car. Max, with eyes squeezed shut, thrust both his arms violently upward and broke Henry's grip. He simultaneously delivered a roundhouse kick with his right leg, which landed on Henry's rib cage. A painful grunt escaped from Henry as he staggered backward.

Max quickly flipped glasses out of his jacket pocket, put them on, and grabbed the right arm of McLister, the nearest incapacitated agent. With both hands, Max gave the arm a quick twist and screamed in triumph as he heard the sickening crack. As McLister was falling, Max snatched the agent's weapon out of midair. All the while, McLister flailed with his left hand, trying futilely to stop him. Max released the safety and aimed the Glock at the agent's head.

"Stop!" Jeremy commanded. Max's fingers squeezed and then reluctantly relaxed. He turned, and together they ran toward the car.

Ellen and Chief Tully had been just out of range of the paralyzing light. Tully had instinctively started to move when the light came on, but Ellen held him back. They would only be effective outside of the rays' range. The entire escape had taken about twenty seconds.

"Halt!" shouted Tully, whose head was slightly above the car. He gripped his pistol with two hands and braced it on top of the car. Max fired at him as he leaped and whirled through the air. The shot skimmed the top of the car, and Tully fell to the pavement.

Ellen fired from her position behind the hood of the car and caught Max in the right shoulder. She shifted to the fleeing Jeremy and fired again, but Max catapulted in front of the shot, caught the bullet in his chest, and crashed to the ground in front of the car.

Ellen jumped up to pursue Jeremy. A hand shot out and grabbed her ankle in a viselike grip, yanking her down to the pavement. Her gun skidded out of reach. All breath left her body. Another hand grabbed her other ankle, and she was dragged on her back toward the car.

As Ellen struggled to regain her breath and her equilibrium, Max rolled his bloodied body on top of her. The moonlight illuminated her defiant but terrorized face as she struggled mightily. He jammed the pistol into her neck. She stilled under the intensity of his demonic stare. Face to face, six inches apart, she was trapped by his body and his strength.

Keeping the pistol pressed tightly under her jaw, the madman moved his face toward hers. She squeezed her eyes shut. Tears of pain and fear were running down her cheeks. He mashed his lips down on hers and kissed her. She blinked her eyes open in astonishment.

Max's face was contorted in pain, but his eyes were ablaze. He let out a garbled scream, and his arms tightened around her with python-like intensity. She could not breathe.

CHAPTER 39

WE WERE STILL ASLEEP when the phone rang. I started to stumble to the closet, but I heard Grace talking on the house phone. "Hi, Joe." As she listened, I had to fight the urge to snatch the phone away from her.

"I'm glad you're safe. Mac told me all about it last night. No, no, we were just getting up. I know Mac wants to talk to you."

She handed me the phone and scooted over, and I sat heavily on the bed. From her face, I could tell that everything had not gone as planned. "Joe, thank God you're okay," I said.

"That's the good news, pal," he said wearily. "Max is dead, but Jeremy got away. We took some major casualties. I don't know how this could have gone so wrong."

I felt a surge of relief. All I heard was that Max was dead. It felt mentally selfish to discount the other casualties, but my family was safe.

Grace touched my back, and I half-turned to her. "Max is dead. I need to talk to Joe. Are you okay?"

She blinked and those precious blue eyes teared up, but she nodded. I kissed her forehead and walked out of the room.

A minute later, I picked up the other phone. "Joe, what the hell happened?" I asked softly.

He sighed. "Best we know from the tech guys is that Lyons activated a military weapon called the Laser Dazzler that, thank God, only temporarily blinded us. I'm not sure if I understand all the technical gobbledygook.

"The design was enhanced with an RF receiver and turned on with a garage door opener–type transmitter," he said. "Lyons had these remotely operated lights covering the area, and the beams hit us right between the eyes. All we saw were green fucking dots. The techs said that the effect centers on the macular vision. It's like someone shot you with the world's most powerful flashbulbs."

Joe stopped to catch his breath. His bitterness and disgust punctuated every word. I almost always see jovial Joe; this one could rip a person apart with his bare hands.

"So how could Jeremy and Max function?" I asked.

"When Jeremy came out of the club, he was wearing these funky glasses. The tech guys said they were probably clear multiple wavelength glasses because they offer the best protection: high ocular density, yet the highest visibility.

"Max didn't have the glasses on, but I saw him squeeze his eyes shut right before the flash, so he had to know it was coming. Somehow he was able to put them on after that."

"What happened to you?" I asked.

"Big fucking hero. I hear grunts and a shortened scream. Shots are fired. I end up on the ground like a crab, trying to grab somebody's ankle. All I managed to do was grab Dean. I was worse than useless."

Words started pouring out of Joe like projectile vomit. "Major has a dislocated shoulder and two broken ribs. Chief Tully got a head wound, but he should be all right. Meanwhile, poor McLister with a shattered right arm, blind as a bat, is stumbling, crawling, and bumping into shit trying to get to Ellen. Finally, on his hands and knees, he bumps into Max."

"So he killed Max?"

"Nah, too late. The bastard bled out while lying on top of Ellen. She's crying, gasping for breath, and McLister is pulling this dead weight off of her with one hand."

I finally let a breath out. "But Max is dead? You're positive?"

"Absolutely."

"Thank God," I said coldly.

"Yeah," he sighed. "Almost like he scripted it, Max dove in front of a bullet meant for Jeremy. In fact, the son of a bitch had two bullet holes in him and still yanked Ellen to the ground."

I shook my head in amazement. "What's the next step with Jeremy?" I asked, trying to keep the disappointment out of my voice.

"His office is locked up tighter than a drum. We not only have the place surrounded with agents, but we are using the new sense-through-the-wall radar imaging technology that the Army developed. There is not a heartbeat in there. So we wait for the first sign of life, and then they either let us in or we force our way in."

"It's strange that he left his offices totally unmanned. It's also not a good sign," I said.

"Well, we won't be lacking firepower. In addition to my guys, the locals are there, along with a SWAT team from hostage rescue and the SEC and the IRS. Guaranteed we will shut his operation down, and there have to be some clues as to where he went."

"I find it hard to be optimistic. Jeremy seems to be at least one step ahead." I felt Joe's silence. I didn't want him to think that my pessimistic outlook was a criticism.

"Okay, pal," I added quickly. "I appreciate the call. It's hard to plan for a military death ray. And Joe, I'm really sorry about your people."

"Yeah," he said, sounding like his adrenaline was wearing off. "Maybe this time I won't step on my appendage."

CHAPTER 40

WITH NO PRELUDE, JOE Sebastiano began. "Jeremy Lyons is one piece of work. You are not gonna believe the crap he pulled."

Absolutely not the way I wanted to start my day. I didn't respond. I closed my eyes and put my hand on my forehead.

"We're gonna get this cocksucker. He's too vain to stay away. And if you detect any jocularity in my dissertation, my shrink told me that it was the only way to prevent me from going mental Chapter Eleven."

My continued silence signaled my acquiescence. I hadn't been sure how Joe would sound or react after what must have been a series of replays and recriminations.

"It's like the whole office suddenly materialized at their desks at seven o'clock. We got movement, heartbeats all over the place. Synchronized swimming was never this precise. Just for grins, we try the door. It was open!"

"Open?"

"You got it, and no armed mercenaries, no enforcers. I've got, like, an army platoon inside the building, and all we see is a hot receptionist. She stands up and says, 'Oh, my!' I look back at my guys and then back at her, trying to figure out if I'm in the wrong building.

"Meanwhile, she steps out from behind her desk, walks directly to me, and extends her hand. I shake her hand, but I'm scanning the room, looking for a trap. She says, 'I'm Vanessa. You look like you're in charge. Are you Agent Sebastiano?'"

"What did you do?" I asked reflexively.

"I nodded like a dummy. It took all of my training to not let my mouth hang open and not act as dumb-assed as I felt.

"Then this Vanessa broad tells us that Mr. Lyons would appreciate it if we would adjourn to the large conference room. She says that she's sorry, but the room won't hold everyone. I motion to the SWAT team and the locals to go baby-sit where we detected other people in the building. McLister, with his arm in a cast and not doped up because he refused the pills, Dean, and Ellen are with me. Only Henry Major is missing; he's in the hospital.

"SEC and IRS guys join us, and we go into this large, ultramodern, over-the-top conference room. She offers us seats, and there's coffee, juice, bottled water, fruit, yogurt, and sweet rolls at our disposal."

"So he's treating you like you're there for a corporate merger. He's pimping you and jerking your chain big time," I said with complete disgust.

"Yeah. I would have ignored this whole scene and just marched through there like Sherman going through Atlanta, but Lyons was obviously way ahead of us. So I just let the farce play out."

"You weren't concerned that they were destroying evidence while you were having tea and crumpets?" I asked.

"Remote. We knew damn well that Lyons wouldn't be there. Whatever play was going on had to be part of his contingency plan. My guess is that this was put into place before my team and I got the dots out of our eyes."

"You're probably right," I conceded.

"So picture this: we are all standing there, staring at a giant TV screen on the wall, with our fingers up our butts.

"Vanessa flips a switch. I make sure that the door is open and that she stays in the room in case there's an automatic release of gas or some shit. Segrum is on the door, weapon drawn.

"Who appears on the screen in high definition and living color but Jeremy Lyons. He's sporting a three-button navy suit, a starched white shirt with the Pat Riley collar, and a blood-red tie. Add horn-rimmed glasses and a meek, embarrassed smile. I almost threw up."

I shook my head while holding the phone.

"You're gonna get a copy of the tape, and I'm not Sam Golden's Kay, but I'll give you the gist. First, he apologizes that he cannot be there with us. He's under a doctor's care because of the trauma of the other night."

"You've got to be shitting me!"

Joe was just getting started, and his voice took on a bitter, prissy tone. "Since no one showed him identification, he had no choice but to flee when those horrible blinding lights came on. And then when the ruffians—yep, that's the word he used—started scuffling with his bodyguard, he was scared to death. He apologized again, saying that he is a financier, not a fighter."

I let what I thought was the final "f--- you" linger. Then I spoke. "Just when you think this asshole has stuck the needle in as far as it can go, he takes a sledge hammer and pounds it in farther!" The heat inside me was reaching a dangerous level.

"Almost done," Joe offered. "He admits sheepishly that if we're watching this, then we must really be men of authority. He wanted to extend his hospitality and hoped that Vanessa would be a good tour guide around the facility."

"Couldn't you have just tasered them when they opened the club door?" I asked in frustration. I instantly regretted my second-guessing and insulting Monday-morning quarterbacking.

Before I could retract, Joe answered. "The Bureau doesn't authorize tasers. I promise you, I've exhausted all of the what ifs, pal."

"I know, Joe. I'm really sorry I said that."

"No problem, Kemo Sabe. Are you ready for the coup de grace?"

"Sure," I said with the enthusiasm of a person responding to his dentist when asked if he is ready for a root canal. "What more could that sociopath do to prove that he's the smartest man on the planet?"

"Stay tuned," said Joe. "Jeremy also tells us that a warrant is not necessary because he has nothing to hide. And he is looking forward to meeting us in the near future. Finally, ever the proper host, he waves good-bye into the camera, and the screen darkens." Joe let it hang. He may have been waiting to see if I was throwing up my breakfast.

"And you got zip when you got on their computers," I speculated.

"Interesting tidbit there. Frank Griffin told us that Lyons had six traders: Milton Peterman, Richard Hwang, three more men, and one woman. When we got to their trading floor, the five men were in their seats, all innocent like, waiting for Jeremy to give them their marching orders."

"So the traders were not given a heads-up?" I asked.

"Apparently not, but their role is difficult to prosecute. It's hard to imagine anyone other than Jeremy deciding what to buy or sell. In your business, are traders responsible for research or coming up with ideas?"

"No." I considered his question. "Spotting trends, analyzing trade anomalies, and responding to breaking news may all be in their wheelhouse, but their primary responsibility is to execute the orders."

"I thought so. Then the $64,000 question is, why wasn't the female trader at her desk?"

"She was hot," I said. It seemed like a logical answer.

"Nope—plain, a hermit, lived in the building. Other than prints, there was no valuable info in her room. She was gonzo."

"Perhaps he took the woman away so that they could spawn a devil child," I offered woodenly.

"Yuck," Joe said. "Anyway, we'll probably figure it out before your grandkids go to college. In your spare time, you can check out killdisk. com; it's a hard-drive eraser. As of now, there's no way to determine who the investors were. My IRS guys confirmed your theory that all of the so-called investors probably made loans, rather than actual investments, so no partnership returns were required."

"It's brilliant," I admitted reluctantly. "My friend's commitment was a loan. No partnership return, no questions. A loan backed by an ironclad guarantee, probably second only to a government loan."

"Let's talk about that for a minute," said Joe. His tone became serious. "This is your area, so maybe you can shed some light on it for me."

I remained warily silent. For some reason, it felt like I was in the principal's office.

"Jeremy's people gave us total access to their prime brokerage accounts at J. P. Morgan—more than $3 billion." He waited, as did I.

"Two withdrawals happened shortly before the planned takedown—one for $30 million and the other for $ billion." More time elapsed between statements, but he could have waited for hell to freeze over before I would volunteer.

Joe went on. "Periodically, Lyons would withdraw massive funds and then put most or all of the money back into the account. It was almost as if he was testing the system. So we figured that the $3 billion withdrawal was definitely initiated by Lyons. What we can't figure out is the $30 million withdrawal.

Why do you think there would be a random withdrawal for $30 million? That's pocket change for Lyons."

I quickly calculated probabilities. First, what was the chance that my call to Rod had screwed up the arrest? Second, what was the probability that Joe would push this issue until it became uncomfortable for me? I played the odds.

By my reasoning, if Jeremy had somehow been alerted to Rod's withdrawal and that had been a red flag for him, he would never have gone to his club that night. He did have an escape route, but too many things can go wrong when agents have their guns drawn.

I wasn't going to take the fall, and I certainly wasn't going to give up Rod. "That probably would not be pocket change for Max," I offered, thinking quickly. "Besides, the fact that it was 1 percent of Jeremy's withdrawal would have seemed appropriate to the mastermind."

Joe waited, probably not buying my explanation, but he got nothing more from me. A loud sigh may have been intended to make me feel guilty. But Joe was too smart to keep banging his head against a stone wall. "Yeah, maybe. I guess we should focus on what happened to the $3 billion."

"That makes sense," I said rapidly but with enough resolve to indicate that further probing would be useless. "He may have more than one prime broker," I added. "I would check with Sam. Also, he probably executes trades with everybody on the street. My guess is that after your audit, you won't find any damaging evidence of an insider trading violation."

"Why not?" asked Joe, sounding confused.

"Think of J. P. Morgan as a warehouse for all the action that ultimately holds all the security positions. They act as a custodian for all the assets, like an omnibus account."

"So if they hold all the assets, tell me again why they can't tell if he's crooked?"

Since I was on familiar ground and had considered this, I exhibited the patience we extend to our clients. Also, I was relieved to be on another subject. "Let me try another example, Joe. Suppose you ask me to buy a hundred shares of IBM and then deliver the shares to your bank to hold as collateral for a loan. The only reason a red flag would appear is if there were a significant corporate event within close proximity to the trade."

"Got it," he said.

"When the SEC or FINRA, the Financial Industry Regulatory Authority, sees suspicious activities on a stock, they issue what's called a blue-sheet request. It's all electronic now, but they want to know the date, time, and particulars of stock trades.

"When there is increased activity around a corporate event, the computers tell them that there may be something fishy. These requests would go to whichever brokerage firm executed the trades. My guess is that this will be a blind alley for you. I think Lyons knew the information well before trades would become suspicious, or you would have heard of him before."

Joe sighed again. "Our guys are pretty convinced that his $3 billion went into cyberspace."

I agreed. "Anyone who is smart enough to set up a fund on a loan basis, thereby eliminating the need for audited partnership returns, won't leave a money trail."

"This may be the only time that I would prefer that you disagreed with me," said Joe.

He paused for a moment. "I'm reluctant to give you this last one, but they may be considering me for an FBI reality show, *Dumb and Dumber*, and I get to play both parts. As soon as we could see straight, we notified the Naples airport to hold all outgoing planes. Of course, we also checked the cab companies because Jeremy left his car behind the club."

It sounded like Joe was going to end up with egg on his face, but his self-flagellation was uncharacteristic. "Most logical would have been for Jeremy to call from the scene, roust his pilots, and head out of Dodge," I said. "Is the airport close?"

"Yep, and the largest plane in his fleet had just taken off."

"So you tracked it," I said, confused as to why this would have a bad ending.

"You got it. Short hop to Miami, reception waiting, surround the plane, and the only inhabitants were two confused pilots. They had been instructed by Mr. Lyons to enjoy a weekend on him in South Beach. In addition, the pilots were told to offer free passage on Monday morning back to Naples for any of the gentlemen in law enforcement."

Joe went silent, and I could almost hear him hanging his head.

I laughed wryly. "He can't resist showing us how much smarter he is than we are. Nothing you can do, pal, when a crook is prepared for every eventuality."

Joe was quiet for a moment. Then he said, "Mac, you've been a hell of a help on this case, and I appreciate it. We did get the bastard that most likely killed your friend. Lyons's operation is closed down. Frank Griffin gave us the names of plenty of CEOs to hammer, and our computer gurus may find some more goodies. We are going to find Jeremy Lyons, and when we do, you damn sure are going to be the first to know."

CHAPTER 41

I CALLED R. J. over the weekend. He was entitled to know everything I knew. Yet he would be sufficiently in sync with my mood to surmise that I wasn't ready for a full discussion. After listening quietly to my dissertation, he simply added, "Thanks for bringing me up to speed, Mac. I'm glad that Max Parnavich is no longer a threat to your family."

Also, I felt obliged to give Danny DeMarco the abbreviated version of events. His initial work on analyzing the lethal pattern of the Washington Group's insurance purchases had been helpful. In addition, this story should be all over the news at any minute, and Danny lives to be ahead of breaking news.

*   *   *   *   *

Monday morning, R. J. motioned for *me* to follow *him* into *my* conference room. The thought of a palace coup flitted in and out of my brain. "Yesss?" I asked with raised eyebrows as I took a seat.

"What level of concern do you have that Jeremy Lyons will resurface and become a problem for you?"

I winced and put my hand on my forehead. It had not been easy to fight my fear of Max Parnavich. I was not sure that I was strong enough to engage in another battle of conversations and self-talk to try and get somewhere close to my usual life again.

"Are you volunteering to be my bodyguard?"

"I'm serious, Mac. This man has been multiple steps ahead of the SEC and the FBI."

The look on his face was disconcerting. I sighed, realizing that he would not let it go unless I focused on this. I collected my thoughts. "I've had this discussion with Joe. His *theory*—and I emphasize theory because, you're right, nobody knows with Lyons—is that hiding from the law is a full-time job for him."

R. J. did not look convinced.

I tried again. "Just like with work," I said, "I assessed the probabilities. I'll give you my logic, but if you disagree violently, I don't want to know."

He nodded, understanding completely, and politely did not remind me that I had previously asserted the low probability of a fifty-five-year-old being dangerous.

"Lyons may not be aware of my involvement. Without Max's visit, that would be almost assured. Yet, other than being scared half out of our minds, there were no repercussions. Next, it seems like there would be higher priorities if Lyons even has a hit list."

R. J. frowned at my uncomfortable reference.

"Ellen Williams, who shot Max. Joe. Frank Griffin. Even Margo Savino. I'm just rationalizing, but I wasn't involved in any of his business dealings. I did not betray him. Finally, I'm not sure that they could ever prove that Lyons committed or authorized murder."

"You've got to be kidding ..."

I raised my hand to stop him. "Wait until we get the tape from Joe, where Lyons paints himself as a victim."

R. J. shook his head as if I had just told him that the world was flat. He thought for a moment. "Okay," he said. "I'm sorry for bringing up an unpleasant subject, but it has been weighing on my mind." He looked at me for a long moment. "Is there anything I can do?"

I smiled, paused, and looked at him as if I were seriously contemplating the offer. "Start packing heat, and pray that I'm right."

*　　　*　　　*　　　*　　　*

The story made the Monday evening news. The fact that the confrontation and resulting death had transpired early Friday morning and had been contained by the FBI made the media coverage resemble a pack of rabid dogs.

Any of the residents of the quiet city of Naples, Florida, who might have heard a shot in the wee hours of the morning chose to roll over and go back to sleep. Neither the police nor the media had received a single call. No pictures or citizens' video were available to give the newscasters an inside look. Consequently, they could only report what had been given to them.

As Heywood Cunningham flipped the channels in the luxurious bar of the Sequoia restaurant in Washington DC, he shook his head at the similarity of the righteous indignation spat out by the media clones. He paused to consider whether the media or Congress had a larger feeling of entitlement. Only Fox News appeared more interested in the story than in the fact that their access had been delayed.

The only photos of the incident were FBI photos. There were no photos or collaborating video from the media. The only local involved was Naples Chief of Police Jed Tully, and he was still in the hospital recovering from a head wound. Even while Heywood's mind, clear due to the club soda and lime in his hand, was rapidly analyzing the possibilities, he thought that it would be interesting to count the cumulative air quotes from the babbling heads.

Heywood's son was due to meet him for a drink in about ten minutes. Normally on a balmy late spring evening, they would meet at the restaurant's riverfront bar. The Sequoia has stunning views of the Potomac River.

During the warmer season, with the expansive patio dining and the outdoor bar, it was the place to be. However, that night, light rain had driven the patrons inside. It was fortuitous for Heywood; otherwise, he would have missed this breaking news, and his response would have been less timely.

As he looked at his BlackBerry, he smiled. You *could* teach an old dog new tricks. Human nature dictates that 99.9 percent of the population focuses initially on their own situation in a time of crisis. Fortunately, this wily veteran always had a contingency plan. It was a damn good bet that most, if not all, of the other recruiters were crapping in their pants at this moment.

Heywood pulled up his e-mail chain and started to type. He looked up at the TV screen to assure himself once again that Max was really dead. The message would go to each recipient, and none of the recipients would know that the same message was being sent to all.

I am shocked and appalled by what I have just seen
on the news. Yet because I introduced you to the Franklin
Corporation, I feel obligated to pursue your interest vigorously
with the authorities. My goal is to have your funds returned

to you with the utmost urgency. Please acknowledge receipt
of this message and inform me if you do not want me to
represent your interests in this matter.

Respectfully,
Heywood

"Make the best of a bad situation" had always been Heywood's motto. It had been almost two years since he had become involved with the now infamous Franklin Corporation. During this time, he had stashed away a million dollars.

Oh, he would bluster and demand the instant release of his $5 million loan, and he would help any of his CEO recruits. But he was smart enough to know that the regulators would hold on longer than necessary to make a point. Still, letters of credit, money in the bank—good as gold. In the meantime, a few of his grateful recruits might slip him a token of their appreciation in the belief that he had actually expedited the process.

Heywood smiled as he considered why he was so sanguine about the death of his golden goose. With the Franklin Corporation exposed, his stipends would end. Well, the next morning, he would go to the FBI agent in charge. Upon receiving a guarantee of immunity and anonymity, he would hand over the secret tapes he had made of all his conversations with the CEOs.

He took another sip of his club soda and smiled again. The undoctored tapes sure as hell would make this old fool sound like he had been totally duped. While his fellow "see no evil" coconspirators were shucking and jiving, Heywood would be volunteering evidence.

The upside of his severe reduction in cash flow was that Max the Psycho would no longer be watching Heywood's every move. As he had concluded and as the news confirmed, Max would gladly have wrung the former senator's neck.

One too many drinks, one incautious comment would have equaled one less Heywood. Just to be sure that his sentiments were clear, Heywood raised his glass and said out loud to the TV, "You intimidating piece of shit, may you rot in hell."

At that moment, Heywood's son, Robert Edward Cunningham, approached his father. "Was it something I said, Pop?" he asked, laughing.

"No. Sit down, Robert E.," said Heywood as he scrambled off his bar seat. "I was just toasting a dearly departed enemy," he added with his patented smile. Although he was the only one who did, Heywood referred to his son as Robert E. because of his admiration for the late general. In addition, it was a habit that had been helpful in his campaigning.

Robert was an environmental lawyer, which might dispel the myth of the acorn falling close to the tree. With a handsome, angular face, Jack Kennedy hair, and his mother's dark brown eyes, he was Heywood's favorite. Not only was he the oldest, but he was also the only kid of the three who had totally reconnected with his dad.

"I'm sorry that you can't stay for supper, son, but I'm glad you're here," said Heywood.

"Family obligations," Robert replied sheepishly. "But I enjoy spending time with you. If I do it enough, I may have to vote Republican."

"Be still, my heart," said Heywood as he clutched his chest. They shared a laugh. "One of those apple martinis still work for you?" The bartender, Justin, was standing at the ready. Heywood was a big tipper.

Robert nodded, affirming to the bartender. While they waited for Robert's drink, they got the family talk out of the way. When the drink came, Heywood toasted to "new beginnings."

Robert looked at him curiously. His father raised his glass to him again.

"In the not too distant future," the senator began, "I'm going to come into a bit of money. I've generally been a horse's ass, not only with you kids but also with my money." He looked fondly at his son and paused for emphasis. "Not this time. When the money comes in, I'm going to have this money man who works with my friend Rod Stanton manage it for me. I'll spend the hell out of what he gives me to spend, but I'm going to leave a bunch for you kids."

"Pop, that's not necessary. We want you to enjoy your life," protested Robert.

"Listen. I screwed up your mother's life, and I wasn't there for you kids," said Heywood, waving an admonishing finger. "It's damn sure necessary for me if I've got any more than a snowball's chance in hell of going to heaven."

Robert laughed and pushed back in mock surrender. "You're the boss, Pop."

The next hour was spent commiserating over the woeful Washington sports teams, with an asterisk to the Capitals; dumb-ass politicians from both sides of the aisles; and the stock market. Robert was as straight as his father was bent, so hot women at the bar were not a topic.

When it came time for Robert to leave, the two men hugged. Then Heywood watched as his son waved and walked away. He sat back down, put his elbow on the bar, and rested his head in his left hand.

After a few minutes, Heywood looked back at the TV screen. Then, for a long moment, he examined the dregs of his club soda. With purpose, he turned and scanned the bar with a practiced eye. Soon, two attractive forty-plus women sitting side by side turned to catch his gaze and smiled.

The old pro gracefully left his bar seat and walked over to the women with a friendly, open smile. Instinctively, he knew that he could lightly put a hand on each shoulder. "I wonder if you lovely ladies might help a former US Senator who served his country faithfully celebrate tonight. I do believe that there is a bottle of Dom Perignon in my friend Justin's cellar that has my name on it."

Heywood pointed at the bartender, who waved in acknowledgment. "But it will remain unclaimed unless you two will share it with me."

Heywood's deep Southern baritone, plus his twinkling eyes and inviting smile, made the subsequent simultaneous smiles and agreeing nods of the ladies a foregone conclusion.

CHAPTER 42

VERY RARELY WOULD YOU find Joey McLister hanging around his Connecticut Avenue apartment in Washington DC by himself on a Friday night. Then again, very rarely would you see him frustrated and feeling sorry for himself. The events of last week marked his only failure with the Bureau.

His arm was broken to shit. He had been disabled by a man twenty years his senior. And the loss of his weapon had almost resulted in the death of the Naples chief of police. What if his actions had gotten his most favorite person on earth killed? By his reasoning, he had every right to be depressed.

When Joey had been a golf pro, in his earlier life, he had certainly known failures. Gagging a three footer, losing concentration, and skying to a round of eighty—he had taken it all in stride. If you play golf, no matter what your skill level might be, you know you're only renting the game. Yet in his chosen career as an FBI agent, just as in the Army, a failure can cost lives.

Everyone on the team had taken responsibility for the botched Jeremy Lyons operation, but Joey couldn't let it go. His damn arm *should* still hurt. It served him right.

With his left hand, he raised his second can of Miller Lite and swallowed the last sip. He was not a real drinker, and he never got drunk, but several more were chilling in the fridge. He was currently waiting for his damn pizza to arrive. After he bullied his way into the raid on Lyons's offices, he was on forced sick leave until Monday, so what difference did it make anyway?

With all this, the main reason he was unable to escape the dark cloud of self-recrimination was that he had not seen or talked to Ellen since that night.

Laying the beer can down, he ran his left hand through his short hair, causing no discernable difference. "Shit, shit, shit, shit," he muttered. He was worried. He had left two messages on Ellen's cell, but she had not returned his calls. If she blamed him, he would leave the FBI. He wouldn't be able to face her disappointment in him.

The doorbell ringing brought him back to the moment. He walked over and looked through the peephole. The pizza delivery person had on jeans and a dark sweatshirt. A baseball cap pulled low completed the picture, and the person's eyes were on the ground.

Although Joey lived in a great neighborhood, he generally erred on the side of caution. The pizza box looked genuine, but pizza delivery people usually presented a tip-wanting face when he looked out. The bell rang again. This time he walked back to the door and opened it awkwardly and painfully with his right hand. In his left hand, at his side, was his recovered Glock.

His opening of the door was greeted by "Don't shoot! I'm just hungry!" The apparently frightened delivery person was now looking him square in the eye with a grin that would make the Cheshire cat look grumpy—Ellen!

Joey's heart leapt into his throat. "If I had two good hands, as my dad used to say, I'd turn you over my knee and blister your bottom." It was hard for him to say anything when he was smiling so hard he thought his face would break.

"Promises, promises," she said as she pushed by him into the apartment. "Didn't you hear me say I was hungry?" came the whiny, little girl voice.

Joey tripped in after her as she plopped the pizza box on his small white-lacquered kitchen table, threw her hat on the sofa, and pulled out a bottle of Merlot from a paper bag that he hadn't even noticed. All this was done with the grace of a ballerina or an accomplished magician. The fact that she was there was magic, or proof that God still did love him.

Ellen gave him a guilty smile and said, "Don't ask me where the wine came from. I knew that you'd have rotgut in this dump, so I brought the classy stuff—like me," she said, giving him her best cute smile. "Now sit your skinny ass down. Where are your glasses?"

Ever since his first word as a child, Joey had never been silent for fear that he might make a fool of himself. Yet, wordlessly, he took two steps, opened a cabinet door, and one at a time removed two wine glasses. He walked back to a kitchen drawer, opened it, and removed two paper plates and two napkins and put them on the table.

He was hoping she would think that his compliant silence was cool, but his frozen smile remained a dead giveaway. In less than five minutes, his life had been turned around.

While Joey was setting the table, Ellen opened the wine. She poured it as he sat dutifully. When they each had a glass, she raised hers up and said excitedly, "To the Supremes and the Temptations."

Joey held his glass with a puzzled look. "Okay. I'll bite. To the Supremes and the Temptations?"

Ellen smiled and took a sip. "Mmmm, good. Now," she said enticingly, "here's the first rule." She raised her index finger in the air. "Me first!" She finished in a rush, and as the words left her lips, she was grabbing a piece of pepperoni pizza and stuffing it into her mouth.

Joey laughed and shook his head. "Williams, you are one piece of work." He followed this by gentlemanly removing a piece of pizza and taking a small, exaggerated, well-mannered bite.

He was on his third Miss Manners–approved bite when Ellen pointed behind him and said with alarm, "What the hell is that?"

About halfway through his head swivel, he knew that he'd been had. When he turned toward her, she was smiling triumphantly and wolfing down another piece of pizza. "You are such a rookie!" she screamed, while her body was bouncing around in her chair.

Joey looked at her, raised a combative eyebrow, and said, "Now the gloves are off." He jumped from his chair, shielded the pizza box with this cast-laden arm, and began shoveling pizza into his mouth with his left hand.

Her laughter mixed with his, and then they convulsed into laughter together. "That's more like it," Ellen finally managed. "Skinny's back!"

After dinner, Ellen asked that they face each other on the couch. She had another glass of wine in her hand, while Joey was still on his first. "Do you think that we'll find Lyons?" she asked.

"If *we* don't, *I* will," said Joey. Just saying that gave him a sense of purpose.

She winced, and he wasn't sure if it was because of his comment or the subject matter. She closed her eyes and then opened them. "They made me go to a shrink for five straight days. I think I'm two inches shorter," she said with a wistful smile. "Now I want to tell my best friend." Joey looked at her wide eyed and touched. He swallowed, and it felt like his Adam's apple hit the top of his chin.

Ellen told him everything she remembered about that night—how helpless she had felt when Max kicked Henry Major and how it took all of her discipline to keep from trying to shoot Max when he grabbed Joey and pointed the gun at his head. She said she was sorry. When Joey started to protest, she gently placed her finger on his lips and whispered, "Shh." With tears in her eyes, she said that if Max had killed him, she wouldn't have been able to live with herself.

Ellen took a calming breath, and then she spared no detail describing how she shot Max and how he grabbed her, kissed her, smothered her with a hug, and then died. "The medical examiner said that Max should have been dead from his chest wound. He couldn't believe Max could summon that superhuman strength after being mortally wounded.

"The shrink said that he was probably fixated on me." She looked down and paused. "In Max's apartment, they found a file on me and an eight-by-ten photo. Fortunately, it was not sticky," she finished with a subdued voice and a grimace. She bowed her head as if in prayer.

Joey was glad that Ellen's head was down because he was clearly tearing up. The warmth and connection that he felt from just holding her hand was indescribable. He had loved her from the moment they met. And he could stay just like this forever. "Are you okay?" he half-whispered to her.

With her head still down, she replied in an even quieter voice. "The doc told me that I have a tough row to hoe if I want to be totally healed." The sadness in her voice was accentuated by the tears in her eyes as she lifted her face to his. "Will you help me?" she pleaded.

"Of course," he stammered. "I'd do anything for you."

She looked at him, and his tears matched the tears in her eyes. "Even if it means breaking FBI protocol?" she asked.

"Screw the FBI! All I care about is you!" he shouted.

Ellen looked at him for a long time. Then she stood up slowly. "Okay. Do you have an iPod dock?"

"Sure," Joey said uncertainly, and he pointed to the table.

Ellen took her iPod from a pocket in her jeans, placed it on the holder, and pushed Pause. She walked back over to him, took his left hand, and helped him up. Her hands caressed his face with a feather-like touch as she looked deeply into his still-tearing eyes. She leaned forward, put her hands behind his neck, and pulled his mouth gently to her lips.

Ellen pulled back from the lingering kiss and looked into Joey's eyes, which were now filled with loving wonder. She stepped away from him, went back to the iPod, and pushed Play. He heard the sweet tones of the Supremes and the Temptations singing "I'm gonna make you love me" as she pressed her lush body into his.

When they came up for air, he whispered in her ear. "Is this the prescribed medicine?"

"Yep," she answered in a husky voice. "Don't get nervous, but the doctor said I'm supposed to take it every two hours."

C H A P T E R 4 3

MY TEAM'S PURPOSE HAS been and always will be to protect and enhance our clients' lifestyles. The ingredients of a good relationship with investment professionals are similar to those of a good marriage—work together, stay together, care for each other, and listen well.

Increasing our asset base is always an objective. Moreover, new clients are an invigorating aspect of the business. Best of all, this year we knew that we would not have a hard act to follow from a previous advisor's performance.

Consequently, I figured that my Friday morning call from Sam Golden was most likely a referral. I had previously written Sam a note thanking him for recommending us to Kay Murrey. In spite of my rare display of petulance at the basketball game, she came in and met with us and decided to have us help her with a recent inheritance.

I had also thanked Sam for his kind and very touching letter to me. Having taken care of the required niceties, I could return to giving him my normal ration of crap.

"Sam the Sham, you must really be sad that I'm no longer your personal operative. And if this is a call to tell me that once I'm in, I can never leave …"

"No, no," he laughed. "Listen, Mac. Check your calendar for next week."

"Mornings or afternoons?" I asked with anticipation.

"Lunch."

Only really big ones begin with lunch. "Just me or should I bring a partner?"

"Just you," Sam answered.

"Hmm. Either Tuesday or Thursday would work. What's the purpose?"

"Lunch with your best pal, Sam."

My enthusiasm waned.

"Tuesday at noon should work," he continued. "If there's a glitch, I'll e-mail you. Come to the White House, bring your ID and a urine sample, and I'll meet you in the president's dining room."

"Wait a minute, you politicking devil! Am I really having lunch with the president instead? Should I not wear my 'Contract with America' button?" Being able to say I had eaten a meal in the president's dining room sounded cool. "Do I need to bring anything, like new account forms?" I hinted without subtlety.

He laughed. "No, just your charming self. By the way, it would have been gracious to at least comment on the urine sample request."

"I wouldn't trust that to be handled by anyone but you personally."

"I'm going to quit while I'm miraculously even. Have a good weekend." Sam hurried off the phone like his mom was calling.

*   *   *   *   *

I had told Artie Cohen about my upcoming lunch date with Sam Golden. Whenever possible, I like to maximize an opportunity. It's sort of like having only one wish and using it to wish for more wishes. You never know until you try. In order to determine if I had any hope of furthering additional agendas, I needed to pick Artie's brain.

Even though the stock market had been in a strong up trend, investors' psychological scars would take a long time to heal. Abject fear dissipates slowly, and for some, nightmares revisited could be terminal. Scams, Ponzi schemes, and fraud will always be around. On the other hand, if the financial system remains broken and easily manipulated by predators, another catastrophe is inevitable. I was ready to cash in a chip with Sam Golden.

"Artie, do you remember my mentioning my friend Steve Mosberg?"

"Yeah, smart guy, arbitrageur in New York."

I smiled because Artie's staccato answer made it sound like I was talking to Mosberg.

Succumbing to the temptation of our trusty cafeteria, we were catching a quick bite while solving the world's problems. "Mosberg used to run a hedge fund. I asked him what strategies were used by the most aggressive of his former brethren."

"And?"

"He said that I insulted him by lumping him in with those scumbags."

"You insult everybody. It's how you show love!"

I smiled. It felt good. "Anyway, I won't bore you with the details, but when the SEC relaxed the rules on short selling, the gloves were off. Our markets have been the victims of some serious manipulations."

"How do you stop it?"

I shrugged. "Who knows? Maybe you throw a penalty flag. Have the refs do an instant replay and reverse the rulings."

"Nice analogy," he said.

"How they force healthy companies down the drain is academic," I said. "Unless the system changes or the hedge funds acquire a conscience, they bring the economic system down."

"I'm losing my appetite."

"Sorry. I'm really focusing on another systemic problem, and I wanted your opinion."

"Shoot." Artie's face rendered both surprise and the fact that he was flattered to be asked something that was normally in my area of expertise.

"Rapid trading causes extreme volatility and creates severe investor anguish. It's three forty-five and the market is flat. Fifteen minutes later the stock market closes, and it's either up or down 150 points. No news, just traders playing games, finding a microscopic anomaly in stock prices, and instantly pushing the pedal to the floor."

I took a breath. "Ready for the clincher?"

He gave me an apprehensive look.

"Mosberg said that *one* group of investors, using only their *own* funds, account for 25 percent of the market's volume."

Artie blinked about five times in rapid succession, and his mouth fell open like I had just told him I was pregnant.

"That's frightening."

"Assume these are all upstanding citizens, just money-hungry billionaires." There was almost a lilt in my voice as I stated this. I let him hold that thought for a minute and then changed to a serious tone. "Now imagine that they're foreign investors who are unfriendly to our interests."

Artie's eyes widened.

I held up my hands. "I have no idea if that's even remotely possible. But I do know that the average holding time for a stock purchased by this particular group is ... three minutes!"

Artie shook his head in amazement. "So if they hold a stock position for ten minutes, should they be considered long-term investors for tax reasons?"

Sarcasm was a new outfit for my friend, but I thought he wore it well. "Here's my question to you because you're the office politico: What would be the temperature in Congress for putting these rapid traders out of business?"

Artie put down his fork and looked at me as he considered the question. Finally, he asked, "What do you want me to do?"

CHAPTER 44

IT WAS ABOUT ELEVEN forty-five on Tuesday morning when I approached the main gate of the White House. Although we work with politicians and members of former presidents' cabinets, I had never been an invited guest there. I felt sort of like Groucho Marx when he commented, "I wouldn't join a club that would have me as a member."

The day before, I had given the Secret Service my social security number and date of birth. After looking at my ID at the gate, they asked me to repeat my birth date. So far, no surprises from our government at work.

Next, I got to walk through a puffer machine like the ones at Reagan National. After they determined that I was a clean, mean, money machine, a very serious-looking young man escorted me to the president's dining room.

I had read about the president's dining room on Wikipedia, and I was particularly amused to read about the decorating changes over the years. After Jacqueline Kennedy, first lady Betty Ford removed the ornate wallpaper and had the walls painted a soft yellow. Then Rosalynn Carter rode into town and reinstalled scenic wallpaper.

During my hero Hillary's tenure, the walls were hung with chartreuse Italian watered silk moiré fabric, whatever the hell that is. Finally, during the second term of George W. Bush, the walls were re-covered in an off-white silk lampas.

I had memorized these vital facts so that I could throw them at Sam if he got too officious in telling me about the history of the room.

Sam was waiting for me with a smile and an outstretched hand. Because there were only a few people around, and thus I could not be accused of reaching across the aisle, I pulled him to me and gave him a brief hug.

When we separated, I noted an excited gleam in his eyes, and my first thought was that they had found Jeremy Lyons.

We ordered iced tea from a very impressive waiter, and I looked at Sam expectantly. He spoke with enthusiasm. "The good news is that we have completely shut down Lyons's operation. Already, seven CEOs have pleaded guilty to insider training, and one CFO also confessed. More are coming. It's another huge black eye for our corporate governance, but the market seems to love criminals getting punished. So far, there has been no structural damage to the market as a result of this."

"But Lyons is still on the loose," I said with resignation.

"Yes. So it's not all good news."

I shook my head and replied with exasperation. "What percentage of the folks who have read about this perfidy consider it a victimless crime—the rich stealing from the rich?"

Sam didn't answer, so I continued. "Put aside for an instant that this man used assassination to increase his return on investment." I took a few breaths. "Think of the money lost by everyday investors, the thousands of people who lose their jobs because of the avarice of assholes like this."

I raised my hand. "Sorry." My voice had risen to an uncomfortable level. I appreciated the fact that Sam had not called that to my attention.

"When stocks are manipulated through false rumors, innuendo, and naked shorts, companies go out of business that should still be in business." I didn't really expect a reply from Sam. I was just venting. I blew out a breath and climbed down off my soapbox.

"Was Frank Griffin the primary source of your identifying the culprits, or were you able to hack into their computers?" I asked.

Sam responded. "Everything we've gotten so far is from Griffin or Vanessa."

"Vanessa?"

"Sorry," he continued. "She acted as the receptionist when our troops stormed the Bastille."

"I know that, but why would she have relevant information?"

"Because she was also one of the 'perfect specimens,'" said Sam.

I looked at him quizzically.

"Joe sniffed this out quickly," Sam added. "By the way, I know that you're aware that he beat himself up pretty badly about botching the operation. But he's too much of an old pro, so he worked through it by redoubling his efforts.

"Anyway, Vanessa was too poised and gorgeous to be just a receptionist in Lyons's office. It didn't make sense that Jeremy would have wasted that kind of talent. Joe broke her down.

"Bottom line, Lyons got a little too big for his britches when he left Vanessa there. All the other girls have disappeared like they never existed. Griffin identified them, but we haven't located them. Lyons's computers may be a dead end. The congressmen that Griffin recruited or coached all lawyered up and pleaded shocked ignorance.

"All this will take time. We may get some jail time out of the computer gurus, but they're playing the 'we were just following orders; we didn't know where the information came from' card."

"I'd like to get some clarity on what happens to the stock positions. Are they just frozen and unmanaged?" I asked.

Sam looked at me sheepishly. "It seems like Lyons was ahead of us there, also. On the surface, it appears that the man actually cared about his clients."

I narrowed my eyes and leaned toward him. "Convince me."

"He left written instructions that if he called the CEO of J. P. Morgan and requested it, the bank was authorized to use their discretion and proceed with an orderly liquidation of all positions."

Sam looked at me. "Tell me where I'm off base here. Since Lyons had already withdrawn the maximum amount of his own funds, what was the benefit to him?" he asked.

I considered his question before answering. However, to me, the answer was easy. "Client retention," I replied.

Sam started to speak, and I held up my hand. "This is the most anal-retentive man on the planet. Meticulous, organized with military precision, he would never leave a loose end. He would hate to be reviled by his clients like Barney Farb has been."

When I paused, Sam said, "I guess that sort of makes sense," although his face said he was not convinced.

I tried another avenue.

"What will the clients that don't get caught think?" The question was rhetorical, so I answered it myself. "He *may* have done those things that he's accused of, but he made me great money, and I did get my loan returned. If someone makes you 20 percent a year for three years, are you calling the SEC to give the money back because he might have massaged the rules?"

Sam nodded. "I get your point."

"Remember that it costs him nothing to request an orderly liquidation of his account," I said. "He had already wired out all of *his* money. And the final piece of the puzzle … " I paused for a moment, realizing with troubling certainty that I was inside Jeremy's mind, "is that the arrogant bastard has a built-in clientele if or when he decides to resurface."

Sam shook his head in astonishment. "Now you've given me nightmares."

"Welcome to my world," I replied grimly. We looked solemnly at each other, and then I changed the conversation. "Get back to the Vanessa connection. I'm missing something there," I said.

"Sure. Let's order first," said Sam. I ordered the grilled salmon with vegetables, and Sam almost knocked me out of my chair when he replied simply to the waiter, "I'll have the same." His response to my gaping open mouth was simply, "I'm eating healthy."

After the waiter left, Sam spoke. "Griffin knew that Vanessa was sleeping with Congressman Floyd Caldwell. So Joe used that, telling her that Caldwell told him that he wasn't her only lover. Consequently, she could be charged as an accessory.

"It sounded mostly like BS to me, but Joe pulled it off. As expected, she lawyered up, but the promise of immunity got her to give up the CEOs about as easily as you can get kids to give up Brussels sprouts."

I nodded. I was still having difficulty celebrating. I looked at Sam. "I have a favor I need from you."

"Anything."

"Reckless answer, but you remember that I need to be sure that Margo Savino is taken care of, as per our agreement?"

He nodded.

"I'm sure her pension has stopped. We need to follow through. I have no idea how you'll get this done."

Sam thought about it for a minute and then responded. "I'll tell you what.

I have business in Sarasota a few weeks from now, and I'll visit her. I'll either hand her a check or wire it wherever she desires."

He returned my steady gaze, and I was confident of the last statement but suspicious of the first. "You could just call her and handle it over the phone, Sam. I don't think it's necessary to see her in person," I replied innocently.

He colored slightly. I had struck a nerve. "I think that it will be more personal if I discuss this with her over dinner," he said primly. "There are some sensitive nondisclosure issues."

I laughed. "If you want her phone number, I will want details."

Much to my delight, Sam looked thoroughly embarrassed, unable to return my gaze. He was vulnerable, so I took my shot. "Let me go another direction and pick your brain."

Sam nodded his assent.

"While talking to a friend of mine in New York who used to run a hedge fund, I ran an idea by him. I then asked the great Artie Cohen to check with his political contacts and see if this idea could become an issue for Congress."

Sam looked up and smiled. Like everyone, he loved Artie.

"Now I need to run it by the former SEC chairman."

"I'm all ears," he replied and sat forward, steepling his hands and resting his elbows on the table.

"The issue is rapid trading on the stock exchanges. I want to make it prohibitive."

Sam looked at me thoughtfully, now totally engaged.

"First, my solution pisses off the people who are trading, the big banks and brokerage firms who are generating the commissions, and the exchanges—a formidable group. Second, it helps every 401(k) participant, every parent using stock mutual funds to save for college education, and, in my opinion, every single investor. No more casino. The stock market goes up and down due to valuations, news, or psychology—nothing artificial."

Sam looked at me intently. "A politician's wet dream," he said quietly. He paused and then leaned even closer. "So what's the solution?"

"A transaction tax, a sin tax. But only on stock positions held for fewer than twenty-four hours. These traders, whom I often think of as computer terrorists, are like the banker who rips off one penny on every customer transaction. I believe that even a 1 percent tax on day trading would put these parasites out of business."

Sam looked at me for a long time. Then his face broke into a grin so huge it was like he had just won the lottery. "My friend," he offered, "what you need is a forum."

He maintained his self-satisfied grin until his BlackBerry chirped. He looked down and, with a start, his angular body unfolded. "Mac, I have to get this. Excuse me." He walked quickly out of the room.

My face wrinkled in annoyance, but I shrugged it off. A BlackBerry in the president's dining room struck me as a bit rude, as was his exit, but I was the guest.

A few minutes later, the waiter brought the lunches—still no Sam. I expected that the plate covering his meal would remain there to keep it warm, but it was removed just as mine was. Do I eat? Do I wait? Do I start getting pissed? Too late.

Just then a very attractive woman approached the table and said, "I'm so sorry, but Mr. Golden will not be returning."

Smiling at me, dressed in a wonderfully tailored navy dress with tasteful pearls, this woman looked frightfully familiar. "Sam thought that I might be a suitable substitute."

She looked at me with questioning eyes and offered her hand. "I'm Susan Bloom, Mr. McGregor, chairman of the Securities and Exchange Commission."

My mouth gaped open. I jumped up, shook her hand, and helped her to her seat. As I pushed in her chair, I said softly, "I'm indeed honored that you've taken the time to meet with me, Ms. Bloom. However, I must inform you that your esteemed colleague, Mr. Golden, will be punished severely for surprising me."

As I took my seat, she said, "We can schedule another meeting if you're not prepared." There was an engaging and challenging twinkle in her eye.

"No, ma'am," I said smiling. "And I assume that the meal was your order and not that of my friend, who is a gastronomical aberration." All my senses were on alert. "I have to tell you that I've been really prepared for this meeting for a long time."

CHAPTER 45

SITTING ON HIS BALCONY, half-mesmerized by the Gulf waters, Frank Griffin took stock. Ice cubes clinking in his bourbon and water reminded him that he was due for a refresher. He looked at the glass, amused by his indecision. At the moment, it mirrored every aspect of his life.

The good news—money in the bank; immunity; ding, dong, the son of a bitch is dead. The bad news—his hot, lesbian gal pal was a fed; no job; no prospects. Jeremy de Sade is still alive, but he has to be in deep, deep hiding.

The femme fatale now known as Ellen had given him a parting gift. She told him that his scars were only badges of shame if he allowed them to be.

Instead, she suggested that he explain them by saying that he was working undercover for the FBI and that criminals had tortured him. But his information was instrumental in bringing them down. Sometimes there is a price for doing the right thing.

"Spin control!" she had shouted. "Learn it and you can be a politician."

Frank sighed. If, like in the movies, he had ended up with the girl, everything would have been worth it.

His reverie was broken by the sound of his doorbell ringing. He was confused. He wasn't expecting anybody, and he had almost no real friends. He pushed himself off of his mesh recliner and walked to the door. Keeping the chain on, he opened the door and peered at his visitor.

"May I come in?" the woman standing outside asked tearfully.

Frank's mouth fell open as he stared. Still beautiful, but dressed in jeans and a sweatshirt, with her long hair tied up in a bun, she looked more like a waif than a model.

"Please," she begged as the tears streamed down her cheeks. "I'm scared. I don't know where to turn."

Although he was still confused, nobility nonetheless won out. Frank nodded, reclosed the door, removed the chain, and motioned for her to enter. From habit, he automatically scanned his apartment. Everything was in order.

"Please sit," he suggested as he motioned toward the couch. "Can I fix you a drink ?"

"Yes," she answered softly. "Bourbon and water?"

Frank raised his eyebrows and said, "Of course." He walked to the bar. He mixed her drink, walked back to the balcony, retrieved his glass, and refilled it.

Carrying both drinks, he moved to the couch and handed hers to her. He took his drink with him to the chair directly across from the couch and sat down.

After she took a grateful sip, Frank leaned forward and asked, "How can I help?"

She responded by inhaling half of her drink in successive swallows. She dried her eyes and looked up at him. "I'm so sorry," she said. "I hate to impose."

Frank looked at her and gave her a reassuring nod and a smile.

"I just didn't know where else to go," she moaned.

As he stared into her eyes still brimming with tears, Frank marveled at how this woman would end up here. Her beauty was so exquisite it was hard to imagine that any man could refuse her anything.

"I know that Jeremy will think I told the authorities about him!" she blurted out.

Although the panic level in her voice greatly increased Frank's own anxiety, he fought to keep his face impassive. "Why would he think that?"

"Because we argued. I told him that what he was doing was wrong! But I didn't tell anyone!" she almost screamed

Beautiful and brave, Frank thought. Somebody who worked for Jeremy actually had the courage to confront him. He envied her. "Jeremy probably just made a mistake somewhere," he assured her. "Besides, I'm sure he's in another country by now."

She buried her face in her hands. Tears escaped through her long fingers as she sobbed. In broken phrases, Frank heard, "He doesn't make mistakes, and he always punishes."

Frank moved to the couch and encircled her with his arms. Leaning down, she burrowed into him, and he felt her warm tears through his T-shirt. She hugged him fiercely. Still holding him with her left arm, she reached under her right leg.

Reflexively, his head turned toward the movement. Quick motion. A sharp pain in his side. Fifty thousand volts incapacitating muscles and nerves. Blackness.

*　　*　　*　　*　　*

Dizzy and light-headed to the point of nausea, Frank felt the iron railing painfully pressing into his stomach. Like a slab of beef, he was slung over the balcony. His hands were secured to the rails with duct tape, as were his feet. And he was naked.

Panic rushed into his brain as he felt pressure on his testicles. "Please do not make a sound of warning or alarm. At the first utterance, I will taser you again, cut the tape, and toss you over the balcony. Nod if you understand." Her voice was calm, unemotional, and eerily professional.

Frank nodded. Tears and mucus ran down his face. "Why?" he whispered feebly.

"I will ask the questions. If your answers are satisfactory, you will still be punished for your betrayal. But we will allow you to live."

Frank's body shivered involuntarily in fear.

"Who else, Judas? Who else?" she asked in a low voice

"F-FBI already knew."

"Who in the FBI?"

He thought frantically and remembered that her real identity was protected. He stuttered, "T-Tracy. Tracy Lane and some guy. I don't know his name. He was the guy who took me down."

She was quiet for a moment. "Who else in the company betrayed Jeremy?"

"I swear I know of no one," Frank rasped.

The woman looked dispassionately at the helpless man. She left him hanging and expertly wiped her fingerprints off of anything she had touched. Then she walked back over and whispered in his ear, "I believe you."

He shuddered with relief.

"You must follow my instructions, or you will die. I'm going to cut your hands loose. After that I will release your feet. You must remain perfectly still."

Frank tensed, willing himself to stop shivering as she cut the tape from his hands, then his feet.

She leaned into him and whispered again in his ear, "Did you feel safe when Max died?"

He nodded tentatively.

"Then you forgot what Jeremy taught us. People are replaceable." With a grunt and a powerful thrust, she threw his legs up over his head.

Sabine watched Frank's ungraceful descent. She walked over to the corner of the balcony, took a deep bow, and smiled. Then she loosened the straps where she had affixed the video camera.

EPILOGUE

LIKE CHILDREN WHEN THEY first arrive at Disney World, Grace and I tumbled excitedly out of the car. We raced each other over the short span of asphalt cul de sac and up the wooden steps, and then we stopped to take a breath. Prudence prevailed, and we walked down the steeper wooden steps together until our feet hit the sand. Kicking out of our sandals in unison, we galloped through the heavy sand until our toes touched the surf.

I reached over and took Grace's hand, and we watched nature's miracle symphony as if it were our first time. The sun sparkled on white-crested waves, and we smiled as they slapped the beach in rhythmic harmony. Rising swells of salt water gained momentum, humping, rising, and then standing to salute us before crashing into the sand. Clean, pure ocean air enticed us to breathe deeply. In our little slice of heaven, depending upon the tides, there is between a half and a full football field of barefoot-friendly sand before the surf.

The week of July 4th is always my absolute favorite week of the year. I look forward to it like a groom looks forward to his honeymoon. For Grace and me, it is an annual honeymoon.

Four of the world's greatest kids join us for the entire week at the beach. They do not bring friends, hang with friends, or hit the bars or clubs at night. We all hang together.

After four months of a rising stock market, investors were starting to allow themselves to exhale. In the past, the public had shown resilience and remarkable recuperative tendencies after severe market declines. In fact, many had bought into the theory that the stock market was like a roller coaster to new highs. Only those who jumped off got hurt.

Pontificating, prognosticating pundits supported the theory. They turned their switch from doom and despair to fragile hope and, finally, irrational exuberance. Unfortunately, this time *was* different—global panic, public companies leaping out of windows, loans made in excess of value, real estate plummeting, excessive leverage, shadow markets with no supervision, misguided politicians, faulty valuations by rating agencies, bailouts, stimulus, brokerage firms on the brink, fraud on a massive scale ... we didn't start the fire.

It may be years before confidence is restored. From my perspective, it felt like our economic system had been shaken to the core. But as we walked back to our house to get ready for the arrival of the kids, I smiled. Friends and family are healthy, the sun is shining, and I am blessed far beyond anything that I deserve.

Grace unlocked the door of our home away from home and turned off the alarm. We continued to wear our giddy grins of anticipation.

Moving with machine-like efficiency, I emptied the car of everything except our two golf bags. Although the elevator was loaded and we could still fit comfortably, we considered it our aerobic duty to climb the stairs.

Grace had gone to the bathroom and then surveyed the bottom floor before returning to judge my packing performance. Predictably, she smiled and then bent down and rearranged.

We climbed the stairs to the third floor, or living floor. An open kitchen, a great room, a glassed-in porch, and a wraparound deck are all on that floor. Two large French doors lead to the front deck, where a mesmerizing ocean view awaits. A door off the small adjoining den leads to the back deck, which catches the sun late on a summer day. There are small decks outside each of the bedrooms. Our grilling deck, a popular favorite, is in the back and adjacent to the kitchen.

We have a large, L-shaped, really comfortable sectional couch in the great room. Surprisingly, it's still in good shape after numerous swan dives and wrestling matches. Not only does it offer excellent TV viewing, but it's also a great place for charades and other family games.

Chock-full bookshelves hold new and old fiction treats, which are passed around like a summer cold. After twenty-five years of investing, Grace and I had bought this lot and designed our dream home.

Even though we all live within fifteen minutes of each other in Maryland, the beach is different. Grace and I greeted each arrival like we had not just seen them a few days ago. By one o'clock, all were present and accounted for. We grabbed a quick lunch and then hit the beach.

*   *   *   *   *

Often, when you expect something to be great, it becomes impossible for reality to live up to your expectations. In this case, our week at the beach had lived up to every expectation. We had all arrived on Friday the third. Now it was Friday a week later.

As customary, we had hung out with Rod Stanton and his family. Their beach home is about two miles south of ours, on the beach, and maybe the largest house in any of the Oceanside developments. Each year, his two girls bring ringer friends to the beach in an attempt to dethrone the real kings of beach volleyball, the McGregors.

Inevitably, the "we're only playing for fun; it's just to get the families together" Stantons leave the beach volleyball court with little pride intact. Keep in mind that unlike some of the Stantons' gargantuan friends, the only six-footer on our squad is yours truly, and that's only if we go by measurements of thirty years ago. There has been no height measurement since then, as I refuse to consider the possibility of shrinkage.

My sons, Jamie and Hunter, have played in beach volleyball two-man tournaments, and Frannie and younger sister, Leigh, have played in some mixed tournaments, but heaven forbid that their brothers would deign to play with them.

We have also played as a family indoors in volleyball leagues. In the winter, our family team, known as "Mac Attack," has consistently been at least respectable. Just like with investing, I prefer the odds to be on my side.

*   *   *   *   *

Because she is a perfectionist, Grace spends more time in the house taking care of things than I would like. As she approached our conclave of beach chairs, I waved and pointed to the chair that I had already set up for her.

Anyone who is familiar with beach chairs knows that it would be above and beyond to get out of the chair whenever a lady approaches. As expected, she readjusted her chair to get maximum sun positioning. The kids were enthusiastic that Mom was here. They always did like her better.

"Just before I left the house, you had a FedEx package delivered," said Grace. "It felt like a book, but I didn't open it."

"Really? In five years that's the first FedEx package ever delivered here. More than likely it's one of my literary clients sending me a prerelease copy."

My son Hunter wasted no time. "Oops! I hope my porn didn't get rerouted."

"If it's porn, it's definitely Hunter's," I said with arms raised in innocence.

"I'll cover for you, Dad, like always," added my helpful son.

I thought no more about the mysterious package and went back to reading my book. After a while, I closed the book and pushed myself up seminimbly from the beach chair.

As I headed back to the house to get first shot at the lunch goodies, I remembered the package. When I entered the kitchen, I saw it waiting for me on the table. It might be a business book sent as a gift, but I didn't know why it would be sent here.

I sat down and opened the envelope. Out tumbled what looked like a normal-sized novel with a slick book jacket and the title *Survival of the Fittest* emblazoned across the front. At the bottom, in letters only slightly smaller than the title, I saw the author's name—Jeremy Lyons.

I dropped the book on the table as though I had received a powerful electric shock. I closed my eyes and breathed deeply. I had to still the adrenaline rush and the jumble of thoughts running through my brain. I picked the book back up, noticed that my hands were trembling, and turned it over. Staring at me with the eyes of Satan, shirtless, every muscle clenched and defined on his sweat-covered body, was indeed Jeremy Lyons.

I could not take my eyes off of the picture. I was in a trance-like nightmare, staring at his incredible arrogance. Once again, I dropped the book on the table, feeling like I should close my eyes and never open them again.

My imagination was going full tilt, and no alternative scenario was acceptable. Why would he send this piece of blasphemous garbage to me? How could this fugitive get a book published?

Unfortunately, the answer was easy: money rules. I felt naked and vulnerable. To shield my family, I took the book upstairs to temporarily hide it in my dresser.

If I were a wiser and more patient man, the book would have remained there until all the kids had left for home. Yet curiosity is a cruel and tempting mistress.

The house was still quiet, so before I relegated the poisoned papers to the bottom of my underwear drawer, I steeled myself and opened the book. On the title page was an inscription in bold handwriting, "To my inspiration—I have enjoyed playing hide-and-seek with you. The next time it will be your and Grace's turn to hide. All the best, Jeremy."

It's a Family Affair

WHEN GIVING THANKS, MY first responsibility is to thank God. From birth, through a tour in Viet Nam, through children and grandchildren, the Lord has blessed me with His mercy.

Next on my list must be my tireless sister, Kay Krug. Through what felt like never ending rewrites, she edited my manuscript. If my investment comments were too obtuse, she told me the she didn't understand, and I made changes until she did. At least someone in the family is not a CNBC-aholic.

Because I am a literary dinosaur, my daughter Cathy typed my prose as I read it from my multiple handwritten steno pads, made countless trips to Kinko's to collate and copy my numerous drafts, and only occasionally grumbled. Both she and my sister were consistently positive about <u>Insiders</u> and, dear readers, I know that you wouldn't want to hurt their feelings.

Other family all stars include Jessica, whose descriptions inspired both Ellen and Sabine, and Brian, whose engineering mind fashioned "Someplace Else." Daughter Cristin I thank for her name selections and her idea that I donate half of all proceeds to charity. Son Jamie I thank for challenging me to write this book, and son Jon I thank for his ideas on character development. And Aubrey's enthusiasm always makes me smile.

I am extremely grateful for my work family. The Capital Wealth Management Group rocks. A.J. is a great partner, a great friend, and a great wordsmith. His brilliant mind was a constant source of ideas, and I shamelessly stole what I needed. Thanks to all of my talented team for allowing me to become an advisor/author.

At the top of my family of friends to whom I owe gratitude must be the wonderfully gifted writer David Baldacci. Demonstrating an inordinate amount of patience, David generously gave me advice and encouragement. Also, my dear long-time friend, the celebrated and courageous author Kitty Kelley gave me inspiration and direction. For delivering brutal, succinct critique as requested, I am grateful to my author friend Richard Gazala.

Bill Miller, who may be the smartest man in the markets, gave me an idea that I quickly claimed as my own. Stuart Bowers gave me great insights on the interworking of prime brokers.

Thanks to the owner of Laser Dazzler and the helpful gentlemen from the FBI. Finally, thank you for choosing to read my book. First-time novelists write, then hope and pray that their work will be well received. I would love to hear your thoughts.

Marvin McIntyre